KU-198-318

PRAISE FOR

BEASTLANDS

'I loved how Jess combines **animal expertise**
with **infinite imagination** to create an
unputdownable fantasy adventure.'
A. F. Steadman, author of *Skandar*
and the Unicorn Thief

'**Hugely exhilarating and wildly imaginative**, Beastlands
is a truly magnificent new fantasy series. Prepare to fall
in love with Alethea, Rustus and Kayla as they embark on
a heartstopping adventure packed full of **intrigue,
twists and a multitude of magical creatures.**'
Aisling Fowler, author of *Fireborn*

'Beastlands is a triumph of imagination and animal lore.
**A non-stop thrilling adventure . . . I could not put this book
down**, and I'm as hungry as a salinka for the next one.'
M. G. Leonard, author of *Beetle Boy*

'Beastlands is a fabulous adventure! **High-stakes action,
gripping storytelling and a multitude of magical beasts!**'
Abi Elphinstone, author of *Sky Song*

'**I absolutely loved this book!** It's perfect for fans of
Skandar and *Fireborn*, with **brilliant world building, great
characterisation, heaps of peril** and a subtle but
knowledgeable **eco angle.**'
Hannah Gold, author of *The Last Bear*

BEAST LANDS

RACE TO FROSTFALL MOUNTAIN

JESS FRENCH

Piccadilly
PRESS

First published in Great Britain in 2024 by
PICCADILLY PRESS
4th Floor, Victoria House, Bloomsbury Square
London WC1B 4DA
Owned by Bonnier Books
Sveavägen 56, Stockholm, Sweden
bonnierbooks.co.uk/PiccadillyPress

A CIP catalogue record for this book is available from the
British Library.

ISBN: 978-1-80078-406-2
Also available as an ebook and in audio

1

Typeset by Envy Design

Printed and bound in Great Britain by Clays Ltd, Elcograf S.p.A.

Piccadilly Press is an imprint of Bonnier Books UK
bonnierbooks.co.uk

*For all the brilliant beasts of our world,
to whom we owe everything.*

NORDGAP

THE SCATTERED ISLES

Hookclaw Point

Port Royal

Frostfall Mountain

Mount Atana

FJORDLANDS

Freyavik

ASHLANDS

THE SHIVERTIPS

SHADOW LANDS

The Silk

VIRIDIAN SEA

SOUTHLANDS

Sophiatown

DRAGHLUND

MAP of THE REALMS of

RAMOA

PROLOGUE

Before there were people, there were beasts.
Before there were beasts, there were plants.
Before there were plants, there was an island.
Before there was an island, there was ocean . . .

In the first age, an island was born. Made from the fiery lava of underwater volcanoes, it rose from the sea in a roiling dance of steam and waves. When the molten rock finally cooled, it formed a mass of land that was barren and lifeless, except for a tendrilous purple fungus that lay deep in its heart. Gradually the fungus sprawled its way up through the earth and over the land, new life sprouting in every place it touched.

In the second age, the plants came, flourishing in the rich volcanic soil. On the slopes of the island's only surface volcano, Mount Ataria, there grew a turquoise jungle, strung with climbers and vines. In the south was a deciduous forest, where the leaves turned red and gold as the seasons changed. And to the west the banks of the watery fjords were colonised by mosses, lichens and enormous flowers.

In the third age, came the beasts. From tiny creepers scuttling over rocks to treetop acrobats leaping from bough to bough, they evolved to thrive across the island's many habitats. Huge winged creatures ruled the skies while colossal ocean beasts lurked in the shadowy seas. Beasts were everywhere; the air was thick with the scent of them and their squeaks and roars echoed through the mountains and forests.

In the fourth age, the first people arrived. They called themselves Lia'Oua – the people of the island – and they named the island Ramoa. They lived alongside the beasts and plants in harmony, taking from and giving back to the land in equal measure.

But in the fifth age, a new wave of settlers came from across the Viridian Sea. They found Ramoa to be wild, unfriendly and filled with monstrous beasts. They brought blades and fire and a hunger to conquer. As they slashed the trees and hunted the beasts they could not tame, the island whispered to the Lia'Oua, prophesying a time of great ruin. Wanting no part in the destruction, the Lia'Oua went underground, making a new home for themselves deep beneath the Shivertips. The settlers never saw the Lia'Oua, but they told stories of a legendary people that crept beneath the earth, whom they called Shadow Ghouls.

Where once the island and its beings had lived in harmony, there grew a divide between humans and all other living creatures. The new settlers created three distinct realms and fortified their cities to keep out the beasts. The Fjordlanders created Freyavik, a city suspended over the water on sky bridges and stilts, the people of the Ashlands made their home in the hot caldera of Mount Ataria, and in the south, where the forests had been totally decimated, the Southlanders built a huge walled city, which they called Sophiatown.

Everything outside of these civilisations became known as the Beastlands, a wild and dangerous place where humans must not roam. The city walls protected their people from almost all beasts, save for the mighty winged creatures who could soar over them. To rid themselves of this final threat, the people of the Realms trained warriors to slay the sky beasts. The Fjordlanders had Tree Wraiths, who fought with poison blow darts, the Atarians had Scorched Ataris, who fought with fire and spears, and the Southlanders had Elites, who fought with bow and arrow. They were all efficient beast-hunters and eventually only two species of large winged beast remained: the warm-blooded pangron and the largest of all flying beasts, the mighty phaegra.

Eventually the Elites found a way to capture and enslave the pangrons, taking their eggs out of the Beastlands and hoarding them in watery caves deep below Sophiatown. They learned to ride the creatures and renamed themselves 'Sky Riders', adapting their bows and arrows into knucklebows, which were worn on the hand and more easily portable on pangron-back. Once the pangrons were

3

tamed, only the most fearsome of the winged beasts, the phaegras, were left.

The realms threw all of their resources into killing the phaegras until finally, on what became known as Vanquish Day, the last phaegra was destroyed. Each realm claimed the victory as their own. But even then, with the threat of the beasts extinguished, the settlers could not rest. They feared the other realms would invade and take over the cities they had fought so hard to build, so they kept their warriors ready, just in case.

Now, centuries later, the winds of prophecy are whispering again, foretelling a time of danger and great change. *Perhaps*, say the whispers, *a sixth age is coming . . .*

1

KAYLA

Sophiatown

'Faro, *wait!*'

Kayla Karakka thundered along the narrow street in pursuit of her pangron, her leather boots smacking hard against the cobbles. Ahead of her, Faro was approaching the end of the street, where market sellers were setting up for the evening's celebrations. He was too big to squeeze comfortably between the stone wall and the stalls, but he showed no sign of decelerating.

'Slow down!' Kayla shouted. 'Faro, stop! You'll break something!'

But she was too late. As he turned the corner, Faro lost his balance, instinctively opening his wings to steady himself. His right wingtip clipped a large pot of spices, sending it crashing to the ground. Yellow powder cascaded over the cobbles.

The spice merchant shook his fist in the air. 'Whose pangron is that?' he shouted. 'You should have that beast under control!'

'Disgraceful,' agreed another. 'All pangrons should be safely locked away in the Academy.'

Kayla grimaced. She knew the rules. Pangrons were meant to be kept under close supervision, not running wild through the city. But Faro needed to stretch his legs and wings.

'He's mine,' she called. 'He didn't mean any harm. I'll pay you for the damage.' She pulled a money pouch from her belt and jogged up to the stall, handing the seller her two largest coins.

'A cadet,' he grumbled. 'Could've guessed it. You need to learn to keep your pangron in check. They're dangerous beasts – someone could get killed.'

Kayla bit her tongue and her hand went immediately to her necklace, a shard of the eggshell Faro had hatched from a year earlier strung on a length of brown leather. It wouldn't help to tell the merchant Faro was the gentlest, most loving creature she had ever known. The other citizens of Sophiatown only tolerated pangrons because they kept the city safe. They were weapons, not companions. Kayla did her best to pretend she felt the same way, but it was hard when Faro was the single most important thing in her life.

'Give her a break,' a nearby cloth seller chimed in.

'If we come under attack, you'll be glad to have our Sky Riders to protect you.'

'With discipline like that they'll be no good to anyone,' replied the spice merchant. He wagged a finger at Kayla. 'If I see your pangron loose again, I'll be telling your wing commander.'

Kayla hung her head. She knew he was right. She loved Faro's clumsiness and boundless enthusiasm, but if she was to improve her standing at the Sky Academy she would have to learn to control him in public. Being the daughter of a criminal was not an easy reputation to shake off. If news of this encounter got back to the Academy, Kayla would be in serious trouble. Wing Commander Barash already used any excuse to criticise Kayla and Faro, but a flagrant rule-breaking episode like this risked getting Kayla suspended, and that would mean losing Faro, which was simply not an option.

'Sorry,' Kayla mumbled. 'You're right. I'll send him back to the stables. It won't happen again.'

The merchant returned to his spices, shaking his head, and Kayla glanced around. Faro was out of sight now, but he had left a trail of yellow pawprints for her to follow. She raced past the rest of the market stalls, lungs burning with the exertion. She could hardly blame Faro for being excited. He had just spent three days locked in an underwater cave in the centre of the city. It contained a secret lake where the pangrons laid new eggs for Academy hopefuls. Earlier in the afternoon this year's prospective cadets had each been let into the cave to swim down and claim an egg of their own. Kayla had only been inside the cave once herself, during her own initiation this time last year. She remembered it to be a dark and mysterious place – for an animal used to flying every day, being shut down there for so long must have been torture. It hadn't been much fun for Kayla either; while her fellow cadets had sat around the watchtower playing cards and chatting, ignoring Kayla, she had taken to pacing the city walls, counting the minutes until Faro's return.

The pawprints led her through a tall archway into the city's walled gardens. On the grass, Faro was standing on all fours with his wings, which doubled as front legs, folded neatly by his sides. Kayla watched as he shook himself, releasing a cloud of dust from his shaggy red coat. He could do with a dip in the ocean to clean himself properly, but since the quarantine rules had come into effect, no one had been allowed to leave the city – even when flying.

As he swung his lean body vigorously from side to side, Faro's jowls flapped wildly, and a string of slobber flew in Kayla's direction, making her duck and squeal. At the sound of her voice, Faro looked over. His head was large and wide, covered in the same red fur as his body. When he saw Kayla, he reared up onto his powerful hind legs and unfolded his wide leathery wings. He looked enormous when he stretched himself like that. Usually Kayla's head reached just below his shoulder, but when he stood up he suddenly seemed about four times larger. Unlike the rest of his body, Faro's wings were totally hairless, the soft skin stretched so tightly over his bones you could see the pulsing of the veins beneath.

The merchant's worries hadn't been baseless; pangrons had the potential to be deadly predators. But Kayla didn't see Faro like that. She was far more interested in the soft dark fur of his belly, which she loved to rub after a long day of archery drills, the vibrations that rumbled through his deep chest as he purred by the fire and the weight of his head as he snored on her lap. Of course, Faro had a powerful arsenal of weaponry at his disposal – sharp teeth and powerful jaws, a whip-like tail and razor-sharp talons – but those things did not define him any more than Kayla's knucklebow defined her.

'You have to stop running off like that,' she said, pushing her right hand into the thick fur of his neck and giving him a scratch. 'We'll get into serious trouble.'

Faro turned to look at her, his golden eyes sparkling mischievously. He lowered his head, as if asking her to stroke between his ears, but when she leaned in he gently headbutted her in the stomach, knocking her onto her bottom.

'Faro!' she protested, swatting him away. He pushed back, leaning over her and giving out a loud snort of hot, stinky air. 'Eugh, fish breath.' She grimaced as he ran his huge bristly tongue over her face, covering her in pangron drool. 'You could have at least cleaned your teeth.'

She didn't really mind, of course. She had spent the first twelve years of her life desperate to have a pangron of her own. Perhaps because of the tales her mother had whispered to her by candlelight when she was young, of

9

incredible sky beasts, freely roaming the skies, or maybe it was simply the desire to have someone she could rely on. Whatever the motivation, now that she had Faro, she wasn't going to take a second of it for granted.

He gave a deep, rumbling purr.

'I missed you too.' She rubbed his cheek roughly with her fingertips. Faro was Kayla's best – and only – friend. She couldn't imagine what her life would be like if she hadn't passed her initiation last year. Getting here hadn't been an easy journey. Considering who Kayla's mother was, nobody had wanted Kayla to succeed. But despite the obstacles the Academy had put in her way, last year Kayla had been one of the fastest hopefuls to retrieve a pangron egg from the Great Lake, and so she was enrolled as a Sky Cadet in Sophiatown's prestigious Sky Academy. Two moons later, Faro had hatched, and now he and Kayla were inseparable. Attitudes to Kayla within the Academy were still frosty, but she was determined to prove she and Faro deserved their places there as much as any other pair.

Kayla pushed Faro off and leaped to her feet. She had promised to take him back to the stables – and she would – but she felt sure they had time for a quick flight first. They wouldn't be long. The Initiation Day celebrations would be starting soon – and wouldn't let up until the end of Vanquish Day tomorrow.

'Are you ready?' she asked. Stupid question. Faro had been ready the moment she had picked him up from the cave.

He took a step backwards and dipped his head, inviting his rider to climb aboard. Kayla ran her hand gently along the mottled chestnut fur of his neck, leaned her weight into his body and swung her right leg deftly over his shoulder. As she tucked her heels under Faro's wings and grabbed his scruff, Kayla felt her body instantly relax. This was so familiar, so comfortable. While she was riding Faro she didn't need to worry about making friends or being expelled from the Academy. She could simply exist.

Faro took a few short paces, then Kayla shifted her weight forward and his gait changed once more. With a couple of bounds he was in the sky, his huge wings spread wide, cutting easily through the crisp air. As they rose, the Viridian Sea came into sight – wide and green. If only they were allowed to fly beyond the city walls.

Buzzzzz.

A small winged hexapod zipped past them, dazzling sapphire wings glinting in the fading sun. It brushed by Kayla's ear then darted in front of her. Kayla pressed her heels gently into Faro's sides, nudging him to chase it. He understood immediately and shot upwards in pursuit.

The hexapod changed direction, darting suddenly to the right, but Faro didn't miss a beat. Kayla leaned into the turn, watching the gap between her pangron and the hexapod grow smaller and smaller. It was almost too easy. There was no creature in all the Realms that could fly like a pangron.

She wondered briefly if the phaegras of legend would

have given them some competition. Presumably not, considering it was the Sky Riders who had wiped the phaegras out in the first place. At the Academy, Kayla had learned how the first Sky Riders had captured pangrons and domesticated them, before using them to fly up to the phaegras' treetop nests and destroy them. Thanks to the valiant efforts of those early Sky Riders, Sophiatown and the rest of the realms were now safe from all beasts.

Faro closed in on the hexapod and Kayla imagined herself as one of those original riders, tearing through the sky in pursuit of a phaegra. She reached out a hand to snatch the hexapod from the air. Not quite close enough. She urged Faro on, stretching her arm as far as she could reach. Her fingertips brushed the fly's buzzing wings. It was almost within her grasp –

'Sky Cadet Karakka, descend immediately!'

The shout from below broke Kayla's attention. *Don't look down*, she thought to herself. Wing Major Flynn, her flying instructor, was forever reminding Kayla to 'look forward, stay focused, align with your pangron'. But it was too late. Her automatic reaction to turn towards the source of the sound had made Faro slow down, unable to read her instructions. The hexapod zipped away out of sight and Kayla cursed under her breath.

She leaned forward, peeking through the gap between Faro's wing and his head, to see a woman in uniform, with a grey-furred pangron at her side, waiting in the walled garden below. Wing Commander Barash. Kayla gave an inward groan and shifted her weight, signalling to Faro to descend. He flapped his wings and turned a loose, lazy circle as he returned to the ground.

Commander Barash's hands were on her hips and she was tapping her foot impatiently. She wore the traditional Sky Rider uniform of leather riding trousers and purple jacket. Her hair was pulled into an immaculate bun. When Kayla graduated from the Academy she would be granted her own purple jacket, but for now she wore the yellow of the cadets. Kayla pulled awkwardly at her jacket's tails, wishing she had pressed it that morning. She didn't want her wing commander to have *another* reason to criticise her.

As Faro landed neatly on the grass, Kayla slipped off his back and stood to attention, raising two fingers to her temple in salute. 'Ma'am.'

'No flying today,' Commander Barash said sternly.

'Why?' Kayla protested. 'The initiation ceremony finished hours ago!'

'I gave you an order,' snapped the woman. 'Back to your quarters immediately. There's a citywide curfew.' She glanced at Faro. 'And stable your pangron until further instruction.'

Citywide curfew? Kayla had never known that to happen before.

'But when will we –'

'So many questions,' Commander Barash interrupted. 'Just like your mother.'

Kayla felt her face flush. She was *nothing* like her

mother. She gritted her teeth and stared defiantly back.

Commander Barash narrowed her eyes. 'To the stables,' she repeated. 'Now.'

Kayla saluted and responded with a polite 'yes, ma'am', but it took all her self-control to do so. She marched back down the cobbled path towards the Academy, Faro padding quietly behind her, until they were back at the marketplace, where he headbutted her in the bottom.

'Thanks for that, fluff brain,' Kayla said. Faro rubbed himself along her side, purring noisily. He knew she wasn't happy. 'It's just not fair.' She scratched his cheek. 'We haven't been flying for days. And why can't Commander Barash see that I'm nothing like my mother? I'm not trying to change anything about the Academy, or the way we use our pangrons. I'm just trying to fit in! It's like she's constantly waiting for me to slip up.'

She leaned into his body and sighed, taking comfort from his purrs, which rumbled right through her. As they stood there together, Kayla realised that the marketplace was unusually – eerily – quiet. When she had been here earlier it had been bustling with people, but now there was nobody. Candles flickered in the evening breeze, casting shadows over the empty stalls. Where had everyone gone? Was this to do with the curfew?

In the distance a bell tolled. Kayla's heart pounded. That was the emergency signal for Sky Riders to patrol the city, all cadets knew that, but outside of practice drills, Kayla had never heard it ring. Had something happened? Was that why she wasn't allowed to go flying?

Maybe one of the other realms was attacking!

She led Faro quickly through the deserted marketplace, passing the now-unattended spice stand, its grumpy merchant nowhere to be seen. Yellow footsteps crisscrossed the cobbles, suggesting the sellers had left the square in a hurry. They headed down a narrow alley, Kayla now keen to get back to the safety of the Academy, until a gust of wind whistled by, carrying voices. Faro's ears flicked up, swivelling in search of the sound. They stopped as whispered words swirled around them.

'. . . can't be true . . .'

'. . . on Initiation Day of all days . . .'

Then words that struck fear into Kayla's heart: '. . . a pangron . . . missing.'

Her blood ran cold. How could a pangron be missing? They'd all been underground for three days and had only been released an hour ago.

More whispers drifted down the alley.

'I heard it was stolen . . .'

Stolen? Surely not. Sophiatown was the most fiercely guarded city in all the Realms. There were no greater warriors than its Sky Riders. Besides, it didn't seem possible that a pangron could be taken against its will. Something didn't add up.

'You're not sleeping in the stables tonight,' Kayla whispered as she turned back to Faro. 'Come with me.' She darted down another alley, glancing nervously around to check they hadn't been spotted.

The Academy handbook was clear that pangrons

should spend every night in the Academy stables, but Faro almost never did. And if there was a chance the pangrons were in danger, there was no way Kayla was letting him out of her sight.

At the end of the alley they approached a huge heap of barrels piled next to a basement door. The distillery – a building Kayla knew all too well, even better than the Academy watchtower where she now lived with the other cadets. After her mum had been imprisoned when Kayla was nine, she'd needed a place to live and a way to earn her keep, somewhere that would give her the best chance of getting into the Academy. Luckily, Padrig Shion, the city's Master Distiller, had given Kayla a job. He had worked her hard but treated her fairly and paid her enough to survive until she had passed the Initiation. She'd spent many an evening hauling barrels through this very door, her eyes always lingering on the towering spires of the Academy over the road.

They were so close – if they could make it across the street without being caught they would be safely back at home.

But suddenly Faro lurched forward, grabbing the tails of Kayla's flying jacket and yanking her into the shadows.

Moments later, a voice rang out. 'I'm just going to check down here. I thought I heard something.'

Kayla turned desperately to Faro, worried he would be seen, but he had already melted into the evening shadows. Kayla pushed herself back against the barrels, hardly daring to breathe. She watched as a city guard took a few steps down the alley then retreated, calling out to his squadron, 'Must have been a mudrat. There's nothing there.'

'Thanks, boy,' Kayla whispered. If they had been caught, the guards would have forced Faro to go back to the stables. 'Wait here.' She gestured that he should stay. 'I'll check the coast is clear. Listen for my signal.'

She scurried past the barrels and poked her head out into the street. A group of guards lingered by the corner, deep in conversation.

'It's the prince's pangron, you know?' one of them said.

Kayla's eyes almost popped out of her head. Prince Ethun was in her year at the Academy. His slender tawny pangron, Ezra, was guarded by the palace's own personal security.

'It never returned from the cave.'

'Some people are saying it contracted the Scourge and the palace is trying to cover it up.'

Rumours about the Scourge, a sickness said to have been spreading through the other realms, had been bouncing around for a while now. Sophiatown had quarantined immediately and there hadn't been a single case inside its walls as a result. Kayla's city had always been selective about who was allowed in and out, but for the last year not a soul had passed through its gates. Even fully fledged Sky Riders had been forbidden from landing outside the walls so they wouldn't catch the Scourge and bring it into Sophiatown.

'I heard the pangron was taken from *inside the city*,' said another. 'That's why they've imposed a curfew. They think the thief is still on the loose.'

Kayla fought to remain calm. A thief in the city? She urgently needed to get Faro into the watchtower, but how in the Realms was she meant to do that with a bunch of guards stood right outside? She hurried back to Faro.

'Bad news,' she said quietly. 'There's no chance we're getting you home that way. We'll have to think of something else.'

Her pangron looked at her with his big golden eyes, and Kayla felt a pang in her chest. Sometimes it was actually painful to love something as much as she loved Faro. How could the other cadets have left their pangrons in the stables? After three days of separation, Kayla didn't want to spend another second apart from him.

She tore her eyes away from her pangron and once again noticed the wooden barrels stacked up outside the distillery. A thought took shape and her skin prickled with excitement. 'I have an idea. Come on!'

2

ALETHEA

Ataria

Alethea Bashoa sat cross-legged on a mat in the Blue District's House of Healing. As she carefully ground rockwood leaves, a young girl watched, slipping into her father's shadow whenever Alethea looked in her direction. The girl and her father had walked for almost an hour to reach Alethea, across rough volcanic terrain peppered with bubbling lava lakes and towering rock columns. It was a long way to travel, but the girl was injured and Alethea was the only healer in the district.

'Lay your head here,' Alethea said to the girl, patting a blue cushion on her lap. 'I'm going to take out your plaits so I can get a better look at the wound.'

'But the webspinners . . .' Panic flitted across the girl's

face and she looked anxiously at her dad. 'Without the cloth I'll have nothing to keep them away.'

The man took his daughter's hand and encouraged her to do as she was told. Alethea gave him an approving nod.

'It's OK,' she said, stroking the girl's hair. 'The webspinners hate the smell of this –' she held up the bowl containing the rockweed paste – 'just as much as they hate the lava mud.'

Like all Atarians, Alethea, the girl and her father had brightly coloured cloths braided into their hair. Alethea gently untied the girl's intricate plait and pulled out a frayed piece of blue cloth. It smelled of fire and rotten vulcanwing eggs, like the lava lakes the city was built around. It was said that the volcanic minerals of the lakes were protective, and for as long as people had lived in Ataria they had dyed cloths in the waters to use for everything from cushions and bedding to clothing and braids. Most recently they had been promised that the smell of the minerals would ward off the obsidian webspinners, whose terrible bite was said to spread the Scourge.

Alethea had never seen an obsidian webspinner in the city – in fact she'd never seen one anywhere. The enormous webspinners lived in the Turquoise Jungle on the slopes of Mount Ataria, out in the Beastlands, and had long been feared by the Atarian citizens. But recently, with so many dying of the Scourge, that fear had intensified. People were not taking any chances and had started covering every inch of their houses and bodies in dyed cloth.

In the Blue District, so named for the colour of its bright lakes, everyone wore dazzling azure clothes and braids, but other districts had different colours; their immediate neighbours in the Pink District wore cloth as pink as ashflowers, those that lived by the croplands wore green, the sacred silver of the holy lakes was worn by the city's leaders, the Ash Bishops, and of course the Scorched Ataris' clothes and braids were bright red.

Alethea cast the cloth from the girl's braid aside. She tried to remember when she had last changed the cloth in her own braids, or those of any of her family. It had been a long time. Perhaps she could do it next week. That said, she wasn't entirely sure how much difference the cloths actually made, or if the webspinners ever truly ventured into the city, so she wouldn't lose sleep over it. It would be nice to spend some time with her siblings though. Since the Scourge had arrived she had been so busy in the House of Healing she hardly saw them.

She uncovered the girl's wound. It was large but not deep. A burn from a fissure eruption – one of the perils of living in a dormant volcano. Luckily the lava was less active on the outskirts of the city, so burns weren't frequent in the Blue District. Unfortunately, though, the bardflies preferred the cooler lava here and liked to buzz around, laying their eggs in the blue lakes. The flies were about the only things in the city that showed a preference for the blue zone– as far as everyone else was concerned, it was the dirtiest, poorest, most undesirable district, and the people who lived there weren't much better.

To Alethea, who had come to know people from across the entire district, this label was grossly unfair. But such was the way of life in Ataria: blue at the bottom.

The girl's wound was superficial and would soon heal as long as it didn't get infected. Alethea made a poultice of rockweed paste, just as her da had shown her. The girl gave a little squeal as the herbs seeped into the wound. Good, that meant they were doing their job. Alethea's fingers moved quickly to secure the poultice with a bandage, well practised from the thousands of dressings she had tied over years working as Da's assistant.

'Come back tomorrow,' she said as she helped the girl up. 'I'll change the dressing and check how it's healing.'

'Tomorrow?' said the girl. 'But tomorrow's Vanquish Day! I want to watch the Scorching.'

Alethea looked into the girl's hopeful eyes. She was probably only a few years younger than Alethea herself, but there seemed a chasm between them. Personally, Alethea couldn't understand the fuss around the Scorching, but she knew that for many the ceremony to initiate new warriors into the Atarian army was the highlight of their year.

'In that case, why don't you come by and see me after it's finished?' Alethea said with a kind smile.

'After? But we'll be at the feast,' said the girl's father. 'Can't we come the next day?'

Da used to say, 'As a healer, it's my job to tell patients what they *need* to hear, not what they *want* to hear.' Alethea knew this meant healers must sometimes be strict with their patients in order to help them. But was this one of those times? She still had so much to learn, and Da wasn't here to help her with those decisions now. She pondered it for a second. The girl's wound wasn't deep or infected and an extra day would probably have little effect on the progress of its healing.

'All right,' Alethea said, thinking of how excited her own siblings were for the celebrations. 'But come here first thing the following morning.'

She hoped she had made the right call.

'Thank you!' The little girl jumped to her feet, already looking brighter than when she'd arrived. 'We love the feast, don't we, Daddy?'

'That we do, sunshine. That we do.' He stroked her head gently and turned to Alethea. 'Thank you for everything, Miss Bashoa,' he said. 'Your da would be very proud.'

Tears sprang to the corners of Alethea's eyes.

'I knew him,' the girl's father continued. 'He was a good man.'

Alethea swallowed. She was still getting used to 'was' instead of 'is'. She rose and ushered them to the door. The man lingered on the threshold, opening a pouch on his belt to remove a handful of something he pressed into Alethea's hand.

'These are for you,' he said, and she felt something dribble down her wrist. She lifted her hand to see a trail of purple juice disappearing up her sleeve. Lavaberries.

'Where did you get these?' Alethea whispered, looking

23

around nervously as she emptied them into a pouch of her own. With so many people sick from the Scourge, most of their crops had failed earlier in the year, and fresh fruit was hard to come by. Atarians were assigned rations at the end of every week, but that was still four days away and they rarely got anything as extravagant as lavaberries.

'Don't worry about that,' the man said with a wink. 'It's the very least I can do. You keep up the good work. The district relies on you now.'

Until her father's death Alethea had just been an extra pair of hands, but now he was gone she had taken over as primary healer. Despite the lessons he had taught her, she still felt totally out of her depth most of the time. But if Blues didn't look out for one another, who would take care of them? It wasn't like the Ash Bishops cared what was happening in the Blue District. Despite their claims to be fair and just rulers, as long as the Reds and Silvers were fed and cared for, the people in charge were perfectly content to overlook the misfortune of the other districts.

'Thank you.'

Alethea imagined her siblings' faces on seeing the delicious purple fruits. Little Digby had never even tasted lavaberries before. And Ma . . . Well, maybe this would be the thing to finally put a smile on her face.

After saying goodbye to the man and his daughter, Alethea retired to the herb larder, which doubled as her office, where she set about tidying the baskets of plants she used for her work. Even in good times there had only been enough space in the croplands to grow a limited number of non-food plants, but with this year's poor crop, her larder was barer than ever. She noticed with a sigh that the firewort was beginning to wilt.

'Blast it,' she said.

Firewort was a rare plant in the tasselbaggia family. Its strong stems were used to make weapons and cooking utensils. Its flowers had round orange bladders with long tendrilous petals, and it was very difficult to grow. Like many Atarian plants, this year's firewort crop had almost entirely failed. Usually Alethea wouldn't be too worried – firewort wasn't a plant she and Da had often used in their healing – but last week Alethea had had something of a breakthrough.

For over a year now, the citizens of Ataria had been plagued by the Scourge. It started small – a puncture wound surrounded by itchy concentric rings on the skin – but soon progressed to fever, vomiting and ultimately death. The exact time it took to run its course varied, but the final outcome was always the same. Da had survived almost three weeks before finally succumbing to the illness, but many other Atarians only lasted days. Before his death six moons ago Da had been desperate to find a cure, and Alethea had carried on that work ever since. She had tried countless salves, tinctures and balms, but to no avail.

Until last week, when a young boy named Tommo had come to her with a fresh Scourge wound and she had decided to apply the liquid from the bladder of a firewort flower. As well as sloughing away the damaged skin, it seemed to have neutralised the toxin. Days later, Tommo showed no symptoms at all. Alethea had been delighted by the success but had soon realised it was limited, because when she tried using the same technique on a patient whose wound was more advanced, the woman had not been saved. Alethea suspected the Scourge had already travelled too far into her body. Firewort clearly wasn't a cure for all cases, but it was the most progress Alethea had made so far, and she was keen to experiment with the plant further.

Turning back to her desk, Alethea glanced at her botany textbook: *A Healer's Guide to the Flora of Ramoa*. It was growing late, she should go home, but she hadn't had a chance to read at all today. How could she expect to find a cure for the Scourge if she didn't keep searching? *Just a couple of pages*, she told herself. *For Da*.

She would start with the entry on firewort. She had read it before, but maybe there was something important she had missed.

Firewort
Member of the tasselbaggia family

Tall herb growing to several strides in height. Has a single stem, scythe-shaped thorns and narrow paired leaves. Grows in volcanic soils, particularly where lava and ash have recently fallen. Begins to bloom in late summer and has bell-shaped orange flowers that may last for many moons. Round bladders directly below the flowers attract hexapods, which, once caught, are digested by the liquid inside.

Leaves: Blood thinner when taken orally.

Stems: Hard and woody. Can be dried and used in building.

Roots: No known medicinal benefit.

Bladders: Contain rich digestive fluid with a strong spicy scent. Useful in removing necrotic or infected tissue. Do not apply to healthy skin.

Only one other plant was listed in the tasselbaggia family: frostwort.

Frostwort
Member of the tasselbaggia family

Native to cold alpine areas, usually at high altitude. Blooms only at temperatures below freezing. Has a single stem, scythe-shaped thorns and paired lance-shaped leaves. Spiky white flower heads with rings of white petals are highly attractive to flying hexapods. Round bladders directly below the flowers contain a liquid that is used to digest small beasts trapped inside.

Leaves: Muscle relaxant and antidote to hypnos snake venom.

Stems: No known medicinal benefit.

Roots: Diuretic with a potent effect on cardiac muscle, causing the heart to beat more strongly.

Bladders: Contain rich digestive fluid with a sweet and spicy scent. Do not apply to healthy skin.

Despite living in vastly different habitats, the similarities between firewort and frostwort were obvious. Alethea wondered if frostwort would work on the Scourge in the same way as firewort. Or perhaps – her stomach gave a little flutter – it would be able to do what the firewort had not been able to: cure all cases, no matter what stage the disease. Not that it really mattered. Frostwort only survived in cold temperatures, so it wouldn't grow anywhere near Ataria. When her firewort ran out, Alethea would have to find another way to treat the Scourge.

She closed the book and rose to her throbbing feet. She had been working since sunrise and really wanted to see her little brothers and sisters before she fell into bed.

As she made her way out of her office, she ran a finger along one of the cracks that criss-crossed the stone wall. The people of her district were too busy trying to protect themselves from the Scourge and feed their families to think about caring for the public buildings, but Alethea was concerned. Where would she treat her patients if the House of Healing collapsed? In the morning she would send another message to the Ash Bishops about the cracks. Not that she expected any reply.

She was still staring at the wall when a voice from behind caused her to jump in alarm.

'Alethea Bashoa?'

Alethea turned, and gasped as she saw who had spoken. The brilliant sheen of the woman's silvery clothes made everything around her look dirty in comparison. An Ash Bishop. Alethea's hand went automatically to the pouch on her belt, where she had hidden the berries. She shoved the pouch nervously into her dungaree pocket.

'You *are* Alethea Bashoa?' the Ash Bishop repeated.

'Sorry,' said Alethea quickly. 'Yes, I am. How can I help you?'

'Can we sit down?' the woman said, inclining her head towards the herb larder. Two plaits interwoven with silver cascaded over her shoulders.

'Of course.' Alethea held the door open for her to enter. What was going on? Alethea had never seen an Ash Bishop in this part of the city before. Something serious must have happened. It couldn't be about the lavaberries, could it? She'd only just been given them. And surely a handful of stolen berries wasn't that serious a crime. She took a steadying breath, then followed the Ash Bishop inside as confidently as she could.

'Will we be disturbed?' the woman asked. Alethea shook her head. 'Very good.' She indicated that Alethea should sit, so she did.

'I've been watching you for a while,' the Ash Bishop said. 'You're a competent healer. Last week you cured a boy of the Scourge, did you not?'

Alethea swallowed. It was true that Tommo had survived, but to call it a cure was a bit of a stretch. After all, it hadn't worked when she'd tried it again. 'Not exactly,' she said.

'Then my sources are wrong and the patient died?'

Alethea fought to stop her brain from drifting into memories of Da lying in this very room, covered in leaves and poultices. 'No,' she said, 'he's alive. But he was in the very earliest stages when I –'

'Alethea,' the Ash Bishop interrupted, 'let me be clear. We don't have much time. The Scourge is ravaging our troops. Our army is dwindling and we are in desperate need of a solution. We have consulted seven healers from across the districts and your patient is the first person in the whole of Ataria bitten by an obsidian webspinner to live to tell the tale. We need to know how it happened.'

Alethea's heart raced. She had often wondered how the other districts had been coping with the outbreak. She'd thought perhaps the Silvers had already found a cure, as she hadn't heard of any of them dying.

'It was a very specific case,' Alethea said. 'The wound was fresh, the rash had barely spread –'

'What did you use?' the Ash Bishop interrupted.

'Firewort,' said Alethea. 'A salve of firewort applied directly to the wound.'

'Do you have more?'

'A little,' said Alethea, indicating the dwindling pile behind her. 'Though it's starting to wilt.'

'Excellent. I'll take it,' said the Ash Bishop, moving towards the plant.

'Take it?' Alethea rose from her seat in shock. 'All of it? But it belongs to the Blue District. I need it for my patients.'

'Our need is greater,' said the Ash Bishop curtly. 'The Scorched Ataris must protect us from the webspinners, otherwise the whole city will fall to the Scourge. They must be treated first.'

Alethea stared open-mouthed as the woman gathered up the firewort greedily. Once she'd tied it all in a bundle, she turned back to Alethea. 'Your city thanks you, Alethea Bashoa. You have done a great service to its people today.'

What about my *people?* Alethea thought. *The people of the Blue District.*

But she didn't dare defy an Ash Bishop, so she simply watched as the woman made her way out the door with her entire supply of firewort. As soon as she was gone, Alethea realised she had never even asked her about the cracks.

Sadly Alethea closed up the House of Healing, wondering what Da would have done in her situation. He would have been angry, sure, but not defeated. One of his favourite sayings had been: 'We cannot choose how the ash falls, only what we build with it.' But what could Alethea possibly build now, with all her firewort gone?

Across Ataria, the evening prayer bells started to toll. The Ash Bishops would soon lead the central districts in evening worship. Together they would pray to the Ash Gods who had created their city. But to Alethea the sound signalled something else: her siblings would now be fast asleep.

As she made her way home, Alethea edged around a gurgling blue lake where a cloud of steam belched from the water, sending a spatter of blue mud across the path. Next to it, on the uneven lavastone, she spotted a single orange flower. Firewort! The Ash Bishop must have dropped it in her hurry. Alethea stooped to pick it up. The bladder was empty.

Her emotions swelled as she looked across the surface of the lava, which was a haze of sulphurous smoke. She thought of the suka-moss nose plugs jammed up her nostrils, blocking the worst of the smell. The plugs were one of Da's ideas, and lots of people in their district made use of them. He'd always had a botanical solution for every problem. If he were still here, she had no doubt he would have found one for the Scourge too. If only he'd had more time . . .

But Da wasn't here now, Alethea reminded herself, and nor was the firewort, there was no point dwelling on it. Blues were still dying of the Scourge and if anyone was going to help them it sure as Ash wouldn't be the leaders of the city, so it was down to Alethea to find another solution.

She picked herself up and forged on to her cave house. When she finally made it to her front door, a fire gecko on the door frame caught her eye. As she approached it scuttled up the rock column and out of sight. Above the door a banner fluttered. In the wonky handwriting of her siblings it said: *Happee Burfday Aleethya*.

In all the strange events of the last week she had totally forgotten. Maybe her siblings would forgive her for missing the celebrations when she shared the lavaberries with them tomorrow morning. She pulled out the pouch and peered inside. More bad news. The berries had been squashed on her hurried journey and were now nothing but a congealed handful of mush.

3

RUSTUS

Ataria

Rustus Furi crept through the Beastlands, spear in hand, his thoughts dominated by the Scorching. Tomorrow, he would graduate from being an Unscorched, a boy whose place in the world was unproven and uncertain, to being Scorched, an esteemed warrior of the Atarian army. Tomorrow, he would climb the tallest rock column in the city, hoping to be fast enough to avoid the streams of scorching ash and gas that spewed from its centre.

All Scorched Ataris went through the Scorching ceremony; some even chose to complete it more than once, making them Twice or Thrice Scorched. Rustus, in particular, had a lot to live up to; both of his elder brothers had scaled Kahanga Rock multiple times. Octus

34

had completed the Scorching five times – matching the record set by their father, Brutus. And Tactus had been the fastest of his cohort to complete the climb on each of his four ascents.

'Don't embarrass me,' Rustus's father had muttered quietly that afternoon before Rustus had left their cave house in the Red District for the Scorching Eve hunting ceremony. 'You're a Furi. There's a certain expectation that comes with that.'

'Of course not, Dad,' Rustus had replied, but his dad hadn't heard him. He had been too busy with his other sons, laughing jovially at some joke one of them had made. He never laughed with Rustus. None of them did. Since Mum had left the Red District a few years after Rustus's birth, no one in his family had shown him much kindness. He was sure that would change if he was successful tomorrow though.

Thoughts of the Scorching and how he could ensure he would be the fastest to complete the climb had consumed all of Rustus's recent thoughts. And this afternoon he had had a lot of time to think. Along with his peers, Rustus had marched the long route from the Red District, up over the rim of the caldera, through the city gates and down the slopes into the Beastlands. It was the Unscorched recruits' first time stepping outside the city, and as Rustus took in the wilderness surrounding him, his thoughts were wrenched from the trial that lay ahead.

Rustus's brothers had told him plenty of terrifying stories about their patrols in the Beastlands. He himself had stared out over the untamed land countless times on lookout duty; from above it was easy to underestimate the jungle – everything looked much smaller from that perspective. But now, deep inside, it was Rustus who felt small, dwarfed by the towering turquoise trees that spread as far as the eye could see. Despite its size, the jungle closed in tight around him and he could sense that unknown beasts lurked in every shadow. It was disconcerting, but surprisingly exhilarating too. Above him, silk strands of web criss-crossed the trees, glimmering silver and pink as the sun flickered through them – a stark contrast to the bare rock of Ataria.

'What was that?' said Hubert, the smallest of their Unscorched band, pulling Rustus out of his thoughts. The boy slapped at something on the back of his neck, panic in his eyes. 'Is something on me?'

Rustus moved Hubert's long black plait to one side and checked the back of his neck for bugs or webspinners. Hubert's plait was woven through with red cloth from the lakes of the Red District, which should theoretically ward off all unwanted beasts, but Rustus understood why Hubert was nervous. The feeling of danger was heightened out here in the wild. Back in Ataria there were few beasts and the air was still; they could see for miles around them. Here in the jungle though there was a constant aura of threat. They could not see further than an arm's length away and they were expecting webspinners at every turn – the fact that they hadn't yet seen any somehow made it worse.

'Nothing there,' Rustus said. 'It's all in your head.' If he wasn't so overcome with worry about disappointing his father, Rustus might have been just as concerned about the jungle beasts, but he had to complete this hunting expedition to be allowed to enter the Scorching tomorrow – and no beast was as terrifying as the thought of what his father would say if he failed to become a Scorched Atari.

'It's not in my head,' Hubert protested. 'There are bugs everywhere. Look!' Hubert pointed to a nearby web, where a worm as long as Rustus's arm wriggled pathetically against the threads that restrained it. Rustus took a step towards the creature to get a closer look, but Hubert pulled him away. 'Stop it! Don't go any closer. The webspinners are probably waiting to pounce. Come on – let's catch up with the others.'

They pushed their way under a web that was half covering the path.

'This is horrible.' Hubert wiped sweat from his brow. The air felt different here too; in Ataria the heat was dry and dusty, but here in the jungle the air seemed to stick to you, warm and humid like a clammy blanket. 'I hope we find these things quickly, so we can fight them and go home.'

'We don't have to fight them,' said Rustus. 'Tactus said if you just spear them through the back of the head then it's over within seconds.' He grimaced a little. When his brother first told him about the pre-Scorching ritual, the thought had turned his stomach. Of course he didn't want to kill a webspinner, but he *had* to climb that tower.

'Easy if you're a Furi,' said Hubert, eyebrows furrowed. 'I don't think I have the strength for it.'

'I don't want to do it either,' said Rustus. 'I don't see why we can't just leave the webspinners alone and focus on the climb.'

'What did you say, Furi?'

Rustus's stomach dropped. They'd caught back up to the group and their instructor, Scorch Knight Itticus, must have overheard them. He spun towards them, plaits whirling. Each braid had two obsidian beads threaded into the bottom, one to mark each successful Scorching, and they glinted in the snatches of sunlight that broke through the canopy. 'You don't see the point in killing the webspinners?'

Rustus swallowed.

'The mighty Furi here has forgotten the importance of culling the webspinners,' Scorch Knight Itticus announced to everyone. 'Anyone care to remind him why our job is so important?'

Aro, a lithe, strong girl who Rustus thought would probably be the first to the top tomorrow, put her hand up eagerly. 'The Scorched Ataris are the sworn protectors of Ataria,' she said. 'They defend the city and its people from any threats they may face.' Scorch Knight Itticus nodded approvingly as she went on. 'We must remind the beasts of the island that *we* are the ones to be feared, not them.'

'Excellent, Aro,' said Scorch Knight Itticus.

'It's not like the webspinners come up into the city though,' Rustus countered. 'Maybe if the Scorched stopped coming into the Beastlands and disturbing them . . .'

Scorch Knight Itticus shot him a furious look.

'Of course they come into the city,' said Aro. 'Otherwise how would they give everyone the Scourge?'

Rustus didn't have an answer. He'd spent an entire year in training, doing perimeter walks and night watches, and not once had he seen an obsidian webspinner. But everyone else, even Hubert, was nodding in agreement.

'Are you scared of killing a webspinner, Furi?' Scorch Knight Itticus mocked.

Rustus shook his head. Scared wasn't the right word. He didn't fear what was ahead, he just didn't *want* to do it. He would happily protect the people of his city, but he wished he didn't have to kill anything in the process. Unfortunately, that was a necessary part of the ritual, and so he tried to push his thoughts to one side and concentrate on how proud his brothers and father would be when he came home and told them he had passed the first part of the Scorching.

'Well, why don't you prove it?' said the instructor. 'I think we've gone far enough. Everyone, have a drink and a quick break. You're going to need it for what's ahead.'

Rustus felt his insides clench. There was no turning back now. He strode away from the group, hoping for a moment of quiet to gather his thoughts before the hunt began.

'Don't go too far, Rustus,' Scorch Knight Itticus called after him. 'You're going first.' As Rustus moved further away, he could just about hear his instructor add, 'We'll soon see what Furi Junior is made of.'

Rustus sank to the ground, placing his obsidian spear, forged in the sacred lava of the Silver District, by his side. He unscrewed his canteen. How did he always manage to say the wrong thing? Why couldn't he be more like his brothers, strutting around with confidence, flexing his muscles and making everyone laugh? He looked up as Hubert approached and patted the spot next to him to indicate that his friend should sit.

'I'm going to fail,' Hubert said morosely, pulling a fire melon from his pack. 'Even if I manage to kill a webspinner, I'll never get to the top of Kahanga Rock.'

As much as Rustus wanted to put his mind at rest and assure him he had nothing to worry about, he couldn't be entirely sure that Hubert *would* pass the initiation. Hubert was around half the size of Rustus and had all the courage of a skittery fire gecko.

'Don't say that,' said Rustus. 'He's just trying to scare us.'

'Well, it's working.' Hubert bit into the fruit, juice dribbling down his chin. 'It's impossible for you to understand. You're the fastest and strongest of all of us.'

Rustus shrugged. 'Try telling my dad that,' he said. 'I think he's expecting me to fail.'

'Not a hope,' said Hubert, a look of wonder lighting up his face. 'Can you imagine if you were faster than Tactus?'

'Wouldn't that be something!' Rustus forced out a hollow chuckle.

'I'm only joking,' said Hubert, nudging him. 'I know

you're not like them.' Understatement of the year. 'No one cares what order we get to the top in, as long as we get there.' He paused then added, 'You could definitely be first if you wanted to though – we all know that.'

Rustus closed his eyes. He wished it were true that nobody cared, but the fact was, it *did* matter. To his father, coming first was *all* that mattered. If Rustus didn't come first, he might as well not pass the Scorching at all. In fact, if he didn't come first, he might as well catch the Scourge. Rustus took a deep, calming breath and noticed the sulphurous stench of their hometown was less intense here.

'Don't you hate the smell of Ataria?' he asked.

Hubert sniffed. 'I dunno. Just smells like home to me.'

Rustus rubbed his nose. 'I can't stand it.' He closed one nostril with his finger and snorted down the other. A congealed lump of bright yellow snot splattered onto the dry earth beside him.

'Where's your handkerchief?' Aro was standing before them, arms crossed. Couldn't she leave him alone for five minutes?

'They've run out,' said Hubert. 'Haven't you heard? Cloth shortage in the Blue District because so many of them have died of the Scourge.'

'Well, the ones that are left should try working a bit harder,' she said. 'Typical Blues – they wouldn't know hard work if it slapped them in the face.'

Rustus rolled his eyes and repeated the snorting process on the other side. Aro was audibly disgusted.

'Stop it!' she shouted. 'It's just common decency.'

'No one asked you to come over here,' said Rustus. 'If you'd stayed over there with your best friend, Scorch Knight Itticus, then you wouldn't need to feel so offended. There's no law against nose-blowing, and I hate the thought of that stuff clogging up my insides. It can't be good for us.' He wished he could somehow plug up his nostrils to prevent the foul stench from entering. Why didn't anyone else seem as bothered by it as he was?

Aro shrugged. 'Doesn't seem to have done your brothers any harm. Not like them though, are you?' she said with a sneer. 'Bit more sensitive.' She rubbed her eyes as if she were crying.

'Nothing wrong with that,' said Hubert. 'Look, have you come over here for a reason or are you just –'

But Aro had already turned on her heel and stalked off.

'She's awful,' Hubert said with a shudder.

Behind Rustus, the vibrant trunks of the turquoise trees rustled and creaked. He looked around, scanning the webs for signs of an obsidian webspinner. He knew they were supposed to be scary, but the truth was they hadn't seen a single one yet despite passing hundreds of webs. The webspinners might have a deadly bite, but they didn't exactly seem desperate to use it.

Suddenly a silvery blue hexapod flew into the web ahead of him. The more it struggled, the more entangled it became. Just as Rustus began to think about rescuing it, a huge webspinner shot out from the depths of its web and grabbed the flying hexapod with its two front legs. Rustus leaped to his feet, his eyes going wide, and leaned towards the web, peering at the delicate markings on the webspinner's bulbous body, which was almost as long as Rustus's arm.

'Don't get so close,' hissed Hubert, tugging him back. 'Did you see how fast that thing moved?'

Rustus backed off a fraction but found he still wanted to look closer. The beast had eight smooth black legs, with two fist-sized eyes on the front of its head and six smaller ones, each around the size of a vulcanwing egg, sitting just behind them. Rustus was horrified and transfixed in equal measure.

'Isn't it beautiful?' he said.

'If by beautiful you mean deadly,' said Hubert, a trickle of sweat dribbling down his forehead, 'then yeah.'

'Look how carefully it's wrapping up its dinner.' Rustus was entranced. 'Do you think all webspinners like the taste of bugs?'

'What?' asked Hubert, dumbfounded by this line of thinking. 'I dunno. What's got into you?'

Rustus watched as the webspinner swaddled the large fly in thick grey strands of silk, twirling it expertly until the whole carcass was covered.

'Rustus, move back.' Without realising, Rustus had leaned in towards the web again. Hubert pulled him by the shoulder. 'I don't think webspinners really think about what they like or dislike. They're beasts. Pure instinct, aren't they?'

Rustus watched as the webspinner hung the parcel neatly in its web. 'Do you think they all have the instinct to catch flies, then?'

Hubert groaned. 'I don't know, Rustus. And I don't really care. Can you please move away from that thing before it turns its attention on us?'

Rustus was about to step away when movement from behind the web caught his eye. He grabbed Hubert's arm. 'Look!'

'What is it?'

Rustus squinted, trying to make out what he'd seen. He could have sworn it was a person, but they didn't have the distinctive red cloth and uniform of his fellow recruits. 'I think it's a webwalker.'

Unscorched recruits who failed the Scorching were cast out of Ataria to live in the Beastlands, and rumour had it many took up an unnatural residence in the jungle's webs, hence the name. Though now Rustus wasn't so sure – whatever he'd glimpsed before had gone.

'Don't say that,' said Hubert, shivering. 'That's bad luck, that is, to see a webwalker on Scorching Eve.'

'Don't be ridiculous.' Rustus moved closer to the web again, trying to peer through its strands.

'Will you stop getting so close to that web!' said Hubert, exasperated. 'You're practically sitting on that webspinner's lap. Besides, you're probably seeing things. There can't be any webwalkers left. They'll all have died of the Scourge by now.'

'Feeling better after your rest, Furi?' The voice startled

them. They spun around to see Scorch Knight Itticus standing right behind them. He was flanked by the rest of the group.

'Yes, sir,' Rustus replied, jumping away from the web.

'Good, because you're about to kill that webspinner.' He jabbed a calloused finger at the beast they had just been watching.

'Right,' Rustus said, glancing back at the webspinner and remembering why he was here in the first place. How had he let himself become so distracted from the important task ahead? The webspinner was sitting still in its web now, probably thinking about the delicious meal it had wrapped up for later. Rustus remembered what his brothers had told him about the first time they had killed an obsidian webspinner.

'Single shot to the back of the head,' Tactus had said simply. 'Send your spear straight through it.'

'Wrestle it to the ground, then break off its legs one by one,' Octus had said, rather more aggressively. 'Show it who's boss.'

It was hard to imagine inflicting such violence on a creature just minding its own business.

'Hurry up!' Scorch Knight Itticus barked. 'We haven't got all day.'

Rustus nodded, his throat growing tight. He didn't need to look behind him to know that the whole group had gathered to watch. His fingers started to tingle, loosening his grip on the obsidian spear in his hand.

Keep it together, Rustus, he told himself. *Do Dad proud.*

He lifted the spear above his head and pulled his arm back, fighting hard to stop his body from shaking.

'Not so clever now, are you, Furi?' the instructor jeered.

Rustus gritted his teeth.

'Come on, Rustus!' shouted Hubert. 'You can do it!'

Then, to Rustus's surprise, all of his fellow Unscorched joined in. Although Aro's voice was notably absent among the crowd.

'Rustus! Rustus! Rustus!'

Buoyed by the encouragement, he threw the spear with all his might. It flew through the air promisingly, but then glanced off the webspinner's swollen abdomen and clattered through the web behind. Though it was wounded by the blow, the webspinner was not killed and instead shot defensively from its web towards where they all stood. Hubert shrieked and stumbled to the ground in his desperation to get away from the beast.

Rustus, realising he had put the group in danger, leaped onto the webspinner and stamped on its head with one forceful blow. It stopped moving immediately.

The instructor curled his top lip. 'All right,' he said. 'Not the most graceful I've seen, but you got the job done.' He pushed the webspinner's body off the path with his foot, leaving a trail of orange goo behind.

Rustus stared at the body in disbelief. Moments before it had been a living, breathing beast. He had watched it gracefully and expertly prepare its next meal – a meal it would now never get to eat. He felt sick to the pit of his stomach. His brothers talked proudly of the rush they had felt after killing the webspinners, but Rustus felt nothing of the sort. He just felt hollow, numb.

'Out of the way, Furi,' said Scorch Knight Itticus, giving him a shove. 'Who's next?'

Rustus stumbled away from the webspinner, trying to hide his disgust at what he had done. The group looked at one another nervously, no one keen to repeat the spectacle they had just observed. Eventually Aro raised her hand and their instructor led them through more trees until he found another occupied web, this one with a much smaller webspinner, which Aro killed easily. One by one, the rest of the group completed the ritual, until only Hubert was left.

'You can do it,' Rustus whispered as his friend stepped forward. He wanted Hubert to pass the initiation almost as much as he wanted to pass it himself. Their mothers had been best friends and they had grown up together since they were babies. He couldn't imagine being Scorched without Hubert by his side – and yet he was ashamed to admit that a part of him hoped another beast wouldn't have to die. That one of the poor creatures would escape.

They were back by the spot where Rustus had killed his webspinner, and Scorch Knight Itticus had tasked Hubert with a webspinner that was almost as big, but in a much more difficult position, half buried in its thick web. Hubert blinked nervously at Rustus, then pulled his spear from the holster on his back. The group was silent, waiting to see what he would do. After a couple of

47

practice movements, he let the spear fly. It arced through the air until . . .

Splat.

The Unscorched erupted with cheers.

Rustus felt bile rise in his throat. 'Well done!' he said, forcing himself to smile and pat Hubert on the back.

Hubert beamed, and Rustus suspected he was a little bit in shock that he'd succeeded.

'That was actually pretty fun,' said Hubert. 'Don't you think?'

Rustus made a noise he hoped came across as agreement. How could he admit to Hubert that killing the webspinner had been the worst thing he had ever had to do? He was about to become a Scorched Atari. Killing webspinners would soon be his job.

It's OK, he tried to reassure himself. *Once you're Scorched, you can just volunteer to scout the perimeter. Everyone hates that job. Just get through tomorrow, prove to Dad you have what it takes and then you can do whatever you want.*

'You're right. That was a bit mean. He didn't have to make you go first,' said Hubert, misunderstanding Rustus's response. 'He's just jealous that you're a Furi and bigger and stronger than he'll ever be.'

Rustus nodded. But what good were his strength and size if he didn't have what it took in his heart? He needed to buck up his ideas before tomorrow. During the climb he would have the eyes of the whole city on him and he couldn't afford to bungle it like he had today.

'All right, we're all done,' yelled Scorch Knight Itticus. 'Let's get moving. And no more rests until we're back in Ataria. It's getting dark now, so watch your step.'

As they turned around, Rustus looked back at the remains of the webspinner he had killed. 'I'm sorry,' he mouthed. Then he pulled his eyes away and tried to push all thoughts of it from his mind.

Returning to Ataria was more difficult than leaving because it required a steep uphill climb, but the rest of the group seemed in high spirits, uplifted by their successful completion of the hunting ritual. At last, sweating and exhausted, they made it out of the jungle and back to the beginning of civilisation. A tall lava-forged fence ran around the perimeter of Ataria – an extra layer of protection from the beasts. At the gates to the city, they were greeted by Cardinal Magmatis, leader of Ataria.

'Well done, warriors,' he said. 'You have passed the first stage of the Scorching. Tomorrow, you will prove your value as our bravest and strongest citizens, joining generations of Reds before you to serve and protect our fine city.'

Rustus looked around at their group. Aro and a couple of others were grinning, but not everyone looked so enthusiastic; Hubert's euphoria had faded, and he clasped and unclasped his clammy hands.

'If warrior fire runs through your veins then neither the climb nor the scorching gases will cause you a problem,' the Cardinal continued. 'But if you fail, you are not worthy of the title "Scorched". And we have no place in Ataria for Unscorched who do not become warriors. If you fail, you will be cast out of the city to live in the swarming Beastlands with the foul creatures you've just encountered.'

Rustus had always been taught that life in the Beastlands would be no life worth living. And yet . . . a small part of him wondered how it would feel to be free from the rules and laws of Ataria. How it would feel to escape the stench of the city and his family's expectations. He shook that thought from his head and refocused on what the Cardinal was saying.

'. . . We'll see you at House Atari when the sun rises over the perimeter. Don't be late.' With that the Cardinal swept up his cloak and marched away.

'I heard that those who succeed in the Scorching are the ones that cast out the failures,' said Aro as they headed back to the Red District. 'It's their first mission. My dad had to do it. There was a girl in his year who failed, and they took her deep into the Beastlands and threw her into the webs.'

Hubert turned to Rustus, the colour drained from his face. But Rustus had his own problems to worry about.

He let the group go on ahead of him, back to their training ground, and once they were out of sight he picked his way between columns of rock and red bubbling lakes until he arrived outside the Steam House, a large round building carved into a column of stone on the edge of the Red District. It was a sacred place for warriors to reflect and worship the Ash Gods.

A billow of steam emerged as he pushed open the heavy door. Inside there was a perfectly circular pool filled with bright red mud that gurgled and murmured, burping clouds of red steam and occasionally flinging scarlet droplets at the stone walls. There was only one other person in the room, an old man with knee-length red plaits, praying in silence near the entrance.

Rustus crossed the central chamber, pausing to look at the murals on the walls. Scorched Ataris were pictured standing up to the most dangerous beasts of the land. At the far end of the Steam House, painted in purple mud, was an enormous and terrifying beast. It had four wings, two legs and an impressive silver ruff around its head: the phaegra, a terrible flying beast the Scorched Ataris had defeated hundreds of years ago, liberating the Realms from its reign of terror. Scorched Ataris surrounded the beast, spears raised in triumph. Tomorrow, Rustus would join the ranks of those elite warriors. He had to.

He strode across to the edge of the pool, kicked off his shoes and knelt on the ground. The smell of sulphur was so strong that it burned his eyeballs. He closed his eyes, pressed both hands to his temples and bowed his head.

'Please,' he said softly, 'give me the strength to complete the Scorching tomorrow.' He paused and looked around, embarrassed to be asking for something that should come so naturally to him, just like it did to everyone else in his family. 'And please . . .' he whispered, almost inaudibly, 'please let me get to the top first.'

4

KAYLA

Kayla scrambled easily up the pile of barrels. Her heart pounded. She hadn't been up here since before she had joined the Academy. Back then, when she had worked at the distillery, she had regularly clambered onto the roof to gaze longingly at the Academy and dream of swooping out over the Viridian Sea on a pangron of her own.

Looking back on those times, she could see how far she had come; though the Academy hadn't exactly welcomed her with open arms, she *did* have her own pangron now. Kayla steadied herself, preparing to leap from the barrels up and over the parapet. Below her, Faro shifted his weight impatiently. Kayla bent her knees, poised to jump, but before she could, Faro leaped past her, apparently too impatient to wait. He landed nimbly on the parapet and dropped down onto the rooftop beyond.

'Faro!' she hissed, wobbling wildly on a barrel. A knock from his tail had unsteadied her and she couldn't regain her balance. If she didn't jump now she was going to fall. 'Arrgh!' she yelled, flinging herself towards the rooftop, where she grabbed onto the parapet by her fingertips and heaved herself over.

She rolled onto her back and stared up at the sky, where the soft glow of the setting sun cast wheeling featherwings into shadow: toebeeks, seeking a scaly snack from beneath the waves. A laugh burst uncontrollably out of her chest, then she rolled over to her pangron and ruffled his ears.

'What were you thinking, you clumsy idiot? You could have got us caught! When are you going to learn a little patience?'

Faro yawned and stretched, his long pink tongue curling behind his fangs. He didn't look as if he felt guilty at all.

Kayla crawled to the edge of the roof and leaned over, checking whether any of the barrels had fallen, which could alert the guards to their presence. But everything was quiet and still – not a single sign that anyone had been there. The guards were still patrolling though, so she and Faro would have to wait a while if they were going to come down the other side without being seen.

A little rest on the rooftop then. If they couldn't be out flying, at least they could watch the skies together. She looked for a place where they could settle down to wait. But no such luck: a plume of dark grey smoke billowed from the distillery chimney and out across the glassy green sea.

'They must be malting the barley,' said Kayla, but she

53

was puzzled – it was a very strange time to fire up the kiln. The wind changed, wafting acrid curls of peaty smoke towards them. Faro's long whiskers twitched as he raised his head to sniff the air, and he sneezed as a ghostly finger of smoke crept into his nostrils. 'We need to get out of here before this roof is full of smoke.' Kayla's eyes darted about. Where could they go?

But Kayla was halted from figuring out their next move by the husky whisper of a man's voice.

'What if they see the ship?' it hissed.

Kayla spun around, thinking someone must have joined them on the roof, but there was no one to be seen. Was it the guards again? Surely not. The voice sounded too close to be coming from the street. She glanced around nervously.

'Don't worry,' a second voice said. 'They're too busy searching the city.'

The sound echoed slightly, as if it was swirling within the smoke itself, carried to them on the wind from . . . the chimney! The voices were coming from inside the distillery.

'But what if they see it from the skies?' asked the first.

'They won't. It's almost dark and the ship has bottle green sails.'

'What if they ask why we're malting barley at this time of night?'

'We'll pretend we have permission from Padrig. Say he needed an extra batch of firewater. They won't question that.'

Kayla gestured at Faro to stay where he was, away

from the smoke, and then she moved closer to the chimney, covering her mouth with her arm to prevent her from coughing.

'The Sky Riders are highly trained though. It's their job to –'

'It's *your* job to go back to the palace and enjoy your generous reward. Don't contact me again unless you hear something useful. Go on, I'll be in touch if I need you.'

Kayla's heart raced. Were they talking about the missing pangron? She couldn't imagine what else they could be hiding. And it made sense. The distillery had a door from the cellars that led directly onto the ocean for easy loading of the barrels onto supply ships, the only building in the city with an unguarded opening to the world beyond the walls. Before the Scourge, Sophiatown had regularly traded firewater for other goods from distant realms. But with the quarantine in place, the supply ships were no longer running. Which meant if there was a ship out there on the water, it was smuggling something important.

If Ezra *was* on a ship then the men were right, the guards weren't looking outside the city walls. An anxious coil twisted in Kayla's stomach. She should go and tell her wing commander immediately, but if she was going to divulge what she had heard then she would have to explain why she had been hiding on the roof. Kayla gnawed at her bottom lip as she weighed up what to do.

Maybe she and Faro could do their own investigation first, just a little reconnaissance mission to see if there was anything worth telling. They wouldn't be gone long and they wouldn't land anywhere. They would barely be breaking any rules. And, she thought selfishly, if she was the one to solve this mystery, it could be the thing to finally change her favour in the eyes of the Academy and show them she wasn't her mum.

'It is the right thing to do, isn't it?' Kayla asked Faro.

Faro didn't respond, but the way he was unfurling his wings told her he was as keen for a night flight as she was.

'I think it's the only solution,' she continued. 'We can't just leave poor Ezra to be kidnapped.' She tried to ignore the voice in her head that said, *And it's a great excuse to finally leave the confines of the city after being quarantined for so long.*

Faro crouched and lowered his wings.

'If we see anything suspicious then we'll come straight back and tell Wing Commander Barash.' She threw a leg over Faro's wide shoulders. 'And if we don't find anything, then no one ever need know that we were gone.' She urged her pangron forward through the grey smoke. 'We need to fly straight upwards, all right?'

Faro tossed his head and picked up his pace, thundering across the rooftop. By the time they reached the parapet he was taking such enormous strides he was practically flying already. With one final bound he pushed off the roof and shot into the dark sky like an arrow. Kayla wrapped herself around his neck, hoping the smoke billowing around them would hide them until they were away from the light of the city lanterns. When she decided they were high enough, Kayla told Faro to level out into a glide.

The night was still, its silence broken only by the occasional flap of Faro's huge wings. The vast ocean rolled out below them, white stripes of froth appearing every time the waves crashed against the city walls. Further offshore, a pod of ocean beasts raced along the surface.

Salty air licked Kayla's face. She tilted her head skyward and raised her arms. Pure freedom. She pulled her hair loose of its tight bun, and it flapped and whipped at her face, the smell of smoke mingling with the crisp scent of the ocean. A cool breeze danced around her and she was grateful for the warmth of her flying jacket, designed by the city tailors to be insulating, cooling and lightweight.

Faro turned his head to look at her and she leaned forward to scratch his neck. She couldn't imagine how she would feel if Faro had been the one taken. Poor Prince Ethun. No one should ever have to be separated from their pangron. They had to find Ezra if they possibly could.

Suddenly Faro lurched downwards and Kayla's stomach somersaulted as she felt only air beneath her body.

'Faro!' she screamed, scrabbling for his scruff in panic until she noticed his eyes twinkling, as if he was smiling at her. He'd done it on purpose!

'Don't do that!' Kayla laughed, her heart thumping.

There was nothing as exhilarating as flying. The feeling

that she could fall at any minute, coupled with complete trust that Faro would never let her come to any harm. She squeezed his shoulders a little tighter and they accelerated onwards.

The almost-full moon climbed higher in the sky, beams of light falling over the ocean like liquid silver, yet still they saw no boat. Kayla was beginning to wonder if her hastily scrabbled-together conclusions about what had happened to Ezra were woefully mistaken. But then she spotted something on the ocean below them: a small green dot bobbing amid the endless waves. She shifted her weight slightly and Faro dived towards it.

As they descended, the scene below them rushed into sharper focus. A large wooden ship with bottle-green sails glided through the waves. The whispering men had been right – it was difficult to spot against the ocean.

'Steady,' Kayla said as Faro soared over the length of the boat. 'Let me get a good look.'

He slowed his pace, hovering over the main sail as Kayla's eyes darted about for signs of a pangron. Nothing.

'A little lower,' she whispered.

Faro looped around, taking them closer.

'Where's Ezra?' Kayla wondered. 'And where are the crew?'

A shout from the quarterdeck drew Kayla's attention there. A figure was staring up at them, a dark hood obscuring their face. They held an unfamiliar weapon, and it was pointed directly at Kayla.

'Uh-oh.' Kayla squeezed Faro's neck with her thighs.

Faro understood immediately. He banked steeply to the left and shot high into the dark clouds while Kayla loaded her knucklebow.

Kayla had never been in a real battle before, but she had completed countless drills: shooting moving targets, evading aerial attacks, aiming while in full flight. She smiled nervously to herself; as much as Kayla loved fighting with her fellow cadets, the Academy's drills had never made her feel quite as alive as this genuine danger.

Whooosh. An arrow flew through the air, narrowly missing Kayla's head. This person must be a good shot. Faro was flying full pelt, and Kayla knew from experience that a moving pangron was a near-impossible target.

'Come on,' she urged. But Faro was already at his top speed. *Whooosh.* Another arrow. Kayla's thoughts raced. Who *was* her attacker? Kayla peered down just as a wild gust of wind knocked down their hood. It was a girl! She had a pale face covered in purple and yellow tattoos. Long snowy-white hair framed one side of her head while the other was entirely shaved. Who in all the Realms looked like *that*?

Faro made a jerking movement with his shoulders and Kayla regained her focus on the mission at hand: finding Ezra. *Don't look down*, she scolded herself. How many times had Major Flynn told her not to look back at her attackers? It was difficult enough for Faro to evade the projectiles without Kayla increasing their air resistance and affecting his balance.

'Sorry,' she whispered, pulling herself tight to his neck again and trying to figure out how she could aim her knucklebow in such bad visibility. But it was too late. Another *whoosh* by her ear, a sudden jolt in Faro's movements and a pained groan told her that her pangron had been hit.

Kayla felt as if her heart had dropped out of her chest. While she wasn't worried about falling – one flimsy arrow couldn't ground a pangron, especially not hers – she hated that her error had caused Faro pain. *Forgive me*, she thought, making a mental note to give him extra scalefish when they got back to Sophiatown. They needed to get out of there. Kayla had seen enough. She was sure Ezra must be on that ship, and Wing Commander Barash needed to know as soon as possible. She urged Faro onwards, back to the city, but something was different. Instead of accelerating and climbing higher, they seemed to be losing both speed and altitude.

'What's wrong?' Kayla asked, panic rising. 'Faro? We're falling! What's happening?'

They were nosediving towards the ocean now, Faro's wings crumpling towards his body. She called to him but he didn't respond. As they fell, Kayla tried to focus on her enemy and looked back at the boat. What kind of arrows did that girl have that they could ground a pangron with one shot? The girl still stood on the quarterdeck, watching their descent, and though she had stopped firing, she hadn't lowered her weapon. The water rushed towards them, closer and closer, and still Faro did not open his wings. In moments they would disappear beneath the waves . . .

SPLASH!

Icy water closed in around Kayla, rushing into the space between her skin and her uniform and crashing over her head. She pushed up to the surface and cast wildly around for her pangron.

'*Faro!*' she screamed, twisting and turning in the water to look for him in every direction. Finally she saw his huge wings outstretched on the surface to her left. He was barely moving. Salty water filled her mouth as a wave pummelled into her. 'Faro!' she spluttered, frantically swimming towards him.

She reached him in a few strokes and raised his head above the surface. He scrabbled at the water, digging his claws deep into her shoulders and forcing her head under.

She coughed as she resurfaced, grateful that Faro had finally stopped struggling, and trod water. Now what? She desperately needed to get him to land, but Sophiatown was just a speck on the horizon. Faro's heavy head lolled onto her shoulder. His outstretched wings were of some help in keeping him afloat, but it was still a struggle to keep them both above the surface.

'Are you OK?' she asked, stroking his nose and noticing his eyes were closed. 'Are you all right?' He didn't respond. 'Faro? *Faro!*'

Kayla ran her hands down his body, searching for the place where the arrow had hit. When her fingers fell onto the shaft, she realised the tip was embedded in his shoulder. Ordinarily she wouldn't remove an arrowhead, but she had a terrible feeling that this wasn't a *normal* arrow. She grabbed it and pulled. A torrent of water exploded from Faro's nostrils and relief flooded Kayla's body. He was alive.

'It's OK,' she said, kissing him on the side of his wet face. 'It's OK, I've got you.'

His eyes flickered open. Beneath his long lashes, Faro's pupils were as round and wide as the moon above. What had that girl done to him?

'I'm so sorry,' Kayla whispered, nuzzling her face into his. 'I shouldn't have brought us here. It's all my fault.'

She glanced up at the boat and saw the girl taking aim again. Except this time her crossbow was pointed at Kayla.

You've got to be kidding me, Kayla thought.

She considered reaching for her knucklebow, but discovered that she had lost her arrows in the fall. Maybe the jackblade in her shoe? No, it would be useless at this distance. She started to swim backwards, away from the ship, as fast as she could, but laden with Faro as she was, that wasn't very fast. The girl drew back the arrow and Kayla braced herself for impact. It struck her right shoulder.

Nausea washed over her almost before the pain came. She closed her eyes and swallowed, trying to shake the feeling. That was definitely not an ordinary arrow. She grunted, still trying to drag Faro along with her while keeping one eye on the boat, which began to swim in her vision.

The shooter was lowering a small boat over the side of the ship. Kayla blinked heavily, unable to take her eyes off the girl's glimmering silver boots as she clambered down a ladder into the boat and took up the oars.

'Stay away from us,' Kayla yelled, as the girl rowed towards them, the words distorted and slurred. She tried to keep swimming, but her limbs were as heavy as lead. She blinked slowly, watching helplessly as the shooter approached. All she could do was hold tight to Faro.

'Stay away,' Kayla murmured, when the girl was almost upon them. 'Get away.'

And then the girl was there, prying Kayla's numb fingers away from her pangron.

'Faro,' Kayla tried to whisper, but the name died on her lips. *Faro*, she thought, powerless and terrified as her beloved pangron was dragged away. *Faro*. Her heavy eyelids closed.

5

ALETHEA

Alethea awoke early and headed straight to the kitchen to help with Vanquish Day preparations.

'Thank the Ash you're all right,' said Grandma, looking up from her knitting to acknowledge her eldest grandchild. By the glow of the oil lamp, Alethea saw relief flood her face. 'I was waiting up for you last night, but I guess I must have fallen asleep . . .'

'I'm fine, Grandma.' Alethea tried to make her smile as reassuring as possible. She didn't need to worry Grandma with what had happened. 'What are you doing up so early?'

'Preparing, of course,' said Grandma. 'It's the most important day of the year.'

Alethea sighed. It seemed everyone in the city but her had caught Vanquish Day fever. She tried to muster some enthusiasm for the Scorching, but it was difficult. While she was sure this was an important day for the

Unscorched hopefuls who would climb Kahanga Rock, for normal citizens, especially those in the Blue District, the Scorching was just a distraction from the bigger issues they faced. 'What's for breakfast? Can I help?'

Grandma stood with a groan and fetched a small chipped plate on which a single fire melon had been cut into eight slices. Their fruit ration for the week. Alethea tried not to imagine how delighted her brothers and sisters would have been to see a handful of lavaberries dolloped alongside it.

'I made you a cake too,' said Grandma. 'But I'm afraid when you didn't come back last night I had to cut it up for the little ones. They were beside themselves and I didn't have anything else for dinner.'

'Oh, Grandma,' said Alethea, shaking her head. 'You didn't need to make me a cake.' But of course she knew that Grandma would. Despite their meagre rations, Grandma possessed the rare skill of being able to create food from the most basic ingredients that was both delicious and nutritious. Ma used to be magic with food too, before Da died.

'I wanted to,' Grandma said. 'Here, I managed to save you a slice.' She passed a thin sliver of dense sponge wrapped in cloth to Alethea.

It looked so good that Alethea bit into it straight away. It melted on her tongue in a burst of sticky sweetness.

'This is incredible. Your best yet!'

'Good,' said Grandma, a fan of smile lines appearing at the corners of her eyes. 'Now . . .' She lowered her voice to a whisper, even though everyone else was still asleep. 'Why were you back so late last night?'

Alethea sighed. Grandma had been so excited when Alethea had explained her success with Tommo and the firewort that Alethea had hoped to avoid telling her the plant had now been taken. She opened her mouth to reply, but a knock on the front door interrupted them, giving Alethea a little longer to find the right words.

'I'll get it,' she said.

When Alethea pulled open the door, a young boy dressed in pink stood with a book in his arms.

'Good morning, miss,' he said. 'Happy Vanquish Day. I have a delivery here for Mr Bashoa. Was ordered and paid for moons ago, but what with the Scourge, it's taken a while to . . . Well, here you go.'

He handed her a weighty leather-bound book.

Alethea was about to explain that Da was no longer here, but decided that this information changed little – and she preferred not to say the words out loud whenever possible.

'Thank you,' she said, nodding politely. 'And Happy Vanquish Day to you too.'

The boy gave a curt nod and continued on his way, heavy sack dangling over his shoulder. Alethea looked down at the book.

A Healer's Guide to the Flora of Ramoa

AN UPDATE BY

Constantine Everhart

66

Da hadn't mentioned ordering it. Before she could have a closer look, a stampede of footsteps told her that her siblings were awake. She turned to sweep them into a big hug.

'Alethea!' squealed Digby.

'What's that?' asked Cassio, pointing at the book in her hand.

'A birthday present,' Alethea said, tucking it away in a nook by the door. 'Come on, let's sit down. It's breakfast time and we've got fire melon!'

The children squawked excitedly and crowded around the table, squabbling over who sat where. Alethea saw Ma appear quietly and take her place at the head of the table. Alethea grabbed nine small plates and handed them out. It wasn't until she passed the eighth plate to Grandma that Alethea realised she had picked up a plate for Da too.

'Did you have your cake?' asked Elvira. 'We saved you a bit.'

'I did,' said Alethea. 'It was delicious, thank you.'

'How was your birthday?' asked Ma quietly.

Alethea placed her hand on Ma's gratefully. 'It was fine, Ma. Thanks for asking.'

'Fire melon!' yelled Digby as Grandma brought the fruit slices to the table. Once everyone had a piece, she took her own seat and bowed her head. The rest of the family followed suit.

'Thank you, Gods of Ash,' she said, 'for blessing the people of Ataria with the fine new warriors you deliver us today, for feeding us and for warding off the terrible beasts that roam outside our city. May Ash be our guide.'

'May Ash be our guide,' they all echoed. The familiarity of the ritual brought Alethea comfort, even if the words themselves did not.

The noise of cutlery on dishes and quiet bickering over the bread basket were the only sounds around the table as the family tucked into their breakfast. Mealtimes were relatively quiet periods in the Bashoa household, but even then, the sounds of chomping and chewing were enough to wake a lavabear from hibernation.

'Who was at the door?' Grandma asked Alethea, suddenly remembering.

'Someone brought her a book!' Padma said. 'For her birthday!'

Before Alethea could stop her, Elvira had jumped off her seat and retrieved the book from its place behind the door.

'A hee-lerrs guide to the flor-uh of Ra-moh-uh,' she read. 'An up-daaay-t by Con-stan-teen Eh-verr-hart.'

Grandma choked loudly. 'What did you just say?'

'It's the title of the book,' Alethea said, giving her a searching look.

'Let me see that.' Grandma grabbed the book from Elvira. Her eyes went wide as she took in the cover and ran her fingers gently along the spine. 'Where did you get this?'

'Da ordered it,' Alethea said, 'but it's taken a while to get here because of the Scourge delays.'

Grandma shook her head in what seemed to be astonishment as she continued to stare at the cover.

'What's it about?' asked Cassio.

'It's about healing.' Alethea took the book back from Grandma, eyes narrowed in confusion.

'What's wrong, Grandma?' Elvira asked.

Grandma took a deep breath and forced out a laugh. 'Nothing, my little ash star. Now hurry up and finish your food or you'll be at the back of the crowd for the Scorching!'

At that, Alethea's siblings all started eating ferociously. The ceremony wouldn't start until late morning, but everyone knew you had to get to Kahanga Rock early if you wanted a good view.

'Do you think anyone will die?' asked Cassio through a mouthful of fire melon.

'They might,' said Elvira. 'My friend Illia said her dad had a bet that *two* Unscorched would die this year.'

'Maybe they won't die in the ceremony, but they'll fall and get cast out into the Beastlands and then they'll get the Scourge and die of that instead,' said Padma.

'Enough of that talk!' shouted Ma, banging her fist on the table and making them all jump. 'Is there not enough death already in this city?'

The table fell silent and Alethea's heart panged. Her siblings were too young to understand Ma's grief. Of course they missed Da too, but it was different for them. They had grown up with the Scourge – to them it was normal.

'I've got the day off,' Alethea said, hoping to dispel the tension that had settled around the table, 'so I can watch the Scorching with you all.' She didn't usually take days off, but she figured everyone would be at the ceremony anyway so it wasn't like there'd be anyone to treat, and it would mean a lot to her brothers and sisters if she was there.

'Yay!' they all squealed, and then one by one scampered off to their shared bedroom to get dressed.

'I'll help the kids,' said Ma, following them through the doorway.

'Looks like it's you and me clearing up,' said Grandma, collecting the breakfast plates and carrying them through to the kitchen.

Alethea set about clearing the table when her eyes once again fell on the book. Maybe she would just have a quick look. She lifted it carefully and slid back into one of the chairs, cradling the book in her lap. This volume felt both familiar and at the same time brand new. Alethea already had the original version – she had been reading it the night before – but this new edition was thicker, longer, clearly crammed with more information. She ran her fingers down the index, searching for 'firewort' and then turned to the page listed. The entry she'd read yesterday was fresh in her memory, so it should be easy to notice if there was anything new. Not that it would help now that her supplies had been taken away – at least not unless it gave instructions on how to grow it double speed with no resources.

As in the previous edition there was an illustration of a firewort plant in bloom, along with a short description

70

of its characteristics. To Alethea's great disappointment, the words and picture looked identical. She moved down to check if there were any changes to the entry on frostwort. Again, nothing new. She was about to shut the book in frustration when she realised that there was another plant listed at the bottom of the page. One she didn't recognise from the previous edition.

Marshwort (formerly known as pickleweed)
Newly classified member of the tasselbaggia family

Thorny perennial shrub growing to moderate height. Thrives in sandy/salty soil. Common on tidal plains and saltmarshes along the coasts of the Fjordlands, Ashlands and Southlands. Has multiple woody stems lined with purple scythe-shaped thorns and paired rubbery leaves. Flowers are tiny, star-shaped and purple, set upon globular purple liquid-filled bladders.

Previously, marshwort was grouped into the arrowroot family on account of its small flowers and arrow-shaped leaves, but recent botanical work has found that it belongs instead to the tasselbaggia family.

Leaves: No known medicinal effect but can be chopped and eaten raw or cooked.

Stems: Can be dried and made into tea, may aid digestion.

Roots: No known medicinal benefit.

Bladders: Contain mild digestive fluid with a sweet and slightly spicy scent. Can be applied to skin as an emollient. Mild enough to be consumed orally to treat indigestion.

Alethea's eyes widened. Could the liquid from the marshwort bladders have the same effect on the Scourge as the liquid from the firewort bladder? It seemed to have a milder action than firewort, as it could be taken as a drink to cure indigestion, but perhaps if it were left on the skin for longer . . . Alethea's heart quickened. This could work.

She read the entry quickly again, taking particular note of where she could find it. Alethea knew there was a beach close to Ataria, because it had been mentioned in *Beastly Beasts and Fearsome Feasts*, a picture book of cautionary tales her parents used to read to her about the monstruous creatures that lived in the Beastlands. If the map in that book was accurate then the coast was probably two days' walk away at most. The only problem was that to get there she would have to leave the city and travel through the Beastlands.

'Did you like the fruit?' Grandma asked, appearing suddenly beside her and grabbing a pile of dirty plates.

Alethea slammed the book shut and leaped to her feet. 'Delicious,' she said, following Grandma through to the kitchen with the rest of the dishes. 'Thank you.' She was glad Grandma hadn't noticed that she gave almost all of her slice away to her siblings.

'You know,' said Grandma, 'I'm very proud of you.' She put the plates onto the surface beside the sink. 'Your da would be too.'

Alethea sank her hands into the lava-warmed water and began washing up. 'Thanks, Grandma.' She tried not to let her thoughts drift to the marshwort that might be growing on the coast. Could it be the answer she was looking for?

'So are you going to tell me what happened last night?' Grandma asked, sharp as ever and unwilling to let anything go.

Alethea sighed. 'I had a visit from an Ash Bishop.'

'An Ash Bishop!' The sound of clinking plates stopped as Grandma paused drying. 'What did they want with you?'

Alethea could feel her eyes boring into her back, but she didn't turn around. 'They took something from me.' She wrung out the washcloth into the sink, continuing to squeeze long after it had stopped dripping. 'Something important.'

'What was it?' asked Grandma.

Alethea stared into the sink and rubbed her nose with one hand. 'My supply of firewort.' She tried to suppress the pain that bubbled up inside her, replacing it with anger at the injustice. 'They're giving it to the Scorched warriors in the Red District. Apparently more of them are starting to fall ill now.'

A short pause.

'Was that the plant that helped Tommo?'

Alethea nodded. 'Yep.' She took a deep breath. 'It means I won't be able to help our people. The Reds might get by, but we won't. I just needed more time to study it and then I could have helped everyone all over the city.'

'By the Ash,' cursed Grandma. She sighed deeply. 'This place . . . It's not your fault, Alethea. Don't blame yourself. You've done everything you can.'

Alethea chewed her cheek. *Had* she done everything she could? Now that she knew there was another plant that might work, wasn't it her duty as a healer to try to source it?

'I've read about another plant,' she said slowly, glancing over to determine Grandma's reaction. 'In the same family as firewort.'

'Interesting,' said Grandma, giving nothing away. 'Do you think it could also be effective against the Scourge?'

'Possibly,' said Alethea.

'What's it called?'

'Marshwort, but you might know it as pickleweed.'

'I haven't heard of it,' said Grandma. 'Do we grow it in the city?'

'No,' said Alethea. 'It grows on the coast. Beyond the Beastlands.'

There was a long pause before Grandma replied, 'You're not going to do something silly, are you?'

Alethea looked at the floor.

Grandma sighed. 'You are truly your father's daughter.'

Alethea thought she glimpsed a smile on her face, but then movement in the doorway caught her eye.

'We're ready,' said Padma, dressed in her best blue tunic. 'Shall we go?'

Grandma gave Alethea a look that said, 'We're going to talk more about this later,' straightened her dress and then bustled through to the main room.

Together the eight of them trundled out of the house and joined the crowds of excited people swarming towards Kahanga Rock. It was far away, in the centre of the city, but the rainbow-coloured rock formation rose so high it could be seen wherever you were in Ataria.

The closer the Bashoas got to the city centre, the more varied the heads around them grew in colour: blue, green, pink, silver and red cloth woven through hair to ward off the webspinners. She supposed the one good thing about Vanquish Day and the Scorching ceremony was how united the city felt, even if the rest of the year it felt like every district for itself.

The children chattered excitedly as they claimed their

spot in the crowd, but Alethea could think of nothing but marshwort.

'Do you know how dangerous the Beastlands are?' muttered Grandma, as if she could tell exactly what Alethea was thinking.

'What are you two scheming about?' Ma came to join them. She looked a bit brighter. Perhaps she was looking forward to the feast. Alethea shot Grandma a warning look. Ma didn't need to be worrying about her going off into the Beastlands; she was delicate enough as it was.

'Just planning the menu for dinner,' said Grandma, winking at Alethea.

Alethea smiled gratefully. It couldn't be easy for Grandma, knowing her eldest grandchild was considering risking her life by venturing out into the Beastlands after she had already lost her only son. Alethea wished she could ask Da what she should do. But she knew that if Da were here, he would already be halfway to the coast to collect the marshwort himself. He had never given up a chance to help people. Take that morning's delivery – one of the last things he had ever done was order a book about healing. Alethea couldn't help but think that maybe its arrival was some kind of sign.

'I know you'll make the right decision.' Grandma took Alethea's hand and squeezed it, but as she did so, the sleeve of her shirt slipped away from her wrist and Alethea glimpsed a series of concentric red rings.

Alethea's eyes went wide and she went to grab at the

sleeve, but Grandma batted her hand away, stepping backwards.

'It's nothing, flower. Nothing to worry about.'

But the healer in Alethea knew exactly what that mark was. And suddenly the importance of finding a cure was greater than ever, because Grandma had contracted the Scourge.

6

RUSTUS

It was the morning of the Scorching, and Rustus and his fellow Unscorched were waiting at House Atari, a large stone building in the centre of Ataria where Ash Bishops met to discuss important issues facing the city. A restless energy bounced around the group. Aro was hopping from foot to foot, Hubert was sat on the floor breathing rapidly and Rustus was standing with his arms crossed, praying silently to the Ash Gods to help him win the race.

When the time came, they strode in ritual formation to a stage specially assembled around the base of Kahanga Rock.

Before they climbed the steps, Cardinal Magmatis stopped them. 'Listen to the crowd,' he said, smiling widely. 'They believe in you. They want you to succeed.' Rustus felt a prickling in his chest at the thought of what lay ahead. 'This is the greatest day of your lives, so breathe it in.' Rustus took a nervous, shuddering breath. 'Are you ready to become Scorched?' He saw his fellow recruits nodding and reluctantly joined in. 'Then take your places.'

As they ascended the steps, Rustus noted that little spurts of steam were already bursting out from all sides of the rainbow-coloured rock. Living in the Red District, he'd grown up beside Kahanga Rock and seen it erupt every day when the sun reached its peak in the sky. Seen from afar, the rock tower was breathtaking, with its multicoloured algae and clouds of brightly coloured gases. Now he was up close, it stole his breath for a different reason: the steam inside the rock tower hissed and fizzed like oil in a pan, firing out from fissures in the rock face. It might be beautiful, but it was dangerous. He would have to climb very carefully.

On the stage, the Unscorched arranged themselves in a row. From somewhere in the crowd a drumbeat sounded. The ceremony had begun.

'Welcome, citizens of Ataria!' Cardinal Magmatis's voice boomed over the crowd of adoring faces and brightly coloured cloths. Everyone was there. The eyes of the whole city were on them. But to Rustus only one pair mattered. Through the steamy haze it was difficult to make out individual faces, which was a relief, because seeing Brutus's scowl would do nothing for his nerves. As long as his father could see him, that was enough.

'We stand here today,' Cardinal Magmatis continued in an exultant voice, 'on Vanquish Day, to honour our history and give thanks to our gracious Ash Gods for the new warriors who have chosen to serve and protect us.'

The crowd began to cheer, but the Cardinal placed a finger to his lips to quieten them. 'Many years ago on this day, Atarian warriors killed the last phaegra. By the will of the Ash Gods, they climbed to the top of the highest tree in the Ashlands, where the only remaining phaegra was roosting.'

Even though the crowd listened to this same story every year, they hung on his words in rapt silence. Rustus wished they could just get on with it.

'The Ash Gods bestowed upon each of those Atarians the strength of one hundred men. Our heroes fought valiantly against the terror beast as it burned them with its acid breath, tore their armour with its claws and tried to flee with its huge wings, but they persevered. After a brave battle, they ripped the phaegra from the skies and stole its final breath.'

Sweat beaded on Rustus's neck beneath his plait as the steam continued to billow from the rock tower behind him.

'The warriors returned from their battle battered and burned but victorious! They had channelled the strength of the Ash Gods and rid the island of the terrible beast that had tormented our people.'

Rustus swallowed and wiped the slick sweat from his neck. The Scorching was meant to pay homage to that first legendary climb. In training they'd spent every day scaling the lookout towers to prepare for this moment, but Rustus still wasn't sure if he had prayed hard enough to the Ash Gods to earn their favour.

'Now it is time to ask the Ash Gods again for their grace, as we have done every year since, to bestow upon us another generation of mighty warriors to protect our city from beasts and peoples that would do us harm. More than ever, this year we ask that they honour us with the truest and strongest to serve and protect us. For we face a new terror. The obsidian webspinners plague our city with their terrible Scourge. We will vanquish them too. Just as we vanquished the phaegra before them!' He turned to face the Unscorched on the stage. 'New warriors,' he said, 'the Ash Gods have called upon *you* to deliver the people of Ataria from evil. Do you promise to serve them?'

Rustus realised they were now into the part of the ceremony where they had to give their vows. He had heard his brothers recite these words at their own Scorchings and had practised them himself countless times over the years. He knew the lines by heart.

'We promise,' said Rustus and his fellow Unscorched in synchrony.

'Do you vow to cut down any beast that dares to threaten them?'

Rustus tried to push the image of the squirming webspinner from his mind.

'We will cut down any beast.'

'Will you rise against warriors that dare to rise against you?'

'We will rise against all warriors.'

'Will you be ready in the hour of darkness?'

'We will be ready.'

Cardinal Magmatis walked behind the line of Unscorched, resting his hand on each one's head in a final blessing. Then he threw his arms up to the sky and bellowed, 'Merciful Ash Gods, in the light of the flame and the heat of the embers, bequeath your power to our Unscorched warriors.'

Rustus held his breath. Would he feel something when he received the Ash Gods' power? At first nothing seemed to happen, then a wind whipped around the stage, just as it did every morning before the geyser erupted. The gust carried ash from the base of the rock and showered it over Rustus and his peers.

'We thank you, all powerful Ash Gods,' the Cardinal gushed. 'Warriors, take the spirit of Ash into your bodies. Feel the strength of the Gods as it surges through your veins.'

Rustus tried hard to feel it, to feel anything at all, but there was nothing apart from a slight stinging in his eyes where the ash had got in.

'At last we are ready.' The Cardinal stopped in the centre of the stage, leaned towards the audience and addressed them in a stage whisper, 'It's time to find out who is worthy.' There was an excited murmuring in the crowd as he continued. 'These Unscorched recruits will have ten minutes to complete the climb. Those the Ash Gods deem worthy will reach the platform before Kahanga Rock erupts. They will henceforth be known as Scorched Ataris!' He shouted the last two words, raising both fists in the air, and the crowd went wild.

Please . . . Rustus closed his eyes and pleaded with the Ash Gods one last time. *Please let me get to the top first.*

'On the third gong,' said Cardinal Magmatis, 'these seven Unscorched will begin their climb.'

A Scorched Atari at the edge of the stage raised a large stick and struck a round bronze disc.

GONG.

Rustus took a deep breath to steady his nerves and moved to his place at the base of the rainbow-covered rock. His heart thrashed against his ribs.

GONG.

A low drone started as a group of musicians blew into enormous rock tubes around the stage – the typical musical accompaniment to this part of the ceremony. The powerful sound reverberated through Rustus's whole body, making the tips of his fingers and toes begin to tingle.

Stop it, he told his body. *Concentrate.*

GONG.

Ahead of Rustus, Aro flung herself eagerly onto the rock. Beside him, Hubert stepped tentatively forward, stretching up to reach the first handhold.

To his back, the crowd thrummed with nervous energy. The districts began to chant their traditional melodies, harmonising with each other to form a haunting musical ensemble.

You are a Furi, Rustus told himself. *You are the strongest of all the Unscorched.*

His body didn't feel strong though. It felt like jelly. But somehow he forced himself to the rock face, and step by step, hand over hand, he began to climb. The chants whirled around him, bringing back memories of watching the Scorchings of his brothers.

Tactus and Octus had made it look so easy, sometimes pausing to turn to the crowd and wave. But nothing about this felt easy to Rustus; every movement took all of his concentration, every breath a battle. Still he continued, thinking of nothing but the repetitive movement of his hands and feet and his father's eyes on him from the crowd. It would all be worth it if his father finally accepted him – the years of feeling like he didn't fit in, the gruelling training, the dead webspinner.

He flinched as a spurt of orange steam shot out from a fissure in the rock. Ouch, that was hot – and was only a taste of what was to come if he didn't get to the top in time. He glanced up at the rock face, noting where there were cracks above him and charting a course to avoid them. As he climbed, the rock became slippier with the moisture, but he persevered. At some point, he became vaguely aware that the pitch and speed of the crowd's chanting was increasing. That usually happened when somebody passed the halfway point. He looked up to see who it could be but could see nobody ahead of him.

Was he . . . *first*?

He looked down and saw Aro racing up beneath him, a determined look on her face. When had he overtaken her? He could barely believe it. Perhaps the Ash Gods had heard his prayers after all. He pushed on harder. Until a small voice below him cried out.

'Arrrggh!'

Rustus looked down to see Hubert far below, hanging by one hand from an outcrop of rock. His stomach lurched.

'I'm going to fall!' Hubert shouted, his eyes meeting Rustus's.

'No, you're not!' Without thinking, Rustus began to descend back the way he'd come. 'Hold on!'

'What are you doing?' hissed Aro as they passed one another. 'Leave him. The Ash Gods have made their decision.'

Rustus shook his head. Leave his friend to fall? To be exiled? Never. It turned out some things were more important than winning.

'I've got to help him.'

'Suits me,' said Aro, and she continued upwards.

'Give me your hand,' Rustus said when he finally reached Hubert's side.

'You were first,' Hubert said, confusion on his face. 'You were going to win.'

'It doesn't matter,' said Rustus, grabbing the boy's flailing arm. 'You OK?'

'I am now,' said Hubert. 'Thank you, Rustus.' His eyes were pooling with tears – from fear or gratitude, Rustus couldn't tell.

'You would have done the same for me,' said Rustus. 'Come on – we haven't got much time left before this tower starts spewing its guts out.'

Together they resumed their climb, side by side.

Strangely, now that the chance of coming first was totally out of his reach, Rustus felt calmer. He even managed to look down at the crowd. They seemed very far away, just a sea of beautiful colours.

They were almost at the top when Rustus heard a strange creaking. A fraction of a second later, a huge crack appeared in the section of rock he was holding onto. He quickly checked on Hubert, but he was further over the rock face, no cracks visible by him. The creaking came again, and this time the chunk of rock Rustus was holding on to broke clean away from the tower. His stomach lurched as his fingers grabbed at empty air, trying to find a way to anchor himself. But it was too late.

'Rustus!' yelled Hubert, open-mouthed in horror.

At first Rustus seemed to hang in the air, then suddenly he was tumbling to the ground. Down he went, past the rainbow algae and spurts of colourful steam, slipping further from victory and ever closer to the stage, the crowd and his father.

7

KAYLA

Kayla's burning eyes sprang open and she gazed blearily up at a cloudless blue sky. She rolled onto her side and spat out a mouthful of salty saliva. Wiping her chin with the back of a sandy hand, she pushed herself up to sitting. Her head pounded. There were a few seconds of disorientated confusion as the ocean roared in the distance and toebeeks called overhead, then she remembered.

'Faro!' she screamed, clambering to her feet.

She looked about and saw that the beach she'd washed up on was wide, flat and empty, with nothing to see but glistening black sand. *Black* sand? She blinked and rubbed her eyes, which were stinging from the salt. The only place where the beaches were black was in the Ashlands. *How* had she washed up here, so far up the coast? And how was it morning already? Faro could be anywhere.

'*Faro!*'

87

Her pangron was nowhere to be seen. She walked to the water's edge and looked across the vast ocean, but there wasn't a boat in sight. She kicked the sand in frustration and ran a hand through her knotted, sandy hair.

'Ouch!' A stabbing pain in her right shoulder reminded her that she had been shot.

She peeled off her yellow flying jacket, which was itchy and stiff from the seawater, to inspect the wound. Not a lot to see except a bloody stain on her undershirt. Why had she passed out? Had the arrow been dipped in poison? She stared at the ocean again and wondered how Faro was feeling – he'd been hit too. Had he woken up yet? Was he on the green-sailed boat? She couldn't see it anywhere. Her instinct was to continue shouting his name, but nobody would hear, so she didn't waste her energy.

Next, her thoughts turned to protection: she was in an unfamiliar land, a different realm. The warriors here were Scorched Ataris who specialised in hand-to-hand combat with obsidian spears. They didn't have pangrons but right now neither did she. She looked down at her fist. Her knucklebow was still attached but her arrows were gone. Maybe they'd washed up on the beach somewhere. She strode along the shoreline, searching the sand and seafoam, but the arrows were nowhere to be found. She wondered briefly if she would be able to buy new ones in Ataria, or maybe a boat to go looking for Faro, before realising her money pouch was empty too. It hardly mattered – a Southlander wouldn't exactly be welcomed into Ataria. She would have to sneak into the city unseen and steal what she needed.

She crouched to pull her jackblade from a holster on her boot; it was all she had to protect herself now, but Kayla had always excelled at close-quarters combat, often scoring better marks for her knife fighting than her flying. She shook her head to rid her ears of water, then drew her hair into an untidy bun. She wouldn't want it flapping around her face if she got into a fray.

The Scorched Ataris weren't the primary threat though. To get to Ataria she would have to cross the Beastlands, and who knew what beasts lurked in the Ashlands' wilderness? Beyond where the black sand of the beach met the saltmarshes, a jungle of tall turquoise plants rose in a foreboding wall that stretched as far along the coast as she could see. She'd always been taught that their pangrons were the mightiest beasts in all the Realms, and so Kayla had never had much to fear, but now, out here alone, far from Sophiatown, she wasn't so certain. She dusted the sand from her flying jacket and put it back on, hoping it might give her a little extra protection.

Oh, Faro, where are you?

She hoped he was safe.

I will find you soon, she thought, fingering her necklace. *I promise.*

She quickly crossed the black beach and began picking her way over the saltmarsh, where purple balls exploded into sticky goo under her feet. It made foamy bubbles where it mixed with the seawater.

'Pickleweed,' she realised.

Back in Sophiatown they used the plant's juice to wash their skin and hair. It grew in abundance along the shoreline outside the city. She considered taking some with her, to wash herself if she found a stream, but thought better of it – she didn't need any extra weight to slow her down and sap her energy.

As Kayla drew closer to the forest, she noticed a dense grey substance woven through the trees. She felt a strange prickling sensation down her spine; it reminded her of the grey strands of web that she sometimes found in the corners of her bedroom. Kayla was tough about most things, but she absolutely hated webspinners. Even the tiny harmless ones that lived in the watchtower had her scurrying to the other side of the room. Luckily Faro had developed a taste for them, so he would soon leap to her rescue and snaffle up the eight-legged creatures before they got too close.

But Faro wasn't here, and Kayla didn't want to think about how big the webspinners might grow in the wild Beastlands.

She squinted at the treeline, fighting the urge to turn and run back to the sea. Nothing seemed to be moving in the webs, but the silken strands stretched across the roof of the forest as far as the eye could see. Sticky tendrils reached down to wrap themselves around the tree trunks, and in some places the webs were so thick Kayla could see deep tunnels disappearing within them. In others, the half-eaten remains of large hexapods dangled in cocoons. Kayla's skin crawled.

'Absolutely not,' she said. 'There's no way I'm going in there.'

But Faro . . . a voice protested somewhere inside – her head or her heart, she couldn't be sure. She stood on the edge of the forest, analysing her options. If she didn't enter, she had no chance of finding a boat, so she might never see Faro again. But if she did enter, she might well end up as lunch for a giant webspinner, in which case she would *definitely* never see Faro again. Not great odds either way.

Suddenly she heard a noise from deep within the webs. She raised the blade in her right hand and sank into a fighting stance.

'Hello?' she shouted. 'Is somebody there?'

There was silence except for a quiet rustling; no doubt the hidden webspinners were watching her from their webs. Kayla peered into the dense grey mass, keeping plenty of distance in case they decided to leap out and attack her. A glimpse of movement ahead of her, through the trees and webs, made her heart race.

From within the forest, something very large was moving towards her at great speed. She took a hurried step backwards, and just in time, as a huge, long-bodied beast barrelled out of the forest, tearing through the webs. It was unlike any creature she had ever seen. In place of fur, its body was covered in slick blue plates, like the skin of a scalefish. It moved rapidly, its long body winding from side to side with every step. It only came up to Kayla's waist but was twice as long as she was tall, and as it approached it opened its wide jaw to reveal a mouth full of enormous fangs, poking in every possible direction. Its gaze locked onto her, ice-blue eyes opening wide, pupils dilating. It paused, as if as shocked to see Kayla as she was it, which gave Kayla just enough time to take in its six squat legs before it threw back its head, let out a blood-curdling screech and charged.

'What the . . . !' She flung herself to the ground and covered her head with her arms, holding her jackblade point up, ready to defend, but the huge animal leaped over her. Its scaly blue body sailed through the air and thundered away across the saltmarsh and down the beach, spiked tail trailing behind it.

Kayla let out a gasping breath and cautiously sat up. *What was that?* She had barely got back to her feet when she heard a voice from within the webs.

'Topaz!' it yelled. '*Topaz!*'

A red-faced man burst out of the undergrowth. If she hadn't still been in a state of shock from the near miss with the beast, Kayla would have laughed at the sight of him. Above a bushy silver beard his face shone scarlet, clashing magnificently with his magenta suit, which was adorned with impressive golden feathers. A collection of glass jars were strung around his waist, and on his head sat a pith helmet, decorated with small golden scales that shimmered and sparkled in the sunlight.

He was so focused on the fleeing creature that he hadn't yet spotted Kayla. Using this to her advantage,

Kayla crept towards him, jackblade firmly in hand. By the time she reached the man, he was bent double, panting with his hands on his knees.

Kayla loomed over him, knife at the ready. 'Who are you?'

The man jumped into the air, clutching his hand to his chest. 'For the love of beasts,' he squealed. 'Where did you come from?' He dissolved into a fit of coughing.

'Was that creature something to do with you?' Kayla asked, pointing her knife towards the saltmarsh.

'Did you . . . ?' the man wheezed, producing a handkerchief from the breast pocket of his waistcoat and dabbing at his forehead, which was sweating profusely.

'Did I what?'

The man raised his hand, still unable to continue.

Kayla had never seen anyone like him. His clothing and voice had an air of the eccentric – certainly nobody dressed like that in Sophiatown – and she was sure she had just seen his beard *wiggle*. He removed his helmet to reveal a mop of white hair plastered to his scalp.

'You look like you're about to have a heart attack,' Kayla said, eyeing his heaving chest and rosy cheeks.

'Yes, yes, possibly,' the man muttered, sinking awkwardly onto a large piece of driftwood to catch his breath. 'Ruddy creature. She keeps escaping.'

'Escaping?' Kayla said, wondering why anyone would want to be intentionally close to that thing. 'You mean you kept her, on purpose?'

'On purpose?' the man replied, rubbing the handkerchief

over his head. 'No, not exactly. Though . . . yes, I suppose so . . .'

'What do you mean?' Kayla asked, growing impatient with his inability to finish a sentence.

The man sighed. 'My name is Marquis Macdonald. I'm a bestiarist.'

Every word that came out of his mouth confused Kayla further.

'A *what*?'

'A bestiarist,' he repeated, as if it were something as obvious as a butcher or a spice merchant. 'You do know what a bestiarist is?'

Kayla shook her head.

'Gracious,' said the Marquis, blowing out his cheeks. 'A bestiarist is someone who writes a bestiary – a book of beasts. A list of all the incredible creatures that inhabit the Realms. It was my mother's work really and her mother's before that. For generations my family have travelled the Realms, learning about the beasts and documenting them. So many of the existing records from the cities are inaccurate and often downright biased against these marvellous creatures.'

'You travel the Realms?' asked Kayla, flabbergasted. Her own mother had told her tales of nomads who wandered between cities, living among the beasts, but Kayla had never been sure if they were truth or legend. It seemed impossible that anyone, let alone this wheezing old man, managed to live their life out in the Beastlands and survive. 'Isn't that dangerous?'

'It has its moments,' said the Marquis, 'but on the whole, no. It's brilliant. Anyway, all that to say, that beast you just let go is my greatest discovery. Nobody has ever seen that species before, not in any records I can find at least. Found her wandering at the base of the Shivertips. I call her a needlejaw. On account of the teeth.' He gnashed his own ferociously to emphasise his point.

Kayla grimaced. Needlejaw was about right. It hadn't looked friendly at all.

'But you said it had escaped,' said Kayla. 'If you were just recording it for your book, why would you capture it?'

'Ah,' said the Marquis, looking a little sheepish. 'I only planned to keep her for a few days. Easy enough for me to do – the wagon is set up for caring for beasts. I was going to learn as much as I needed for the bestiary and then I was going to release her. But then someone in my network told me about a naturalist working in Port Royal. We made contact and she asked me to bring Topaz over there to confirm whether she really is a completely new and unidentified species – a needlejaw – or a beast that has always existed but which my family has never before seen.'

Kayla wondered why anyone would care so much about what type of beast it was. As far as she was concerned, the Realms would be better off without any beasts at all. Except pangrons of course. Kayla couldn't imagine her life without Faro or a Sophiatown without pangrons. And yet that was what her mother had campaigned for: to stop the keeping of pangrons completely. It was what had eventually landed her in prison. Kayla would never be able to understand why she'd believed pangrons would be better off without riders. The concept was just cruel.

'And did I hear you right in saying that you keep beasts in your wagon?'

The Marquis nodded enthusiastically. 'Yes, I have a whole host of animal companions.' He beamed. 'A real motley crew.'

Before Kayla could express her horror at living with a wagon full of creatures from the Beastlands, something scuttled over her feet. Her automatic reaction was to kick out, and she saw a flash of pink and orange as the many-legged creature flew through the air, landing a stride or so away from them on the sand. 'Eugh!' she exclaimed. 'Is that a webspinner?' She backed away from the beast with her knife raised.

'A webspinner?' The Marquis guffawed. 'Of course not. That's a stained-glass scuttleclaw. They've got delicate shells, so you've got to be gentle with them.' The scuttleclaw had righted itself and was moving back towards them, scuttling sideways on more legs than was acceptable and holding two large pincers aloft, ready to attack. 'Adorable, aren't they?'

Kayla regarded the Marquis with disgust. 'It's trying to bite me!' She hopped and jumped away from the scuttleclaw as it continued towards her.

'Nonsense,' said the Marquis. 'They're totally harmless in the day, look.' He moved closer to the scuttleclaw and plucked it up by a pincer, lifting it gently into the air. It didn't resist. He moved it a few paces up the beach then placed it down again, giving it a little shove to encourage it to move off in the other direction. 'Best not to be around them at night though.'

'Why?' asked Kayla, not sure she actually wanted to know the answer.

'Night is when they hunt,' said the Marquis. 'They move together in large groups eating everything in their path, be it alive or dead. Plant, animal . . .' He looked at Kayla and licked his lips. 'Person.'

'Person?' squealed Kayla. 'Would they really eat a human?'

'They'd give it a good go,' said the Marquis. 'My father made the mistake of falling asleep on a beach in the Fjordlands once. By the time he woke and got himself away from the scuttleclaw, he'd lost his big toe!'

Kayla wasn't sure if that was a joke or not, but either way she didn't fancy spending any more time than necessary in the scuttleclaw's company.

'Another reason to get off this beach as soon as possible,' she said, keeping the scuttleclaw firmly in her eyesight.

'Very good idea,' said the Marquis. She saw him glance at her jacket. 'What's a Sky Cadet doing outside of Sophiatown without her pangron anyway? Don't tell me you've lost it!'

Kayla glared at him. 'I haven't *lost* Faro,' she snarled. 'He was *taken* from me.'

The Marquis's smile faltered. 'You mean you really

have lost him? Crumbs.' He made an awkward face. 'That was a bit careless.'

Kayla felt a lump rise in her throat.

'If you tell me what happened, I might be able to help you,' the Marquis said, more kindly this time. 'I'm something of an expert at tracking down elusive beasts.'

Kayla sighed. What did she have to lose by telling her story? Maybe this unusual man *could* help her find Faro.

She briefly explained what had happened the night before, though her exact memory of the events was clouded by the effects of the poison. She knew Faro had been shot down, but, try as she might, she couldn't form a picture of their attacker. One thing she *was* sure to make clear was how hard she had fought to save Faro – and how dangerous his captors must be if they had poison that could down a pangron.

After she finished her story, the Marquis looked thoughtful. 'A ship,' he said, stroking his beard. 'Could be headed to the beast market in Port Royal. I'll get someone to keep a lookout.' He cleared his throat and placed his hands to his mouth before making a loud squawking noise. There was a rustling in the trees and a white feathered beast flapped its way out of the forest.

'Milabar!' said the Marquis as it landed on his shoulder. 'My beautiful girl. Take a message to Aquamarine for me, would you?' He stroked the beast's long neck feathers. It squawked, which the Marquis seemed to take for assent, as he took it carefully into his hands, looking it directly in the eyes. 'Start message,' he said. 'Aquamarine, I'm looking for information about a boat with green sails. May have a pangron or two onboard. Do you know if it's headed to Port Royal? Stay safe, and I'll see you in a few days. Finish message.'

Once he had finished speaking, the creature repeated the words to him, mimicking his voice exactly.

Kayla's eyes went wide. 'That was . . .' she said, searching for the right words. It felt wrong to say that a beast was clever or impressive, but she was taken aback by what she had just seen. 'Really weird.'

'Isn't she brilliant?' the Marquis replied, grinning adoringly at the beast. 'She's fast too, so we should soon know whether that ship is headed to Port Royal.'

'Port Royal,' said Kayla. 'That's the other side of the Shivertips, isn't it?' She recognised the name of the city – it didn't belong to any realm. She'd heard it was a lawless, unruly place.

The Marquis nodded. 'Indeed. Six days by foot, longer if you dally.'

Kayla's heart sank. 'Faro could be long gone by then.'

'Agreed,' said the Marquis. 'He could be totally lost. But I have a proposition for you.' He twirled the ends of his moustache thoughtfully.

'What's that?' Kayla asked, eyeing him warily.

'If you came in the wagon with me –' *and the beasts*, thought Kayla – 'I could get you there much faster.' Kayla narrowed her eyes. Why was he offering to help her? 'Naturally,' he continued, 'I couldn't be expected to take you there for nothing . . .'

There it was. A knot formed in Kayla's stomach. He wanted payment, but she had lost her coins in the fall and had nothing to offer him. 'I don't have any money.'

'That's all right,' he said. 'It's not money I'm after.' He pointed along the beach, in the direction of the runaway beast. 'I need to capture Topaz and it would be much easier if I had another pair of hands to assist. If you can help me to get her back into my wagon, I'll take you to Port Royal.'

Kayla pictured the huge fanged beast and gave another nervous glance towards the grey webs ahead of them. 'Do you think she's gone back in there?' she asked, trying not to show how much the sight of them terrified her.

'Not sure.' The Marquis shrugged. 'Might have. We'll just have to follow her tracks and see.'

Kayla gulped. This was the best chance she had of ever seeing Faro again. She didn't really have much choice.

'All right,' she said. 'It's a deal.'

The Marquis held out his hand for a handshake, but Kayla grimaced and stepped backwards. 'For all I know, you've got the Scourge.' She hadn't spent all that time locked up in Sophiatown, safely protected from the disease, just to catch it from the first new person she met.

The Marquis laughed. 'Even if I did, you wouldn't catch it from shaking my hand. You Southlanders – you think everyone is out to hurt you.'

'Judging by recent events, it seems we're right,' Kayla countered.

The Marquis chuckled, heaved himself to his feet and

dusted the sand from his bottom. 'All righty then. We'd best start tracking.' He marched off down the beach, following the huge three-toed prints the creature had left in the sand.

Kayla watched for a moment, barely believing what she was about to do, then followed close behind.

8

ALETHEA

The crowd gave a collective gasp.

The chanting had stopped abruptly. Everyone watched as a large crack laced its way up Kahanga Rock. This had never happened before. A huge section looked as if it was about to fall to the ground – and one of the climbers was going to fall with it.

'I told you!' screeched Elvira. 'I told you someone was going to die!'

Ma was in too much shock to scold her. 'Oh no,' she whispered, wringing her hands. 'That dear boy. Ash be kind.'

'It's Rustus Furi,' whispered Cassio. 'His brother broke the all-time speed record last year. He was meant to *win*.'

Murmurs rippled through the crowd like a seismic wave as everyone turned to speak to their neighbour, but Alethea couldn't tear her eyes away from the rock. There was a loud creaking and the chunk of the tower slowly broke free. Conversations quietened as the crowd watched the rock and its climber plummet towards the ground. Moments later there was a loud crash. The rock shattered, leaving Rustus Furi lying motionless in the centre of the stage. A deathly silence settled over the audience.

'Is he dead?' Padma asked after what felt like forever.

'I don't know,' whispered Cassio. 'Maybe.'

'No,' said Padma, 'he's moving. Look.' The crowd started murmuring again.

'What will happen now?' Elvira asked.

'He'll be cast out into the Beastlands.'

Alethea knew what her sibling said was true. But a Furi? *Outcast?* She couldn't imagine it.

'What will happen to him in the Beastlands?' asked Lillian. 'Will he become a webwalker?'

'Will he die?' asked Cassio.

Alethea didn't know. She didn't see how anyone could survive out there for long, fabled webwalkers included. She had heard tales about the Beastlands, and from her understanding there were far more dangerous creatures out there than webspinners. She didn't want to dwell on that thought though. After all, she'd be making her own way out there soon.

'I think he'll be just fine,' she said, trying to convince herself as much as her siblings. 'He's strong and smart and I'm sure there are plenty of other webwalkers out there to look out for him.'

Two Scorched Ataris had made their way onto the stage and were carrying Rustus Furi out of sight.

Alethea wondered briefly what the Red healer would use to treat his injuries. Ashflower for the bruising, fire thistle for the nerves, perhaps a tuber of taxacum for the pain . . .

She shook the thoughts from her mind and refocused her energy on the task at hand. If she was going to go in search of marshwort, then this was the perfect opportunity to slip away – everyone was looking back to the summit of Kahanga Rock to see who would make it to the top before it erupted. She looked at her brothers and sisters and tried to imagine their faces if she didn't make it back from the Beastlands. Could she really leave them? Never in her life had Alethea been so conflicted. She wanted to stay and protect her family, to shield them from more heartache, but what about Grandma? Now that Alethea knew she had the Scourge, could she live with herself if she didn't try to save her? She knew the answer.

Alethea backed slowly away, imprinting this moment in her memory as her family held each other tightly, gasping in awe and excitement as they watched the remaining climbers. Out of the corner of her eye she saw Grandma fix her with a questioning gaze.

Alethea swallowed. She had hoped to slip away unnoticed without telling any of them where she was going. She shook her head and mouthed, *I'm sorry*. Grandma paled, but gave a resigned nod. Alethea knew that if she didn't leave in that moment she wouldn't have the courage to do it at all, so she wrenched her eyes away from her family and hurried off through the crowd.

As she rushed through a group of Pinks, a huge cheer rang out. Alethea glanced at the stage and saw the six remaining Unscorched standing at the top of Kahanga Rock. Apart from Rustus, they'd all made it to safety. That meant the eruption was imminent. Soon, brightly coloured clouds of steam would burst violently from the sides of the rock, obscuring the Unscorched warriors from view. Once the gases had cleared, the climbers would make their victory descent, the ceremony would be over and the crowd would disperse, back to their districts for the feasts. Alethea needed to collect her things from home before that happened. She pushed through the throngs of people with a renewed determination.

When she arrived at the cave house, she found the last remaining firewort flower and placed it carefully next to Grandma's knitting needles, as a symbol of hope and a promise that she would return with a cure. Next, she grabbed her satchel and thrust in a few essentials: a couple of pieces of flatbread, a water canteen, a cloth sack to hold the marshwort, an old worn blanket and the *Healer's Guide* she had been given that morning.

Then she went to the House of Healing, where she strapped a blue pouch around her waist and placed into it a collection of botanicals and dressings, along with a knife and a pair of plant shears, desperately hoping she would not need to use the healing herbs but knowing the importance of being prepared in case. She also grabbed a square of blue cloth, which she dipped in oil of ashroot. Finally she spritzed herself with blue lake water, hoping there was some truth in the belief that it would discourage the webspinners from getting too close.

Once she was ready she made her way to the edge of the city and climbed the sloped sides of the caldera to reach the city gate. It was manned by a single Scorched Atari, the only person in the whole city – aside from her – who wasn't at the Scorching.

He stepped forward as she approached. 'No citizens allowed on the perimeter,' he barked. 'Return to your district immediately.'

'I'm so sorry to bother you.' Alethea dipped her head to avoid his gaze. 'I was sent here by a colleague of yours. He said to give you this.' She held up the blue handkerchief.

'Oh, brilliant,' the guard said, raising the handkerchief to his nose. 'Been needing this all morning.' He blew out loudly, filling the handkerchief with yellow snot. Alethea watched intently, hoping for some kind of signal that her plan had worked. For a moment there was nothing but then, without warning, the guard crashed to the ground, unconscious.

She rushed over and turned him onto his side, checking his pulse and airways. 'You'll be OK,' Alethea whispered. 'It's only oil of ashroot. It will make you sleep for the next few minutes, but as soon as I'm gone you'll start to come round, I promise.'

Once she was satisfied he'd be fine, Alethea heaved the heavy metal gate open. She lingered briefly at the boundary, looking back over the city. Kahanga Rock was still spewing plumes of ash into the sky as the crowds of brightly coloured people milled around, no doubt cheering for their newly Scorched warriors. She thought about all the things she wished she had said to her family. She pictured the rash on Grandma's wrist. Who would treat her and all the other citizens if Alethea didn't make it back from the Beastlands? The Ash Bishop said nobody else in all the city had cured a case of the Scourge. Alethea *had* to survive and return with the marshwort – their lives depended on it. She tried not to think about the fact that she could be wrong and the marshwort might not even work.

'I'll be back soon, Grandma,' she whispered. 'To fix you.'

Then she shut the gate behind her and stepped into the Beastlands.

The ground dropped steeply away towards dense turquoise jungle, just as it fell towards the city on the other side. Alethea hurried towards the treeline. As she drew closer she saw the webs criss-crossing their way between the plants, wrapping every cane and leaf in a silvery blanket. The path Alethea was on led right into the forest and through the webs, and she saw no alternative but to follow it. She marched forward without hesitation.

As she stepped between the first trees, the sky disappeared and the world seemed to close in around her. Beside her something chirruped. She turned towards the source of the sound as a large orange hexapod leaped out of the underbrush and onto the path ahead.

What's that? she wondered, stepping carefully around it.

The only creatures that lived in Ataria were the fire geckos that sunbathed by the mud pools, the vulcanwings that were farmed for meat and eggs and the bardflies that buzzed around the lava fields. The small beast jumped towards her again, attracting the attention of some predatory beast perched up in the canes. It soared down and snatched the bug from the ground, coming to land a little further down the path from Alethea. It held its pale spotted wings over the hexapod in a protective shield, to prevent any other creature coming to steal its prize. Alethea was startled by its agility and stealth and quickly hurried past it, giving it as wide a berth as she could. She was sure she could hear it murmuring happily to itself as it feasted.

As she continued through the jungle, she marvelled that when people talked about the Beastlands they described the webs and their creators but never mentioned the plants that provided the framework for the webspinners' constructions. In Alethea's opinion that was a travesty, for the plants were the foundations of the whole ecosystem. In particular she noted the turquoise pyro canes, which of course she'd read about in *A Healer's Guide*, but had never actually seen up close, despite living only strides away from an entire forest of them. They were incredible plants, stretching as high as trees but actually categorised as grasses. Little was known about the canes' potential uses in healing because harvesting them was taboo. Da had confided in Alethea that he suspected the healing benefits of pyro cane were many, and she vowed that on her way home – should she survive – she would take a sample to learn from.

She had been striding along for several hours without incident when she came to a wide, flat clearing. A small stream ran through it, which Alethea knelt beside to fill her canteen. The water was like nothing she had tasted in Ataria; it was cool and sweet, without the slightest hint of sulphur. She wondered if the air was fresher here too and decided to remove her suka-moss nose plugs.

Alethea took a tentative breath, followed by a deeper one. The air *was* sweeter here – not so dry and dusty. There was an earthy edge to it that reminded her of her herb larder. She stooped to lift a handful of earth. It was nothing like the dry volcanic ash of Ataria, but instead was rich and soft, teeming with life and bursting with nutrients. She was engrossed in the soil when a movement ahead caught her eye. There, walking to the centre of a large vertical web, was a huge bulbous-bodied webspinner. It moved slowly, testing the silk with its long slender legs before proceeding. Though it was unnerving to look at, Alethea didn't feel threatened. The webspinner wasn't interested in her at all. Even as it turned and she caught a glimpse of its two long curved fangs she felt only awe, not fear.

Wait. Two *fangs? That's strange*, she thought. All of the Scourge wounds she had seen, including the one on

Grandma's wrist, had only one puncture mark. If the webspinner had two fangs, why would it only use one of them?

Truth be told, Alethea had never been entirely convinced by the Ash Bishops' insistence that it was the webspinners spreading the disease – on account of the fact that nobody had ever seen one in the city. Da had felt the same. Alethea remembered a day when he was lying feverish in his bed as she stroked his hair and tended his wound.

'I just don't think it can be the webspinners, LeLe,' he had said. 'Why would they come into the city? I think it's something else.'

'Like what?' Alethea had asked. 'What else could possibly cause it?'

'I don't know,' Da had said. 'There must be a piece of this puzzle I'm missing.'

Alethea knew exactly how he had felt. The more she tried to solve the mystery of the Scourge, the more questions it seemed to raise.

She marched on, making Da a promise as she went.

'I'm going to solve it, Da. I'm going to save Grandma. And I'm going to learn the truth.'

9

RUSTUS

'Sit down,' said Cardinal Magmatis, pointing at an empty chair in front of him.

'When will I go out into the Beastlands?' Rustus asked as he took the seat. 'Will I get to speak to my family first?'

'Just wait there,' said the Cardinal, looking flustered. 'I need to go and make some arrangements.' He strode out of the room, leaving Rustus alone.

Rustus sat quietly, thinking about the events that had unfolded. His whole body ached and he had a long scratch on the side of his head – would the healer be along soon to treat that? He didn't know how it had happened. He and Hubert had been nearly at the top. Rustus hadn't been on track to finish first but he was definitely going to pass the initiation. Maybe he should have left Hubert to fall. If he hadn't gone back to help his friend then maybe he wouldn't have climbed over that particular piece of rock. But then again, maybe he would have. And if he hadn't helped Hubert, then *he* might have been the one cast out. Was that any better?

'Where is he?' The sound of his father's voice echoing through the empty corridors of House Atari snapped Rustus out of his spiralling thoughts.

Rustus winced, wishing the floor would open up and swallow him. He had fantasised about this conversation many times, imagining how his father would proudly acknowledge Rustus as his son and finally declare him worthy of the Furi name. He had prayed that the Scorching would change everything. He supposed in a way his prayer had been granted.

Brutus Furi burst into the room, his quivering face so flushed that it was almost impossible to tell where his red woven plaits ended and his forehead began. Rustus watched him approach, a lump forming in his throat.

'Don't you look at me, boy!' Brutus roared. 'How could you do this to me? You've humiliated me in front of the whole city.'

Rustus found himself unable to make a sound.

Brutus kicked over a chair. 'I always knew there was something wrong with you.'

At that moment his brothers rushed into the room.

'What happened?' asked Tactus, looking directly at Rustus.

Rustus imagined that Tactus and Octus looked exactly as Brutus must have thirty years earlier. Rustus was just as tall as them, despite being years younger, and had the same dark eyes, but people always remarked that he looked far more like his mother than his brothers or his father. From what Rustus could remember of his mother, he thought he agreed, but it was hard to be sure. Since she had left the family home to live in the Silver District, his father had removed all traces of her and didn't like to be reminded of her existence.

'You were doing so well,' Tactus continued.

Rustus heard his other brother scoff at this, while their father continued to seethe quietly.

Rustus shrugged. 'I just . . .' His throat was scratchy and dry. What explanation could he give that they would accept?

'It doesn't matter what happened out there,' interrupted Octus. 'It's what happens now that counts. We need to denounce him from the family before he leaves the city. We can't let this tarnish our reputation.'

'Obviously,' said Brutus, his huge hands clenched into fists. 'I should have done it years ago. He's been a blight on this family since the day he was born.'

At his core Rustus had always known that his father felt this way, but he'd never heard him say it out loud. The words struck a more powerful blow than any punch.

Tactus watched Rustus, eyes searching for an explanation. He lacked the cruel streak of their father and elder brother; while he would laugh when they joked about Rustus's shortcomings, he would never offer up insults himself. 'Do we really need to go that far?' Tactus said. 'He's already being exiled.'

Rustus leaned forward, feeling a surge of gratitude. A tiny flame of hope reignited in his chest.

'Of course he has to go,' bellowed their father. 'Furis have served this city for generations. What good is a warrior that can't pass the most basic of tests?'

Rustus grabbed his chair in exasperation. He had been trying to help Hubert. Why was nobody acknowledging that?

Tactus shuffled his feet awkwardly.

'Think about your promotion, Tactus,' said Octus. 'Do you think you'll still get it if you share a name with him?' He jabbed a finger at Rustus.

Rustus lifted his head a little so that he could see Tactus's face. Despite everything, Rustus was still his brother, and that had to count for something. But Tactus's blank features were difficult to read. Rustus had no idea what he was thinking.

Eventually Tactus opened his mouth. 'I suppose you're right,' he said, nodding at his father and older brother as if Rustus wasn't even there.

Rustus's heart fell through his chair. He couldn't believe it. His whole family were agreed. Rustus would no longer be a Furi. He tried to catch Tactus's eye, but his brother would not look in his direction.

'I'm sorry,' Rustus said quietly. 'I'm sorry that I've failed you all.'

'*Sorry?*' yelled Brutus. '*Sorry!* Well, so am I. Sorry that I didn't cast you out into the Beastlands as soon as your mother spewed that stupid prophecy.'

Rustus's stomach fluttered. His father had never spoken about why his mother had left them. He only knew about her visions from what their elderly neighbour had told him.

'She's a seer,' Mrs Vesta had insisted. 'Knows what the Ash Gods are thinking. It's no good someone with that kind of talent sitting around here in the Red District. They need her in House Atari. She'll be of great use there, as a spiritual guide for the Ash Bishops.'

Since Mum had left, she'd never been back or even written to them, and Rustus had certainly never heard about any prophecy to do with himself.

'What do you . . .' Rustus started to ask, but his father and brothers were already leaving, chatting animatedly between themselves, not giving so much as a backwards glance to the family member they had just deserted forever.

Rustus sat in silence for what felt like a long time. His head was stinging.

'You have another visitor,' said Cardinal Magmatis.

Rustus started, not realising the man had returned. 'Who is it?' he asked, his voice quiet, but the Cardinal didn't deign to respond before he ushered the visitor in and left them to it.

When the woman entered the room, Rustus could hardly believe his eyes.

'Mum?' he rasped out, taking in the unfamiliar silver cloak she wore.

She stopped just before his chair and knelt, staring at

him intently, drinking in every detail. 'Hello, Rustus,' she said with a sad smile.

Her sweet voice met his ears like the sound of a familiar instrument playing a long-forgotten melody. How he had missed her. Had she missed him too? Was that why she was here? Was there something she could do to stop him being cast out? After all, the Silvers were in charge of all the decisions regarding the running of the city.

'Have you come to save me?' he asked hopefully.

She took his hand in hers, tears pricking the corners of her eyes. 'My sweet boy,' she said, avoiding the question. 'You were always different.'

'Can you stop them from sending me into the Beastlands?'

She shook her head sadly. 'Kahanga Rock chose you,' she said. 'The island has made its decision.'

Rustus felt tears in his eyes too. His body and limbs felt icy cold and heavy as lead. They had all made their decisions; Kahanga Rock, the Ash Gods, his dad, his brothers – none of them believed he deserved to be Scorched. Any fire that had burned inside him before the ceremony was well and truly extinguished now.

'What will happen to me, Mum?' he asked, his voice quivering. He tried hard not to cry.

'I can't tell you that,' his mum said. 'But I know that this is your path.'

Was this what his father had meant about the prophecy? Had she always known he was going to fail?

She pushed a lock of hair away from his face. 'Since the

day you were born, I have known you were special, Rustus.'

'Was it my fault you left us?' he asked. 'Dad said there was a prophecy . . . about me.'

She nodded. 'It's true that I saw your destiny was not in Ataria.' Rustus felt betrayed. Why had nobody warned him? Why had they let him attempt the Scorching if it was doomed anyway? 'But it wasn't clear where else you were meant to be.'

Out in the Beastlands with the webspinners apparently, Rustus thought bitterly. Where else was there?

'I don't want to leave,' Rustus said. 'I want to stay here, to be Scorched.'

'I know,' said his mum, soft lines of concern furrowing her brow. 'But this is not your place, Rustus. You have a different role to play.'

'What if I find a way to come back?' he protested, pushing himself to standing. 'To prove to you all that I am worthy.'

She regarded him intently. 'You are not a Scorched Atari, Rustus, and you should stop trying to be one.' Another painful blow.

'But what else is there?'

She took both of his hands in hers. 'If only you knew,' she said, mouth turned up in a half-smile. 'You are going to be so much more.'

He couldn't understand how she could look even remotely happy at the prospect of her youngest child being sent out to become a webwalker.

'Don't you care about me?' he asked.

'More than anything,' she replied. 'All these years I've watched you from afar, wishing I could be there beside you, showing you that there is more to life than Scorchings and spears. But I wasn't allowed to stay with you, Rustus. They made me leave.'

The door to the room opened and she started to whisper quickly and urgently. 'There's more,' she said. 'I thought we would have more time.' Cardinal Magmatis strode towards them. 'You won't be alone,' Mum hissed. 'There are others like you.' Cardinal Magmatis came up beside them and took Mum by the arm. 'You must find them before the return of the –'

'Enough!' bellowed Cardinal Magmatis, pulling her away and frowning at Rustus. 'It's time to go. The others have completed the Scorching and will escort you out of the city before the feast commences.'

Rustus's mother bowed her head to the Cardinal and shot Rustus a final glance. 'Goodbye, my boy,' she said. 'I'm proud of what you did today. Don't forget what I said.' She shot him a meaningful look and Rustus felt a searing pain in his chest.

He looked at the floor, trying to focus on the throbbing in his head instead of the ache deep in his heart. Once she was gone, he realised he hadn't even said goodbye.

As the scent of his mother faded, the sound of chattering voices approached. Aro was the first to enter, and then the others shuffled in behind her, keeping their distance from where Rustus was standing. It pained him to see how they looked at him. They were now Scorched: official city protectors whose job it was to remove anything or anyone that threatened Ataria, starting with him.

'I know what you have to do,' he said to break the silence. 'And I don't blame you or anything.' It had been a long morning and he was ready for it to be over.

None of them met his eye, instead fidgeting and shifting from foot to foot. Even Aro looked uncomfortable.

Finally Hubert stepped to the front of the group. 'This is wrong,' he said, his face pinched. 'It's not Rustus that should be going. It's me.' Rustus could see from the obsidian beads on his braids that he had made it to the top in time.

'You did it!' Rustus said.

Hubert's eyes met Rustus's. 'I'm sorry,' he mouthed.

'For the first time ever, I actually agree with Hubert,' said Aro, and Rustus was almost shocked out of his misery. 'He doesn't deserve those beads.' The surprise gave way to resignation – nothing had changed.

'Enough talking,' said Cardinal Magmatis. 'You –' he pointed at Rustus – 'get behind me. Then the rest of you in single file.'

They carried out his orders wordlessly, even Hubert and Aro, whose protests died on their tongues at the Cardinal's fiery tone. Rustus wished he could think of something to say to comfort Hubert, who looked sick with guilt, but he had nothing.

As they marched out of House Atari and through the city, they passed the bubbling lakes and cave houses that Rustus had seen every day of his life. Would he ever return to see these familiar sights again? His mind whirled. This couldn't be it, could it? Surely there would be a chance for redemption.

'You can't leave,' squeaked Hubert as they marched past Rustus's street.

'It's OK,' Rustus replied. 'I'll be OK.' His mind was running through all the ways he could try to earn back his place in the city. His mother had been wrong – he did belong here.

The crowds who'd gathered for the ceremony now lined the path to watch as Rustus was escorted through the streets. They averted their eyes, as if his bad luck was catching. His neighbours, former teachers, not one of them could bring themselves to look at him.

I'll be back, he wanted to shout at them. *I will find a way to prove you all wrong and I will come back!*

Eventually they reached the city gates. A tall Scorched Atari stood on guard, with a red welt on his forehead. Next to him was Scorch Knight Itticus.

'What did I say, Furi?' He smiled cruelly. 'Not cut out for Atarian life. I wasn't at all surprised to see you fail.'

Rustus looked at his feet and ground his teeth.

'Scorch Knight Itticus will accompany you out of the city,' said the Cardinal. 'Good luck. You're going to need it.'

Before they departed, Scorch Knight Itticus took great pleasure in commanding Rustus to remove the red cloths from his hair.

Rustus forced his hands to his head to unravel the

braids he had so carefully tied just that morning. As he pulled out the cloth, his hair fell loosely over his shoulders. He felt ashamed. He had worn red proudly his whole life and had longed for the day he would prove himself worthy of it. That day had come at last, and he had failed. He stared sadly at the pile of red cloth at his feet and tried to remind himself that it was just a bunch of old rags he was leaving behind. But it felt like so much more – his dreams, his family, his hope.

Once it was done, they left the Cardinal and the city behind and marched out into the Beastlands. Ahead of them the shivering pyro canes rustled and whistled in the breeze. Rustus couldn't believe he had walked this path only yesterday; then it had felt like the beginning of the rest of his life. Today it felt like the end. Somehow he would have to find his way through this sprawling wild and dangerous land and hatch a plan to get home. On the plus side, at least with every step they took away from Ataria the stench of sulphur dulled.

After some time, they reached a clearing, where Scorch Knight Itticus barked for them to stop.

'I guess this is it then,' Rustus said.

Hubert sniffled and Rustus saw that his red rimmed-eyes were full of tears.

'I'll be all right,' Rustus reassured his friend. 'You don't need to worry about me.'

'That's enough chat,' said their old instructor. 'Time to go.'

Hubert sniffed again.

'Pull yourself together, for Ash's sake,' Scorch Knight Itticus said. 'Unless you want us to leave you out here too.'

The boy took in a sharp breath and fell silent.

'I suggest you find a place to make camp and stay there,' Scorch Knight Itticus said to Rustus in what seemed like a rare display of kindness – until the man's face morphed into a cruel smirk. 'There's more than webspinners in the Beastlands.'

Rustus nodded, not wanting to show his fear, and then watched as the group he'd trained with for the last year began to file out of the clearing. A couple of them shot him helpless glances but they all continued back towards the city.

Hubert lagged at the back of the line, lingering in the clearing. When the others were completely out of sight, he turned to face Rustus. His dull wet eyes spoke a thousand words and his face was full of pain.

Rustus lifted his hand so that his open palm faced Hubert. He wasn't sure what it was supposed to mean. *I don't regret what I did? I'll find a way to come back to march beside you? I'm sorry? Goodbye?*

Hubert returned the gesture.

'Keep up, boy,' shouted Scorch Knight Itticus in the distance.

Hubert turned to follow the others, then stopped. 'I didn't mean for you to help me, you know,' he said quietly, voice breaking.

'I know,' said Rustus, nodding. 'Go on. It's all right.'

And then Hubert was gone too.

Rustus looked about the empty clearing. Now what? Find a place to camp – that was what his instructor had suggested. Perhaps he should head down to the coast. His brothers had told him there was a beach. There would be fewer webspinners down there, and the air would be much clearer.

He started to pick his way through the forest. At one point he came across the bodies of the webspinners they had killed the night before. What a pointless waste of life that had been. He should have known then that this was going to be the outcome. He'd never had what it takes to become a Scorched Atari. Not inside.

He fell into a rhythm, listening to the sounds of the jungle and trying to forget the awful things his father and brothers had said, and after a while he found himself in another clearing, where a hissing in the surrounding trees caught his attention.

There's more than webspinners in the Beastlands.

He knew the Beastlands were full of terrible creatures – it was in the name after all – but his brothers had never mentioned seeing anything but webs, webspinners and the occasional webwalker.

The hissing grew louder and more high-pitched, and Rustus started to wonder if he should run. Then the hissing stopped. He stumbled backwards as a bright blue head popped out of the trees, its mouth open to reveal needle-sharp fangs that pointed out at all angles and dripped with something red.

A bead of sweat rolled down Rustus's forehead. He took a slow step back, keeping his eyes trained on the beast. Then a twig cracked beneath his foot and the beast lunged towards him. Rustus gave up on moving slowly and turned and fled.

As the edge of the clearing grew closer Rustus knew he would soon have to choose between turning to face the ferocious beast bearing down on him or running straight into the webs. He looked over his shoulder. Tough choice, but right now one of those options seemed infinitely more frightening than the other. Leaping into the dark grey webs, he made his decision. He chose the webspinners.

Rustus ran full pelt into the webs, feeling the fibres rip and tear as he was immersed in their sticky strands. He coughed and spluttered, pulling the threads from his nose and mouth so he could breathe. All was suddenly silent. Where was the creature that had been chasing him? He ripped the silk from his eyes and looked over his shoulder to discover the web had closed behind him and he was now buried within it.

He needed to get out of there before the webspinners descended on him. He tore at the strands ahead of him; if he kept on moving, eventually he would have to reach another clearing.

At last he broke through and rolled across the ground, coming to land on a woven silver blanket.

'Hello,' said a voice.

Rustus scrambled to his feet. He found he was in a

room of sorts, bordered on all sides by silvery webs. In the centre of the room stood a person dressed in grey.

'Hello,' Rustus replied, as it seemed the natural thing to do and he had no idea what else to say.

And then, before either of them could say anything more, something enormous and blue crashed through the webs and onto the earth beside them.

'Quick,' yelled the webwalker. 'On your feet! How are you at wrestling?'

10

KAYLA

The beast's tracks had been easy to follow on the wet sand of the beach, but to Kayla's horror they had soon led back into the webspinner-infested forest. And when they had, the hard earth there had given Kayla and the Marquis few clues as to where the creature had gone.

Now, a few paces ahead, the Marquis was crouched in a squat, peering down his nose at a small beast on a leaf. He seemed totally unperturbed by the wall of webs around him. It was not the first time he had acted this way. Kayla had watched impatiently as he had inspected leaves, sniffed stems, rubbed his fingers over the ground and countless other things that seemed totally unrelated to their quest. As Kayla waited, she batted at the air with her hand; the forest buzzed with flying hexapods and the heat and humidity made it feel as if invisible creatures were crawling all over her. It was horrible. What was more, she was losing faith in the Marquis's abilities as a tracker and starting to regret her decision to join him.

'You must see this!' he said, beckoning Kayla closer.

Thus far Kayla had managed to stay away from the webs, and she wasn't keen to change that. 'No, thanks,' she said. 'I'll just stay here on the path.'

Even from her protected position, she couldn't help looking around nervously every few seconds to check she wasn't too close to the webs. Something pricked her wrist and she batted furiously at empty air. 'Eugh. What have you found anyway? Is it a clue? Is the razor whatsit close?'

'The needlejaw?' the Marquis asked. 'No, this is nothing to do with Topaz. Look! It's a geyser hopper.'

Kayla squinted over to where the Marquis was pointing. A pale green hexapod with huge, spine-covered back legs sat on the plant in front of him. He pressed a finger to his lip, urging her to stay quiet.

'They're very flighty,' he said. 'Come on, come over here. Just have a quick look.'

Kayla leaned fractionally closer. The geyser hopper's long antennae danced in the air. She had to admit it was beautiful – its long wings curled up like paper scrolls over its back and its eyes were brilliant orange – but while it might have been nice to look at, it was a distraction from their mission.

Kayla moved a little nearer to the Marquis, then loudly remarked, 'And how exactly is this helping us to find the needlejaw?' At the sound of her voice the geyser hopper immediately leaped over their heads, opening its wide orange wings as it glided away to safety. In its wake it left a strong scent of peppermint.

'Why did you do that?' The Marquis shook his head sadly. 'You may never get the chance to see one of those again. They're extremely rare.'

'Maybe you've forgotten,' replied Kayla, 'but we're not here on a bug-spotting expedition. We're here to search for your missing needlejaw. And when we've done that, you've promised to take me to find my pangron.'

He looked set to huff right back at her when a small figure dressed in grey appeared ahead of them. Kayla reached for her jackblade.

'Marquis Macdonald!' the boy yelled. 'Have you lost one of your beasts?'

The Marquis pushed a section of web aside and squinted towards the boy. 'Yes, lad!' he shouted. 'Have you found one?'

'We have, sir! We've got it! In The Silk! Come quick!'

'What's The Silk?' Kayla asked, lowering her knife.

'You'll see,' said the Marquis. 'Come on!'

'Will you at least tell me where we're going?' she asked. The Marquis did not reply. Kayla looked back at him, or at where he had been standing just seconds before, to find that he had disappeared.

'Where did you go?' Kayla said in alarm.

Once again there was no response.

'Hey!' shouted Kayla. 'Marquis Macdonald! Where are you?'

She took a small step towards the webs and peered in.

The Marquis was nowhere to be seen.

'He's gone!' she said to herself disbelievingly.

Suddenly a pair of hands reached out of the webs and grabbed Kayla by the shoulders.

'Arrgh!' She writhed and kicked as she lurched towards the webs. 'Get off me!'

The sticky strands wrapped themselves around her arms and face as she was dragged through. Her stomach heaved and her skin crawled as she imagined the webspinners creeping all over her.

'Let go of me!'

She kicked and thrashed in panic until, finally, the arms did let go and she fell to the ground. It was much darker here, and it took a while for Kayla's eyes to adjust to the low light. A rotund figure leaned down and offered a hand. She did not take it.

'Sorry about that,' said the Marquis, as Kayla clambered to her feet. 'Maybe I should have given you a bit of a warning.'

'You think?' Kayla said, brushing threads of web off her leg. 'That was revolting.' She rubbed at an itch beneath her sleeve. Was it in her head or had something bitten her? The skin did look a little red, but it was probably just from scratching.

'First time is the worst,' said the Marquis. 'You'll get used to it.'

'Why would I ever want to get used to climbing through webs?'

'It's the only entrance to The Silk,' said the Marquis

with a smile. 'The city within the pyro canes.'

Kayla looked around again. Entrance to a city? It wasn't like any city Kayla had ever seen. Not that she had seen all that many, having lived in Sophiatown all her life. Nonetheless, this seemed unusual. Where Sophiatown was entered through a large wooden drawbridge at the base of an enormous stone wall, this city's entrance was a tent of grey silk no bigger than Kayla's bedroom.

'I didn't think anyone lived in the Beastlands,' said Kayla.

The boy who had called to them stepped out of the shadows and gave a little chuckle. 'And we like to keep it that way,' he said. 'Come on.' He wandered to the far side of the chamber and disappeared through the silken wall.

Kayla blinked in confusion, watching closely as the Marquis followed the boy.

'Are you expecting me to walk through that?' she asked, hoping they could still hear her.

'That's right,' said the Marquis from the other side. 'Calm and confident. That's the best way.'

Kayla stepped forward and reached out a hand to touch the silk. It wasn't as solid as it looked. In fact, it seemed to be made of thousands of hair-thin strands.

'Where are the webspinners?' she asked.

'We have a mutual agreement,' the boy replied. 'We don't bother them, and in return they don't bother us.'

It didn't entirely answer Kayla's question or completely settle her nerves, but she believed him enough to push the wall's strands apart and walk through.

'Did the webspinners make the city?' she asked as

she emerged on the other side, turning to see the strands knitting back together as if they had never parted.

'The webspinners?' The boy chuckled. 'No. They make the silk, and then we harvest it and use it as we like.'

Kayla found herself in a new, much larger chamber. It was lighter too; sunlight streamed through small star-like holes in the domed silk roof, making the lustrous walls glimmer like oil on water. Never in Kayla's wildest dreams had she imagined that webspinner silk could be made into anything so beautiful.

'This is pretty impressive,' she said begrudgingly.

'Thanks,' said the boy with a smile. 'It's a lot of work, but we're proud of our home.'

Looking at him again, Kayla realised that his grey clothes shimmered in the same way as the walls.

'Your clothes,' she said, 'are they made of webspinner silk too?'

The boy nodded.

'Amazingly versatile material, webspinner silk,' said the Marquis, stroking the wall. 'Waterproof, fireproof, sunproof, acid-proof, strong, soft . . .'

They walked through a series of tunnels and chambers, passing curtains, hammocks and swings all made of webspinner silk. In one room there were hundreds of fat turquoise caterpillars.

'Ashworms,' whispered the Marquis in Kayla's ear. 'Larvae of the astral ashmoth. Their bodies are packed full of luciferins.'

'What are they?' Kayla asked suspiciously. 'Poisons?'

'No,' the Marquis replied, shaking his head and chuckling. 'You Southlanders, you think everything in the Beastlands is out to kill you. Luciferins are chemicals that make them glow in the dark.'

'Oh,' said Kayla. That was pretty cool. But she was a little put out by his comment about Southlanders. That fear was precisely how they had stayed alive for so long – and the whole reason they were the only city not yet to have succumbed to the Scourge.

Finally they came to a room full of people dressed in grey, some standing, others seated on squat pyro-cane stools. A woman stood up as they approached.

'Welcome to The Silk,' she said, dipping her head. To Kayla's surprise, she saw that webspinner silk was even woven into her hair. 'I am Tas, spokesperson of the webwalkers.'

'Hello, Tas,' said the Marquis, opening his arms to gather her up in a hug.

'Great to see you, Maltheus,' Tas replied, returning the gesture. There was a squeak as they embraced and a small whiskered nose poked its way out of the Marquis's beard.

Tas smiled. 'Hello, Lillypeg!'

Was that a beast in the Marquis's beard? Kayla knew she'd seen something moving in there earlier!

'It's been far too long,' said the Marquis.

'That it has, Maltheus,' said Tas. 'But next time you drop by, please try to keep the man-eating monsters *inside* your wagon, rather than allowing them to rampage wildly through the forest.' Her scolding broke into a laugh and deep creases appeared around the corners of her eyes and mouth.

The Marquis laughed sheepishly. 'Topaz isn't man-eating, she's just . . . flighty. I hope she didn't get hurt?'

Tas turned to the crowd of people behind her, who moved apart to reveal the needlejaw trapped beneath a strong net of webspinner silk. Kayla wouldn't go as far as to say she was pleased to see the beast, but at least it meant they could get out of this forest and be on their way to Port Royal.

'Topaz!' shouted the Marquis, rushing to the creature's side. 'Oh, thank goodness. How did you find her?'

'She found us. Stumbled right into The Silk. What is she anyway?'

The Marquis unwrapped Topaz's bindings and she cooed happily. 'I call her a needlejaw,' he said. 'I think she's a new species.' He stroked Topaz's head tenderly and she gave her scales a little shiver. 'You're all right,' he said softly, pulling a rope leash from his waist and slipping it over her neck. He turned to Tas. 'She just needs a bit of affection.'

Tas raised an eyebrow at Kayla. 'Tell that to the lad she was chasing. Poor boy had just stumbled into The Silk himself when she came crashing through behind him. Luckily he had a strong set of arms and wrestled her to the ground.'

'Thank the Skies for that,' said Kayla. 'We've been looking for that beast for hours.'

'It's not the Skies you should be thanking,' said Tas. 'It's our new friend, Rustus!'

A tall boy stepped out from the crowd. Unlike the others, who were all dressed in grey, his waistcoat and trousers were brilliant red.

Kayla immediately recognised the uniform, which she had learned about at the Academy. Instinctively she sank into a defensive position. 'You're a Scorched Atari,' she said, hands raised.

'Er . . . no,' Rustus said, shaking his head.

'Unscorched?' Kayla asked.

Rustus sighed. 'Technically, no. I failed the Scorching this morning.'

Kayla looked him up and down. His bare arms were broad and muscular. He looked very strong. She wondered why he had failed and whether it had something to do with the cut on the side of his head.

'What about you?' Rustus asked. 'You look like a Sky Rider.'

'I am,' Kayla replied, rising to her full height and straightening her yellow jacket proudly. 'I'm Kayla Karakka, first-year cadet at the Sky Academy.'

'What are you doing in the Ashlands then?' asked Rustus, looking confused.

'I didn't *intend* to be here.'

'What do you mean?' said Rustus. 'Surely a rider doesn't come to the Ashlands by accident.'

'If you must know,' Kayla snapped, 'I was attacked while I was out investigating an enemy ship. My pangron was shot down with an arrow and my attacker left me for dead. I washed up on the coast here.'

The boy looked shocked. 'Your pangron was felled by an arrow?' he asked. 'I'd heard they're pretty hard to kill.'

A red mist descended over Kayla. 'It was a *poisoned* arrow,' she said. 'No pangron would have stood a chance. Faro is the strongest, most –'

'Shh,' hissed Tas, her expression deadly serious. A web of lines criss-crossed her face as her features buckled in concern. 'This is unheard of. You're *certain* that a pangron has been taken?'

'Yes,' said Kayla. 'Actually, two pangrons.' She explained how Ezra had been stolen from Sophiatown and how she had followed the clues to find him. She emphasised the heroics of her role and carefully left out the bit where she should never have left the safety of her city in the first place and could not for the life of her remember what their attacker looked like.

After hearing the story, Tas wrung her hands together. 'So it was a calculated attack on Sophiatown,' she said. 'With the sole intention of stealing a pangron.' She sighed heavily. 'This is very worrying news.'

The Marquis appeared over Kayla's shoulder. 'I know that face,' he said to Tas. 'You're thinking about the prophecy again, aren't you?'

She gave him a knowing grimace. 'I can't get it out of my head, Maltheus.'

'What prophecy?' asked Rustus.

'Don't encourage them,' interrupted Kayla. 'There's no such thing.'

'Of course there is,' said Tas. 'Seers have existed since the first people came to the island. They've foretold all the great events of our history.'

'And I suppose they've told you something is about to happen involving a pangron,' said Kayla.

'Not a pangron,' said Tas thoughtfully, 'but another winged beast.'

'The lord of the skies,' said the Marquis with an earnest stare.

'Lord of the skies?' Kayla scoffed. 'I think you'll find that *is* a pangron.'

'This is no joke, Kayla.' Tas and the Marquis both looked very serious. 'It has been prophesied that the phaegra *will* return, and when it does, the Realms will be broken beyond repair.'

Kayla rolled her eyes. She had no time for prophecies.

'What do you know about the phaegra, Kayla?' asked the Marquis.

Kayla shrugged. 'It was a winged scaly beast that liked to eat people, until it was wiped out by the Sky Riders.'

'The Sky Riders?' countered Rustus quickly. 'It wasn't the Sky Riders that defeated the phaegras, it was the Scorched Ataris!'

How dare he! 'They clearly don't teach you history in Ataria, otherwise you'd know it was the Sky Riders. And if the phaegras do come back, then the Sky Riders will kill them off again, like they did last time.'

'Not if the Scorched Ataris get there first,' Rustus fired back.

'Well, you wouldn't be much use, would you?' snapped Kayla. 'Considering you couldn't even pass your own initiation.'

'Enough bickering,' said Tas. 'This issue is bigger than inter-realm disputes. And if you must know, all of your realms played an equal part in the destruction of the island's wildlife.' Kayla was ready to argue this point, but Tas forged on. 'If it's true that the phaegras will soon return, then the safety of all the Realms is at stake. It cannot be a coincidence that now, of all times, a pangron has been taken.'

Kayla struggled to see how the two things were related, but either way, the quicker she got her pangron back, the quicker this would all be over – prophecy or not.

'There's a lot to discuss,' said the Marquis. 'Perhaps over some refreshments . . . ?' He shot a hopeful smile in Tas's direction.

'Of course.' She indicated a table upon which sat a teapot and a plate of silk tumblers.

'No!' said Kayla quickly. 'We can't stay. We need to get to Port Royal.'

'Not tonight,' said the Marquis. 'It's almost sundown and the bardebeests can't navigate in the dark.'

Kayla didn't even want to ask what bardebeests were, so instead she said, 'So when exactly were you planning to leave?'

'We'll have to set off early in the morning.'

Kayla growled. *Tomorrow morning?* Faro could be anywhere by then. The Marquis wasn't taking this seriously. Maybe she should have just gone alone.

'Did you say you're going to Port Royal?' Tas interrupted her thoughts.

Kayla nodded. 'We think that's where the boat was headed. We're waiting for his featherwing to tell us for sure.'

'Be careful up there,' Tas said. 'They say it's where the Scourge originated.'

'The Scourge?' Rustus said. 'You mean the illness you get from an obsidian webspinner bite?'

Kayla glanced quickly at the Marquis. He hadn't shared that information when she'd suggested the Scourge was spread from person to person – *or* before dragging her through a whole forest of the beasts.

Tas snorted. 'From the webspinners? Is that what they're telling you up there? Nonsense. They do have a mild venom, yes, but the wound clears up within a couple of hours. Besides, they almost never bite, as long as you treat them with respect. The Scourge is something different entirely. We've been lucky here in The Silk – only a few of our people have been afflicted, and only when they've left the city on patrols.'

'You're wrong,' said Rustus. 'The webspinners cause the Scourge – everyone knows that.'

He seemed pretty upset, although Kayla couldn't understand why. She for one was relieved that the beasts they were surrounded by in the forest weren't about to kill them.

'What does cause it then?' she asked Tas. In Sophiatown they had told her that the Scourge was spread by contact with infected people. That was why they'd shut the city gates. She wasn't ready to completely discount that theory yet.

Tas shook her head. 'We're not sure. All I know for certain is that the webspinners are the least of your concerns in the Beastlands. That's why you should camp here for the night. I insist.'

The Marquis beamed at Kayla. 'That's great news, isn't it?' he said. 'Thanks, Tas. We can get a good night's rest and leave bright and early tomorrow.'

Kayla couldn't believe her ears. 'Absolutely not!' she exclaimed. 'I'm going to keep going. I can't just wait around here while Faro is taken further and further away from me.'

The Marquis's face fell.

'Come, Kayla,' said Tas. 'It's not safe to be out in the Beastlands after dark. And besides, you won't be able to navigate – the jungle canopy is too thick to see by starlight.'

'I don't care!' shouted Kayla. 'Faro needs me and I can't help him if I'm sat around here drinking tea!' She kicked out at the table, knocking the tray of tumblers to the ground.

Everyone in the room stared at them, but Kayla was too angry to stop. Why didn't anyone understand how desperately she needed to find Faro? She held tightly on to her eggshell pendant, breathing heavily.

The Atarian was the first to respond. 'It must be really hard,' said Rustus, eyeing the way her fingers gripped her necklace, 'being ripped away from someone you love like that.'

Kayla let her hand drop and regarded him with suspicion. His face looked sincere, but he was probably mocking her. She'd made that mistake before. When she had first joined the Academy, some of her fellow cadets had asked her to join a group called the Association of Pangron Lovers. They had made her believe they cared about their pangrons just like she did. It was the first time she had ever felt wanted and included by her peers and had been one of the happiest days of her life. Until they had given Kayla her badge, all watching eagerly as she unwrapped it from the box. When she had lifted it from its packaging, the badge had read 'The Association of Pangron Losers'. 'Did you really think we were anything like you?' the children had sniggered. 'There's nobody else like you, you pangron-loving freak. You'll be trying to set them all free soon, just like your mum.' Their taunting laughter still rang in her ears.

'Of course it is,' she snapped. 'Faro is a part of me. We don't work without one another. You couldn't possibly understand what it's like to be separated from your pangron.'

'That's precisely why we can't let you get gobbled up by a lavabear,' said Tas, putting a hand on Kayla's

140

shoulder to calm her. 'Faro needs you too. We only want what's best for you.'

'What's best for me is to be with Faro,' said Kayla forcefully, recoiling from the woman's touch.

'But we're not even sure where he is,' the Marquis pointed out.

Kayla scowled at him. 'I thought you said he was in Port Royal.'

'I said that was probably where the boat was headed,' said the Marquis. 'We'll know more when Milabar returns.'

'What we really need to know is why someone would want to take a pangron in the first place,' said Tas. 'And I can't help but think it's somehow tied up with the phaegra.'

Kayla was still seething, but she considered the webwalker's suggestion. 'If people think the phaegra is coming back, maybe they want a pangron for protection.'

'Could be,' said the Marquis, nodding.

'What if the phaegras never fully died out?' said Rustus. 'What if they're hiding somewhere, like at the top of the Shivertips, and someone wants to use the pangrons to find them?'

Tas considered each of the options thoughtfully. 'Whatever they want the pangrons for,' she said, 'a monumental change is sweeping across the Realms and I fear the worst is yet to come.'

'The worst has already happened to me,' said Kayla. 'My pangron is gone. And you promised we would

141

go straight to Port Royal.' She glared at the Marquis accusingly.

'And we will,' the Marquis insisted. 'Tomorrow.'

'Which route are you going to take?' asked Tas.

'The coast road,' said the Marquis. 'It's the only option with the wagon. At first light we'll be on our way.' He looked at Kayla for some kind of agreement. She was still glaring, but what could she say? She didn't have a clue where she was going and she didn't fancy stumbling into a webspinner in the dark. She gave the tiniest of shrugs.

'Excellent,' said Tas. 'I'll instruct the chefs to prepare a feast.'

11

ALETHEA

As Alethea got further from the city the path grew narrower until eventually there was no path left at all. This made things trickier. Without the track to guide her, Alethea found it difficult to know if she was walking in a straight line or going in circles. The webs were denser this deep in the forest too. Sometimes she had to use her knife to cut her way through.

Whenever she saw the webspinners, they were sitting quietly in their webs, minding their own business.

'How did they convince us that you were responsible for the Scourge?' she said, as she passed by one particularly bulbous beast with two brilliant blue wings hanging from its jaws. 'You don't seem in the slightest bit interested in me.'

As she continued through the forest she imagined what she and Da could have discovered here together, exploring the plants of the forest. Why had the people of Ataria been prevented from leaving the city? Who knows what solutions to the problems they faced could be discovered in this place.

She paused to look at a patch of pink cup-shaped mushrooms that a scarlet slug was munching on. Alethea had noticed the same kind of fungi being eaten by a similar-looking slug an hour or so ago. Had she been here before? Or was this another patch that looked the same? She needed to find a way of marking her tracks so she could see where she had come from and where she was going. She ripped off the sleeve of her shirt, tore the fabric into strips and tied one of them around a thick pyro-cane stem.

She pushed on through the forest, forcing her way over, under and through the thinnest areas of web she could find, marking her way with the cloth strips as she went. Once she had used up the fabric of the first sleeve, she cut off the other and used that too. After a while she realised that many of the pyro canes had a crusty purple lichen growing on one side of their stem. She wondered if, like suka moss, this lichen only grew on the north-facing surface. She started to use the lichen as a wayfinder, keeping it always on the same side, hoping her theory was correct.

She didn't know how many hours had passed when she got the first whiff of salty air. The smell urged her on and she sped up, hoping her nostrils weren't deceiving her.

At last, through a gap in the canes, she got her first glimpse of the ocean. The vastness of it was breathtaking.

A perfectly straight line cut across the horizon, separating the green-tinted water from the sky, and there, right in front of her, a carpet of low woody shrubs with lime-green leaves and large purple bladders fringed a wide beach. If her legs hadn't been so exhausted, Alethea might have skipped clean into the air with excitement.

Instead she conserved her energy and hurried towards the plants. The calm ocean still seemed a long way off, but the tide was coming in. Where the marsh didn't reach the sea, a thin film of water coated the compacted black sand, turning the whole beach into a perfect mirror. It was beautiful.

Alethea crouched to take a closer look at the plants and pulled her book out to consult the entry on marshwort.

Moderate height. Check!
*Multiple woody stems lined with purple
    scythe-shaped thorns.* Check!
Paired, arrow-shaped, rubbery leaves. Check!
Tiny star-shaped purple flowers. Check!
Globular purple liquid-filled bladders. Check!

This was it! A surge of relief washed over her. She had done it! She had found the marshwort! And it had been so much easier than she had expected. She couldn't believe she had made it to the coast in just one afternoon. If she cut the marshwort now and then spent the night on the beach, she could be back in Ataria by tomorrow evening. Her brothers and sisters would barely notice she had gone.

She hadn't imagined there would be quite so much of it growing here either – enough to fill bags and bags. If this worked, nobody would ever need to die of the Scourge again. It was a big if, but Alethea was too happy with her find to dwell on that for long.

Just then, a large pink and orange creature scuttled between the plants, its transparent shell allowing her a view of its inner organs.

'Hello, little one,' Alethea said. It was a scuttleclaw. There were pictures of them in *Beastly Beasts and Fearsome Feasts*, but in that book they had been characterised as terrible monsters. Alethea had never imagined that in real life scuttleclaws could be so unthreatening or so colourful. At the sound of her voice, it scuttled away into the shelter of the plants.

She slipped off her shoes and walked further out into the saltmarshes. The sun was low in the sky now and fiery colours danced across the wet sand as the last of its rays kissed the black beach. The large white moon had already risen and hung heavy in the sky. Tomorrow it would be full. She breathed deeply and her lungs were flooded with fresh sea air.

She approached an abundant patch of marshwort. This was where she would do her collection. From what she had read, it was best right on the edge of the water, where the ocean danced over its stems. She stepped into the shallows, salty water lapping around her ankles, and pulled out her plant shears. She hummed to herself as she clipped the stems, comforted by the familiarity of the task.

Soon a mist rolled in over the salt flats, cloaking them in a milky haze. The beach that had felt so enormous moments before felt suddenly small and quiet, like a blanket had been draped over it, keeping out everyone but Alethea.

Once her bag was full, she sat back on the sand and watched the waves at the shoreline. Her eyelids drooped. She would soon need to make camp for the night. Her stomach gurgled – she also needed to eat. She pulled the final piece of flatbread from her bag and eyed the rubbery leaves of the marshwort. Her book had said they were edible . . .

She picked a couple of leaves and sliced them thinly, placing them between two halves of the flatbread.

'Ooh,' said Alethea as she bit into it. It was delicious! The texture was soft and buttery, the flavour fresh and salty. She quickly finished the sandwich and was excited to try the other parts of the plant. She picked up a purple bladder and used her knife to cut a slit near the top. She held it to her nose. It had an inoffensive, slightly spicy scent, nothing like the harsh odour of firewort. She pushed her tongue into the hole and dipped the tip of it into the liquid. A little bitter, but relatively mild.

A worried thought crossed her mind. Would something so mild be able to treat the Scourge? If the firewort had an incomplete effect, would the marshwort have any effect at all? Her thoughts were interrupted by the little scuttleclaw returning.

'Hello, friend,' Alethea said. Behind it were two more,

appearing as if by magic out of the fog. The three beasts moved as one, scuttling in spurts and then pausing.

'Look at you all,' said Alethea. 'Are you hungry?' She threw them a tiny piece of bread. They jumped on it immediately, devouring it in seconds. 'Yikes. You're greedy little things.'

As the three scuttleclaws moved forward, Alethea realised there were even more of them behind. Where had they all come from? She glanced up the beach and saw a long line of them making their way towards her. She put her plant shears into her bag and rose to her feet, stepping backwards slowly. The movement seemed to alarm the creatures, causing those closest to her to lift their pincers in defence. The action was copied by the others, travelling through the approaching group like a wave.

Alethea took another step back, trying to steady her racing thoughts. The scuttleclaw at the front scuttled forward again, its eyestalks moving side to side inquisitively.

'I don't want to hurt you,' Alethea said, raising her palms in submission. 'I just want some marshwort and somewhere to sleep for the night.'

But the scuttleclaws weren't interested in what she had to say. They couldn't understand her. What was the best course of action here? If she ran, would they chase her? How fast would they be? Where would she go?

Suddenly, as if they had received some sort of invisible signal, the scuttleclaws all darted forward. Alethea stumbled several paces back, before tripping and falling to the sand while they scuttled towards her faster than ever, clambering up onto her.

'Get off!' she yelled, kicking out at them, but the scuttleclaws were not deterred. Then she felt the first nip, down by her ankle. A sharp pain like someone had sliced her with a scalpel. 'Stop!' she cried. 'Help!' She prayed someone would hear.

What about the webwalkers? she wondered. *Or the Scorched Ataris? Where was Rustus Furi now?* But the Beastlands were enormous and nobody knew Alethea was here.

12

RUSTUS

The people of The Silk were excellent hosts. They treated Kayla, Rustus and the Marquis to a hearty feast of foods Rustus had never encountered in Ataria, including bright pink mushrooms stuffed with gloopy green jelly, long white beans on warm crusty bread, a blue jam Rustus guessed was made of lavaberries, wedges of sweet orange cheese, and beakers of delicious warm tea.

'How are you able to cook such a feast out here?' Rustus asked. 'This is the best meal I've had in years.'

Tas smiled. 'There's a great deal you don't yet know about the Beastlands.'

Rustus looked around. They were in a huge chamber inside The Silk, seated at a long table decorated with flowers and leaves from the forest. It was less humid inside the city and the air was full of the sweet smells of the feast. Tas was right. His world had been turned upside down.

'There are all kinds of treasures hidden in the

Beastlands,' she said. 'We might have fewer people and lack the farms of Ataria, but we have our initiative and the will to try. You will find it's often not the resources that limit us in life, Rustus, but what we are open-minded enough to do with them.'

The people of The Silk had certainly put their resources to good use. Ataria could learn a thing or two from them, especially as supplies were running so low in the city. Rustus considered briefly whether returning with these delicious foods would be enough to win back his father's favour. But no, it needed to be something monumental. An act of enormous bravery and strength. Although, when he returned, he would be sure to take some food back with him too.

'Were you born here in The Silk?' Rustus asked Tas, tucking into a hunk of cheese.

Tas shook her head and smiled. 'No,' she said. 'I was born in Ataria. I came here the very same way you did. Many, many years ago.'

Rustus wondered if she had ever tried to return.

After they had eaten, the webwalkers took Rustus and Kayla to three beds they had prepared in a small dark silken chamber. By the light of the ashworms, whose rotund bodies glowed green at the tail end, Rustus could see that the Marquis (who had left the meal early, blaming Topaz for giving him the runaround all day) was already tucked under a silk blanket, snoring loudly. By his side, the needlejaw had made a nest on the ground and was also asleep, her head tucked between her legs.

Since the Marquis had arrived, Rustus's fear of Topaz had turned to fascination. Close up, her fearsome jaws seemed less frightening and more cumbersome. How could she possibly catch her prey with all those long teeth pointing in every direction? As Rustus watched, a bright red slug slimed across the silk towards her. He was startled when the beast he'd thought was snoozing suddenly lifted her head, sniffed the air, located the slug and slurped it up with a loud slap.

'Totally gross,' said Rustus, surprised to find himself grinning. He turned to check if Kayla had seen. She was sat on her bed with her head in her hands. 'Are you all right?' he asked, turning his attention away from the beast. The prickly Sky Cadet had barely said a word at dinner.

'Fine,' said Kayla, looking distinctly otherwise.

'Faro will be all right,' said Rustus. 'The Marquis will find him.' Rustus had only known the man a matter of hours, but he could tell he was someone who could be relied on.

'*I* will find him,' said Kayla, swinging her legs up onto the bed and lying down with her back to Rustus. Apparently the conversation was over.

Rustus lay back on his own bed, staring up at the glowing hexapods above him. How had he grown up in Ataria for all these years not knowing there was a whole other city out here in the Ashlands? He had been led to believe that life was terrible outside the city gates, that the Beastlands were dangerous and frightening and that the webspinners carried the Scourge. Even when he'd wandered through the forest himself, he hadn't allowed himself to notice the potential of the place. Maybe because he'd always been told there was nothing good to find there he simply hadn't looked for it.

Back in Ataria, he had felt sorry for the exiles who were sent out into the wilds. He hadn't believed for one moment that the webwalkers could be living in such splendour, eating and drinking delicious foods, sleeping in soft beds. Everyone here seemed so happy too. Why did the Ash Bishops pretend this place didn't exist? What other secrets might they be keeping from the people of Ataria? Had his mum been telling the truth when she had said he belonged outside the city after all?

Then his thoughts turned to the prophecy Tas had spoken of. He had been strangely pleased to know that his mum wasn't the only seer, that other people had prophesied things too, but he was more than a little concerned about the prospect of the phaegras returning. Could it possibly be true? He knew he should trust in the Scorched Ataris – they had defeated the phaegras before, he was sure they could do it again – but Tas had made it sound like prophecies were never wrong.

His thoughts raced for what felt like hours, but he must eventually have fallen asleep, as he was rudely awoken by loud shouts from somewhere within The Silk. He rolled out of bed and rubbed his eyes. As he came to, he could just about make out the words.

'Healer! Quick! She's been attacked by scuttleclaws!'

Rustus's heart raced and he looked over to see if they were talking about Kayla. But she was there, sat up in her bed, knife aloft, ready to fight. A grunt from the other side of the room told them the Marquis had heard the voice too. He rolled regretfully out of bed.

'I guess we'd better go and see what all the fuss is about,' he said.

Together they followed the panicked voices to a large chamber, where Rustus was confused to see an Atarian girl, dressed in blue, being carried by a webwalker. Her long blonde plaits were draped over the webwalker's shoulder and both sleeves of her shirt had been ripped off. As they approached, Rustus noticed the girl had blood around her ankles and a long straight cut across one cheek.

'I'm fine,' she said as the webwalker put her down. 'Just a couple of little cuts. I don't need a healer. But thank you for rescuing me. If you'd got there any later I don't know if I'd have made it.'

'What happened?' asked Rustus.

'She was attacked by stained-glass scuttleclaws,' said a webwalker. 'She's lucky we found her when we did.'

'Told you, didn't I?' said the Marquis to Kayla, whose face was pale. 'Nasty little blighters at night.'

'Why did they attack her?' Rustus asked.

'They were probably hoping to eat her,' said the Marquis plainly.

Rustus was horrified. Scuttleclaws sounded terrifying.

'Where am I?' asked the girl, looking around her in astonishment.

'You're in The Silk,' said a webwalker. 'The city within the webs.'

'It's beautiful,' she replied. As she took in the room, her eyes fell on Rustus and her mouth dropped open in surprise. 'You're Rustus Furi!' she said. 'What are you doing here?'

Rustus was taken aback. How did she know his name? 'I could ask you the same question,' he replied.

'I suppose you could,' said the girl. 'I'm Alethea Bashoa. I was collecting marshwort on the coast.'

Rustus couldn't believe his ears. 'You left the city on purpose and travelled alone through the Beastlands?'

She nodded and was about to speak when Tas entered the room. The leader of the webwalkers looked Alethea up and down. 'Where did *she* come from?' She pursed her lips thoughtfully. 'All these visitors. Something's afoot.'

'We found her on the beach while we were foraging for moonblooms,' a webwalker said. 'She'd been accosted by the scuttleclaws. Luckily we rescued her in time.'

'Thank you,' said Tas. 'Girl, what in the Realms were you doing on the beach at night? Of all the dangerous situations to put yourself in!' She shook her head.

'You forget how little they understand,' said the Marquis, gesturing at Alethea, Kayla and Rustus but speaking to Tas. 'They know nothing of the world outside their walls. Such is life in the cities.'

'I was collecting marshwort,' Alethea said defensively, pulling a cloth bag out of her satchel. At their confused expressions, she added, 'Pickleweed – to treat the Scourge.'

Tas stifled a snort. 'You believe pickleweed can get rid of the Scourge?'

Alethea's cheeks went red. 'Well, maybe,' she said. 'Like firewort, pickleweed is in the tasselbaggia family. It might work in the same way firewort does.'

'Firewort?' Tas looked surprised.

Alethea nodded. 'A salve of firewort made some difference in one of my patients. I wouldn't call it a cure exactly, but it helped.'

'Your patients?' Rustus asked. Was she a healer?

'Yes,' she said, blushing again. 'My da used to be the healer in our district. Before he died I worked as his apprentice. When he passed there was no one else to take over so . . .'

Rustus was impressed. He didn't know they made kids work in the Blue District.

'And your first great challenge is to save your people from the Scourge?' said Tas. 'A big responsibility to be borne by such small shoulders. I admire your efforts, but I'm afraid pickleweed is much milder than firewort, so if firewort only had a partial effect, then pickleweed won't be any better. All it's good for is getting rid of heartburn.'

'And for using as shampoo,' added Kayla.

Alethea's eyebrows twitched together. She looked like she was processing this new information. 'Maybe it just needs to be applied in a different way,' she said. 'Eaten, or perhaps even burnt and inhaled?'

'Dear child,' Tas said gently, 'we are a resourceful people. We've used pickleweed in every form you can imagine. We've chopped the leaves into salads, emptied the bladders into tea, burnt the stems to freshen the air . . . and none of those things has the power to cure the Scourge.'

Rustus believed her. After eating the feast made from things foraged in the Beastlands, he could imagine the webwalkers experimented in hundreds of ways with every new plant they found.

'Do you know what does cure the Scourge then?' Alethea asked desperately. 'If I don't find a cure, my grandma and my people are going to keep on dying.'

Rustus vaguely remembered hearing that more people were dying in the Blue District than in any other. With a pang of guilt he remembered being grateful that the Red District didn't seem to be so badly affected.

'I read about this plant and thought it could be a remedy, so I left Ataria to search for it. If it doesn't work . . .' She didn't finish the sentence.

'I'm sorry,' said Tas. 'I wish that I could help you, but we're out of ideas too. We're lucky to have had only a few people succumb, but those who did we sent to Frostfall Mountain.'

'Frostfall Mountain?' Alethea asked. 'What's there?'

'A hospital,' Tas explained. 'The doctor there is said to be chasing a cure for the Scourge.'

Alethea's forehead wrinkled as she digested the information.

'Surely not!' said the Marquis. 'Frostfall Mountain is a cold and desolate place. I tracked an injured snogart up there once. It's no place for healing.'

'Well, that's the rumour,' Tas said. 'Though none of the people we sent there has yet returned. The only other option we have at the moment is to stay here and wait to die, so I know which I would choose.'

Alethea chewed her lip. 'I can't go back home without a cure.' Her face set in grim determination. 'I'm going there.'

Rustus stared at her in disbelief. What was she thinking? She had the opportunity to go back to Ataria and she wasn't taking it. Didn't she know how lucky she was? Even though life in the Beastlands had been better than expected so far, Rustus would give anything to go home and be given another chance.

'I don't see any other option,' she said. 'My people are depending on me.'

The corners of Tas's mouth turned up ever so slightly and her eyes twinkled fractionally more than usual. 'It's not an easy journey,' she warned. 'It's a difficult climb, or a very long walk. A perilous quest with an uncertain outcome. Only the bravest would even attempt it.'

The bravest. A sudden thought occurred to Rustus.

'I'll go with her,' he said, blurting out the words before he had a chance to fully process what he was offering. 'Just tell me where to go and I'll take her there myself.'

If Alethea needed a strong warrior to help her find the cure for the Scourge and take it back to Ataria, then it should surely be him. And if Rustus helped bring the cure back to the city, then perhaps his father and brothers would finally see that he was worthy.

Alethea looked shocked by the proposal. 'That's ever so kind,' she said. 'My little brother Cassio won't believe me when I tell him that Rustus Furi personally escorted me through the Beastlands.'

Tas regarded the pair of them with interest. 'How are you at climbing?'

Alethea glanced at Rustus quickly and he wondered if she was remembering his failure on Kahanga Rock. He wobbled his head from side to side.

'I'm OK,' he said.

'You look strong enough.' Tas gave an approving nod. Her face turned serious. 'You'll need to travel through the jungle to the very edge of the Ashlands. From there it will be easy to identify Frostfall Mountain as it's the tallest of all the Shivertips. The hospital is at the summit. The most direct route up is via the east face. It's the shortest way, but also the hardest – it's pretty much a vertical climb.' Her voice was calm and measured, but Rustus sensed underlying concern. 'And that's not the only danger. There are beasts on the cliff too.'

The Marquis nodded. 'Nasty ones at that. Cliffcreepers – armoured reptillites that will throw you off the cliff face.'

'Isn't Port Royal just the other side of Frostfall Mountain?' Kayla interrupted.

Tas nodded. 'Yes, in the unclaimed territory between the Fjordlands and the coast.'

'Then surely it's quicker for me to climb over Frostfall Mountain too,' said Kayla, 'and come down the other side to reach Port Royal, than to go around the coast road like *you* suggested.' She shot an accusatory look at the Marquis.

'I can't take the wagon up the mountain,' he explained.

'Of course you can't,' snapped Kayla, 'but *I* can climb up there.'

'As I said, it's a treacherous journey,' Tas warned. 'It would be much safer to travel with –'

Kayla didn't wait for her to finish. 'If these two Atarians can make it up there, then I definitely can.' She turned to the Marquis again. 'Take us all to the foot of Frostfall Mountain.'

Rustus recoiled at her rudeness. The Marquis was doing her a favour, yet she was treating him like a servant.

'I'm happy to do that,' he replied nervously, looking at Tas for reassurance. She shrugged. 'But it's awfully dangerous up there.'

'I don't care about danger,' snapped Kayla. 'I care about getting to Faro as fast as I possibly can.'

'Well, there's no need to make your mind up yet,' the Marquis continued. 'We'll pass the foothills of the Shivertips on our way out of The Silk and towards the coast road, so you can decide when we reach that point.' His hesitance made Rustus nervous about what lay ahead.

'I've already decided,' Kayla said. 'Just you worry

about getting us there as fast as you can. In fact, as we're all awake anyway, why don't we get on the road now?'

The Marquis looked to Rustus and Alethea, as if to get their approval. Despite his apprehensions, Rustus nodded – it was his only choice. Alethea nodded too.

'All right, Kayla,' said Marquis Macdonald. 'You've got your wish. Tas, could you show us out please? I'll just nip back and get Topaz.'

KAYLA

Kayla felt exhausted as they followed Tas out of The Silk. Her joints ached all over. She figured it must be the after-effects of the poisoned arrow.

'Do we have to go through that again?' she asked, as they came to a stop in front of a messy mass of webs, so different to the combed and cleaned webspinner silk that made up the city's internal walls.

The Marquis nodded. Topaz stood patiently by his side, a rope leash hanging loosely around her neck. 'It's the only way.'

Kayla grimaced, remembering how it felt to pass through the sticky tendrils.

'You'll be fine,' Tas said, holding out her hand to shake Kayla's.

'She doesn't shake hands,' said the Marquis. 'But I do.' He extended his hand to take Tas's and then pulled her into a hug.

'Be safe out there,' Tas said, breaking away and fixing him with an intense look. 'Keep your wits about you.'

'I'll keep an eye on this lot,' he replied, as she bid goodbye to Rustus and Alethea too. 'Don't you worry.' Then he grunted as he bent to clamber through the webs, contorting his body to keep hold of Topaz's leash. 'Thanks for your help, Tas. I owe you!' He gave Topaz a tug and the webs closed behind them, obscuring them from view.

Kayla took a deep breath. She knew she had to follow him, but every muscle screamed in protest.

Come on, she told herself. *It's the only way you'll get back to Faro.* She braced herself and tried to choose a path. Ahead of her a half-eaten hexapod twitched in the web. 'Eugh,' she groaned.

'Take my hand,' said Alethea, clearly not having heard the Marquis's warning about handshakes. 'I'll help you through.'

Kayla looked at the Atarian girl's outstretched hand. Her face was kind, but Kayla instantly felt prickly. People didn't help you unless they wanted something in return. And Kayla didn't need help. Instead, she closed her eyes and decided to fight her way blindly through the webs by herself. For a few seconds, the fibres encased her, then somehow she found herself on the path outside, just as Rustus emerged beside her. Ahead of them stood the Marquis, stroking the needlejaw and whispering to it quietly.

'That was disgusting,' Kayla said, rubbing at an itch on her wrist. 'I never want to do it again.'

Alethea emerged last. In the gloom her features were hard to make out, but she didn't look like she had particularly enjoyed clambering out of The Silk either.

'Are we all here?' asked the Marquis.

Kayla nodded.

'Great, the wagon's that way.' He started off through the forest, motioning the others to follow him.

Kayla tried not to begrudge the fact that they were giving the Atarians a lift to the mountain too. After all, if it hadn't been for the Marquis's kind nature, Kayla wouldn't have a lift at all. Even so it was hard to shake a lifetime of conditioning that the people of the other realms were her enemies. She decided to focus on the positives instead: she was on her way to find Faro, she had a lift to the fastest route and thus far she had avoided being eaten by webspinners. She tried to ignore the little niggle of doubt: *But what if you don't get there in time?* Or worse still: *What if Faro never went to Port Royal and you never find him?* Then she recalled the prophecy Tas had told them about: *What if someone wants to use him to fight a phaegra?* Well, there was no point worrying about those things now, she reasoned. She had chosen her course of action and all she could do was hope upon hope that her instincts had been right. *I'm coming for you, Faro*, she promised, fingers clasped tightly around her necklace.

A little further down the path Kayla saw the Marquis stop, pluck something from the pyro canes and pop it into one of the jars on his waist. Another new animal companion, she imagined.

As they walked the canes began to grow less dense, as if they were reaching the edge of the jungle, until they thinned out completely and were replaced with low woody heathland. Far off in the distance, she thought she could just make out the jagged peaks of the Shivertips. Much nearer though, and just ahead of them on a path, Kayla could see the outline of what she guessed was the Marquis's wagon.

It was enormous, easily as long as two houses, round-topped and covered in a patchwork of patterns and symbols. As they drew closer Kayla could see four golden-haired beasts tethered nearby. They were magnificent, with long, muscular legs ending in gleaming silver hooves. Large T-shaped horns protruded from their foreheads and each beast had two stout trunks dangling from its face.

'What are they?' Rustus marvelled.

'Bardebeests,' said the Marquis. 'From the Southlands.'

'My realm?' asked Kayla. 'I've never seen them before.'

A loud noise erupted out of one of the beasts – it was a cross between a hoot and a honk and seemed to have come from the hollow horn on the creature's head.

The Marquis took no notice. 'You wouldn't have,' he said, rubbing the bardebeest on the shoulder while feeding it a handful of nuts. 'Your people hunted them practically to extinction.'

The bardebeest shook its twin trunks and stamped its foot, asking for more.

Kayla felt an odd sense of guilt as she tried to imagine these majestic beasts wandering the barren plains outside

Sophiatown. It would certainly brighten the place up a bit, though she didn't fancy waking to that call too early in the morning. The toebeeks were noisy enough.

'I'm sure you know that the Southlands were once covered with forest,' said the Marquis.

Kayla's face must have given away the fact that this was new information to her.

'Goodness, don't they teach you children anything these days?' asked the Marquis.

Kayla scoffed indignantly. 'They teach us plenty,' she said. 'My days are full of classes: battle drills, archery, flying, weapon maintenance, navigation –'

'Mm-hmm,' he murmured, patting the bardebeest on the neck before grabbing Topaz's rope and striding to the other end of the wagon. 'Nothing useful then.'

Kayla growled under her breath as she followed him to the base of a short wooden ladder that led to a door in the back of the wagon.

'In here,' he said, beckoning her to follow. He pulled on Topaz's leash and the needlejaw climbed the ladder, her sinuous blue body winding left and right as she clambered the steps, large clawed feet grasping each rung in turn. Rustus followed, leaping up easily. Alethea was next, but she hesitated at the bottom to look at a small red flower growing by the edge of the path.

'You first,' she said.

Kayla didn't argue – they needed to get on their way. She moved forward and placed a foot on the bottom rung. Her arms and back ached terribly – she must have

166

hurt herself more in the fall than she'd realised.

The ladder was old and rickety, worn smooth through years of use. As she ascended, Kayla was engulfed in a toxic cloud. The foul stench of animal dung billowed out of the wagon, filling her mouth and nostrils with a smell so dense she was certain she could taste it. She coughed and covered her mouth. And she'd thought the pangron stables smelled bad!

As she clambered inside she was met by a cacophony of animal sounds. The Marquis's wagon was full to the rafters; every possible gap was stuffed with cages big and small, making the space seem both claustrophobically tiny because there was barely space to move, yet also impossibly large on account of how many creatures it contained.

'Down here!' shouted the Marquis, from somewhere she couldn't see.

She pushed her way along a gangway in the centre, passing cage after cage of incredible creatures, until she reached a ragged floral sofa, where Rustus was already seated. He was staring around the wagon in open-mouthed astonishment. Kayla took a seat beside him, sinking into the soft cushions.

'Isn't this amazing?' Rustus asked. 'I've never seen anything like it.'

Nor had Kayla. She had seen more beasts today than in the last thirteen years.

The Marquis reappeared then, panting and sweating. 'Topaz is a little feisty today.' He wiped a red pearl of blood that had sprung up on his forehead.

'You can say that again,' said Kayla. 'Have you seen how many teeth she's got?'

'She's harmless enough,' said the Marquis. 'Just not a big fan of staying in her cage.' He lit an oil lamp hanging precariously above one of the sofas, and warm, orange light flickered into the hidden corners of the wagon, revealing even more new creatures.

'Where did you find her?' Rustus asked.

'In the foothills,' said the Marquis. 'By the edge of the Shadowlands.'

'Wow!' said Rustus. 'Shadow Ghoul territory. You really have been everywhere.'

A shout rang out from further down the wagon. It was Alethea.

'We're up here!' Rustus yelled.

Moments later, she emerged wide-eyed as she took in the beasts surrounding them.

'Alethea, dear,' said the Marquis, 'please take a seat.' He gestured towards an armchair before rummaging about in a large wooden crate, muttering to himself. 'Now where was it . . . ? Aha!' He brandished a large paper bag. 'Here,' he said, throwing it at Rustus and Kayla. 'Try these.'

Instinctively Kayla snatched the bag from the air. 'What are they?' she asked, pulling out a handful of pink beans.

'Varja beans,' said the Marquis. 'From the Fjordlands. Try them, they're delicious!'

Kayla eyed them warily. And then her stomach rumbled loudly. Rustus laughed.

'I'm hungry,' she said, shooting him a scathing look. 'I didn't trust any of that food last night.'

'What?' he exclaimed. 'That was the best meal of my life.' He grabbed the bag of beans she was still holding gingerly.

'I'd never met those people before,' said Kayla. 'How was I to know they weren't trying to poison us?'

'Well, clearly they weren't,' said Rustus. '*We're* all still here.' He groaned contentedly as he chomped on the beans. 'You have to try these,' he said through a very full mouth.

Kayla's stomach grumbled again. She would have to eat something if she was going to make it up the mountain, so she popped two beans into her mouth and chewed. Rustus wasn't wrong – the beans were sweet and creamy with a hint of smoke.

'That's not bad,' said Kayla, nudging Rustus to pass them over to Alethea.

'Sorry,' Rustus said, reaching forward with the bag so Alethea could take a handful.

'They're even better when they're warm.' The Marquis turned his back to them, pulled a copper kettle down from a hook attached to the ceiling and started to rummage through the crate again, muttering something about spare mugs.

'Will it be much longer till we go?' said Kayla, frustrated at the Marquis's lack of urgency. She'd thought he was just getting them settled so they could leave, not making them a whole meal.

'No, no,' he said. 'Nearly there now.'

Kayla felt her feet moving restlessly as she fiddled with her necklace. She wanted to get on the road. She wanted to be with Faro. Even eating a snack without him felt wrong – normally she couldn't munch on anything without him lurking hopefully for a piece.

'I bet Faro would like varja beans.' She didn't even realise she'd said it out loud until Rustus spoke.

'Faro is Kayla's pangron,' he told Alethea through another mouthful.

'I guessed that,' said Alethea. She looked directly at Kayla. 'It must be very hard for you to be away from him.'

'It's torture,' Kayla said honestly, scratching her prickling forearm.

'I'm sure you'll be back with him again soon,' said Alethea kindly.

Kayla hoped she was right. 'Are we going yet?' she asked, peering at the Marquis over an untidy pile of books.

'Not long now, not long.'

He had located an odd, mismatched collection of mugs and was pouring steaming water into them. When they were full, he plonked them onto a lopsided bronze tray, carried them over to the children and passed them each one.

'Drop some beans into the water,' he said.

They did as he instructed and a sweet and smoky aroma crept into the air, overpowering the stench of the animals' faeces. Rustus lifted his cup to take a sip.

'Wait!' bellowed the Marquis. Kayla wondered what in

the Realms had happened, as the Marquis leaned towards Rustus with a hard star-shaped object in his hand. 'Break that open and mix it with your hot varja before you try it.'

'Ashstar!' said Alethea, staring as the Marquis handed her an ashstar too. 'I haven't had one of these for years, not since the droughts.'

'You haven't?' asked Rustus, staring at the fruit incredulously. 'We still get them every week.'

'Aren't you two from the same city?' asked Kayla, confused.

'We are,' said Alethea, a furrow between her brows as she looked at the fruit in her hand. 'But from different districts. Some of us are less . . .' she paused to search for the right word, '*important* than others.'

Rustus stared intently into his mug, looking a little embarrassed.

Kayla cracked the hard skin of the fruit over her mug and a clear pink liquid dribbled out. It had a sour flavour that complimented the sweet and smoky taste of the varja perfectly.

'I think this might be the best thing I've ever tasted,' said Rustus.

'That's what you said about the meal last night,' said Kayla, raising an eyebrow. Alethea giggled. Kayla had to admit it was tasty though.

They all sat quietly, sipping their drinks. A Sky Cadet, a nomad, an Unscorched Atari and a healer sharing a moment in a wagon full of captive beasts. What would Wing Commander Barash have made of that?

After a while, a small pointed nose and six long whiskers poked their way out of the Marquis's beard.

'What is that?' said Rustus, looking at the emerging beast.

'You mean *who*,' said the Marquis. 'This is Lillypeg. She's a tamaranian. I hand-reared her and I've never quite been able to release her back into the wild.'

'She's lovely,' said Rustus as Lillypeg scurried onto the Marquis's shoulder. 'Where's she from?'

'The Fjordlands,' said the Marquis, smiling like a proud father.

'Do you know everything about every beast in all the Realms?' asked Rustus.

Kayla started to grow aggravated. They were still no closer to being on their way and she'd found herself sitting around drinking and chatting again without making any real progress.

'Every beast ever known to have existed in the Realms is listed in there.' The Marquis indicated a huge leather-bound book beside Alethea's chair. It said 'Beasts of Ramoa' in gold lettering along the side, and Kayla recognised it as the book the Marquis had told her about when they'd first met.

'That's so cool. So you keep track of them all?' asked Rustus.

'So what?' snapped Kayla impatiently. 'Can we get on the road now?' She saw Rustus and Alethea share a look and knew she had probably come across as foul-tempered, but she didn't care. She was here to get Faro back, not to make friends, and her head was banging, probably from the smell inside the wagon.

'I suppose you're right, Kayla,' said the Marquis, standing up again. 'We should make the most of the daylight. Just one last thing . . .'

Kayla growled. She really would have been better off walking at this rate. This had better be something important.

The Marquis reached up to another ceiling hook and pulled down a metal cage. Inside there was a flutter of silvery wings. A small creature clung to the bars. It was entirely silver, save for the crown of bright red whiskers on top of its head and the scaly red tip of its tail.

'What is that?' asked Rustus, unable to take his eyes off it.

'I thought you might like it,' said the Marquis. 'It's a kind of reptillite.' He looked at the children to check they understood. Alethea and Rustus's expressions were as blank as Kayla's.

'Back to basics, I see,' said the Marquis. 'OK, while warmbloods, such as people and pangrons, have four limbs, reptillites have six.'

Kayla squinted into the cage. The Marquis was right. Unlike Faro, who had two legs and two wings, this animal had four squat legs *and* two narrow wings.

'Like fire geckos,' said Rustus. 'And Topaz.'

'Precisely,' replied the Marquis. 'They also have scales and rely on external sources, such as geysers, hot springs, lava lakes and the sun, to keep them warm.'

'Was the phaegra a reptillite?' asked Kayla, thinking

back to the tapestries that adorned the walls of the Academy, in which a purple six-limbed beast was defeated by Sky Riders.

'I'm not sure,' said the Marquis. 'The bestiary entry about the phaegra is patchy. I know it had orange eyes, powerful venom and could fly, but beyond that I don't know much else.'

'Phaegras have four wings and two legs in all the pictures I've seen,' said Rustus.

'Same here,' said Kayla. On this, if nothing else, they could agree.

'If that's the case, then I suppose it would have been a reptillite, yes,' said the Marquis. 'By the time my grandmother started the bestiary, many of the biggest and most impressive beasts, like phaegras and salinkas, were already extinct. She had to rely on stories passed down through the generations to fill out their descriptions.'

'I guess we'll know for sure soon,' said Rustus. 'If the prophecy is true.'

'What prophecy?' asked Alethea. Kayla realised Alethea had not been there when Tas had told them about the supposed return of the phaegra.

As Rustus explained, Alethea's eyes grew wild. 'Do you think it's true?' she asked, directing the question towards the Marquis.

He shrugged. 'The seers are not usually wrong about that kind of thing.'

Kayla saw a worried look flash over Rustus's face. She didn't want to fall back into discussions about the phaegra, and was about to tell the Marquis they should be on their way when Rustus pointed back at the silvery beast in the cage.

'What's this type of reptillite called?' he asked.

'That's a draggard,' the Marquis said. 'Watch this.'

From his waist he pulled a jar that contained several small webspinners – that must have been what Kayla had seen him collecting earlier – and shook the contents into the bottom of the draggard's cage. It caught sight of the webspinners immediately and started to stalk one, eyes fixed and unblinking. After a few seconds of silence, it opened its mouth and out shot a jet of steam. There was a fizz and a pop as the webspinner crumpled into a heap, before the draggard began to munch happily on its meal.

'Wow,' said Rustus breathily. 'Can I hold it?'

The Marquis's eyebrows shot up. Even Rustus looked surprised at the words that had come out of his mouth.

Kayla did not have time for this. What was wrong with these people? Had they forgotten the objective of their mission already?

'No!' she yelled. 'We need to leave. We're not here for a bestiary lesson, we're here to find my pangron.' She scratched at her wrist again. The skin there felt as irritated as she was. 'Faro could be anywhere by now.'

'Right you are,' said the Marquis, hanging the draggard's cage back on its hook. 'Let me just hitch up the bardebeests and we'll get on our way.'

'Arrgh!' she growled, pushing herself up off the sofa. 'You said the draggard was the last thing!'

Everyone stared at her. Didn't they understand the gravity of the situation? Faro was slipping further away with every breath.

'Excuse me,' Alethea said quietly after a few seconds, 'but do you realise you have a wound there?' She pointed at the underside of Kayla's arm where she'd just been scratching.

Everyone's eyes went to the red mark on Kayla's wrist.

'Oh dear,' said the Marquis, pulling on his moustache. 'Is that what I think it is?'

'What?' said Kayla, confused by the concerned looks on their faces, especially when they all exchanged glances. 'Don't just look at each other,' she snapped. 'What is it?'

The Marquis rubbed his nose awkwardly.

'It's . . . er . . .' Rustus hesitated.

'It's the Scourge,' said Alethea simply.

'What do you mean?' said Kayla.

'The Scourge, it's a dis—'

'I know what the Scourge is!' Kayla interrupted. 'What I mean is how can I have it? I only just got here. And Tas said the webspinners don't spread it.'

Kayla had never seen anyone with the Scourge before. Sophiatown's high walls had kept it out. For the millionth time she cursed herself for chasing that ship. Why had she ever left the safety of her city?

'I don't know how you got it,' said Alethea, 'but that's definitely what it is.'

As much as Kayla didn't want it to be true, it made sense – the aches, the banging head, the tiredness . . . An angry mist descended over her. 'One of *you* must have given it to me!' She tried to think back to when any of them had touched her.

'People don't spread the Scourge,' said Alethea, echoing what Tas and the Marquis had told her yesterday. 'That's not how it works. It's definitely a bite of some kind. Look.'

Kayla looked at the wound. She couldn't deny that it had the appearance of a puncture, as if something had bitten her.

'That's not what I've been told,' said Kayla, though she felt less certain now. 'I was told it was carried by people. And that we were safe in Sophiatown because we locked out the infected and prevented them from bringing it in.'

'And we were told it was caused by the webspinners,' said Alethea. 'But I don't believe it is.'

'It's not,' said Rustus, who also looked like he was struggling to come to terms with this revelation. 'Tas told us.'

'Well, there you have it,' said Alethea. 'Don't you see? Either nobody actually knows what causes the Scourge, or they've been lying to all of us.'

'Or both,' added Rustus.

The three of them looked at one another. Kayla pulled her sleeve back down. She didn't want to believe that her instructors might have been feeding her untruths. That was exactly what her mum had always accused them of, and look where that had got her – thrown into jail.

'I don't have time to have the Scourge,' she said. 'I need to get to Faro. I'll have to deal with it later.'

The Marquis shook his head solemnly. 'The Scourge is no joke, Kayla. Untreated there is a high likelihood you won't make it.'

Kayla gritted her teeth. She knew what they said about the Scourge. That it was a death sentence. But she simply couldn't die. What would Faro do without her?

'What are you suggesting?' she asked.

'That you're going to have to make a detour to the hospital on the mountain too.'

'I can't,' said Kayla. 'Faro needs me.'

'You'll be no use to him dead.'

'Are you saying I have no choice?'

'Not if you ever want to see your pangron again,' said the Marquis solemnly.

Kayla's breathing quickened and she paced up and down in front of the sofa. Her eyes fell on Alethea and she was struck by inspiration. She pointed at the satchel by the girl's feet. 'Didn't you say the pickleweed could fix it?'

Alethea rubbed her face. 'I thought it might,' she said. 'But Tas seemed pretty sure it wouldn't.'

'Well, why don't we test it?' asked Kayla.

Alethea hesitated, looking from the bag to the wound uncertainly. 'I suppose it wouldn't hurt to try,' she said. 'Give me a second.' She rummaged in her bag and plucked a bladder of pickleweed from the stem. 'OK, give me your arm.' She tucked some loose strands of hair behind her ears and busied herself rubbing juice from the plant bladder onto the wound on Kayla's arm.

'Ouch!' squealed Kayla, pulling her arm away.

'Sorry,' said Alethea. 'Try to hold still.'

The wound was sore and it hurt when Alethea touched it, but the pickleweed itself felt like water.

'Am I supposed to feel something happening?' Kayla asked, wincing as Alethea continued to rub the liquid in.

'Hmm,' said Alethea, trying to hold Kayla's arm still to get a better look. 'I'm not sure.' She continued rubbing.

'It's not working, is it?' Kayla asked after a few more minutes. They were wasting time. Tas had been right; pickleweed was useless. As far as Kayla was concerned it was nothing more than a good shampoo. This girl clearly didn't have the first idea about healing.

'Not yet,' said Alethea, avoiding eye contact.

'What happened when you used the other plant?' asked Rustus. 'The similar one that you said worked a little bit.'

'Firewort?' asked Alethea. 'It burnt away the affected skin.'

They all looked at Kayla's arm.

'Maybe it just needs longer to work,' said Alethea, trying to sound upbeat. Kayla remembered what she had said about this being the only hope for her grandma. 'I'll bandage it up and we can check on it later.'

'Good idea,' said Rustus. 'It will take a while to get to the mountain. If it hasn't worked by the time we reach the top then you can come with us to the hospital, and once you're fixed we can all go to Port Royal together.'

'I don't need your help,' Kayla snapped, noticing that Alethea didn't seem too pleased with that plan either; she needed to get back to Ataria. 'I can find Faro myself. Whatever happens, I won't be staying on Frostfall Mountain. Now can we *please* get on the road?'

There was a long silence in the wagon. Even the squawks and squeaks of the animals seemed to momentarily subside.

'Right,' said the Marquis, apparently finally realising the urgency of the situation. 'I think it's time to leave. Lillypeg, down!' Kayla glanced up as he sat the small furry beast on the arm of her sofa, then squeezed his way past the children, saying, 'Hold on to something. It can be a little bumpy out back.'

Rustus leaned over to get a closer look at Lillypeg, grinning as she wagged her pink-striped tail excitedly from side to side.

'Do you think she's friendly?' he asked.

Kayla shrugged sullenly.

Alethea sat down opposite them and tucked the pickleweed back in the bag. She chewed her lip, her expression downcast.

Outside they heard the Marquis muttering and then grunting as he heaved himself up into the driving seat. There was a whistle, a shout and then the wagon gave a lurch. They were on the move.

14

ALETHEA

They had been bouncing about for what seemed like an eternity. Kayla's face had gone almost totally green, Alethea couldn't feel her right bum cheek and, opposite her, Rustus cradled the bestiary, poring over its pages. He was quite unlike any Red she had ever met – though admittedly she had only spoken to a handful. Still, she thought she would be hard pressed to find anyone in the city who would believe that, when faced with hours on end in the back of a wagon, a Furi's chosen activity would be to read a book about beasts, and that he would look quite so delighted about it.

For the first few hours of the journey they had tried to make conversation, but finding a topic in common had proved difficult. So instead Rustus had read excerpts from the bestiary out loud. It had been fascinating to hear about the beasts of the Realms, from the long extinct salinka ('this green beast has only ever been seen by the

Shadow Ghouls, who describe it as having "a mouth full of scalefish"') to the venomous shadowy stinger ('despite being as large as a lavabear, the venom of the shadowy stinger is relatively mild, similar in action to that of the hypnos snake, and only used to defend itself in exceptional circumstances'). But after a while Rustus became so consumed by the book he stopped reading out loud. After that there were only the sounds of the animals to entertain them. Everyone was uncomfortable, tired and pretty fed up. Everyone, that was, except the Marquis.

'How are you doing back there?' he called chirpily from the front of the wagon.

'Still alive,' yelled Kayla, gripping the arm of the sofa tightly. 'Are we nearly there yet?'

Alethea had been watching Kayla carefully for signs the marshwort might be working, but if anything the Sky Cadet looked worse than before, although that could just be down to the bumpy road.

'Nearly,' came the reply. 'Hold on, bend ahead!'

The wagon lurched precariously to the left, and everything tilted violently, sending cages clattering and setting animals squawking and screeching. Alethea's stomach flipped and she let out a little squeak.

'I wish he wouldn't do that,' growled Kayla.

'I could do with some fresh air,' said Alethea. The smell inside the wagon might be even worse than the smell in Ataria.

'Me too,' Kayla said, before shouting to the Marquis, 'Can we have a toilet stop?'

Almost immediately the wagon screeched to a halt. The unexpectedness of it bounced Alethea right out of her chair.

'Perfect timing!' yelled the Marquis as his passengers groaned and rubbed their bottoms and elbows. 'Come on out!'

The back doors of the wagon were flung open, sending shafts of light down into its guts. Outside, the day was bright with the rays of the midday sun. The children picked their way past the assorted cages, trying to avoid being scratched, bitten or grabbed, and emerged into the daylight.

'I think we could all do with stretching our legs,' said the Marquis. 'Welcome to no man's land. We're currently in the foothills of the Shivertips, somewhere between the Shadowlands and the Ashlands. No people here, only beasts.'

'Is it safe?' Alethea asked, stepping off the bottom rung of the ladder. Kayla and Rustus had already clambered down and were contorting their bodies into all sorts of interesting shapes to stretch out their cramps.

'Of course,' said the Marquis. 'That's why I stopped here and nowhere else. Now wait a second, I need to grab someone.' He hurried up the steps.

'Did he say some*one*?' asked Rustus.

Alethea laughed. When it came to the Marquis, nothing was surprising. She took in their surroundings. They were far from Mount Ataria and the pyro cane jungle now and the view took her breath away. A wide heathland of spiky arrowsedge rolled out ahead of them, its fat fluffy seed heads quivering pendulously in the breeze. Beyond, a magnificent wall of mountains rose up, slate-coloured at their base and towering to jagged snow-covered peaks: the Shivertips. She wondered what plants might grow on their slopes. Needle trees, obviously, hare's bane, snowroot, ice thistle . . .

Thinking of all these alpine plants reminded Alethea of frostwort. *Native to cold alpine areas, usually at high altitude. Blooms only at temperatures below freezing.* It would definitely be below freezing up there. Could *that* be the cure the doctor had found? Why else would they situate themselves somewhere so remote and difficult to access? Alethea felt a little surge of pride that she might have been thinking along the right lines all along and encouraged that she could soon be returning to Ataria with the cure.

'Look.' Kayla pointed at a huge mountain that reached even higher than those surrounding it, piercing the sky with its needle-sharp tip. 'That's –'

'Frostfall Mountain.' Alethea nodded. It had to be. The mountain's peak was draped with snow, giving it the appearance of a vast frost-tipped spear. 'How do we get up there?'

'I'll take you to the base,' the Marquis said, lumbering back out of the wagon while pulling a snuffling, snorting beast behind him. 'Then you'll need to climb the rock face on your own. I'd love to come with you.' He guffawed a little at the thought of it. 'But I can't leave the wagon and all the beasts. Besides, I need to get Topaz to Port Royal to be properly identified.'

'What's that?' Rustus asked, pointing at the spotty beast straining at the end of its leash, nose buried in a patch of orange flowers.

'This is Ernie,' said the Marquis. 'He's a grunthog. I forgot to let him out to stretch his legs before we left.'

Ernie was a squat pale-skinned beast with wiry white hairs, round black spots and two corkscrew tusks.

'Hello, Ernie,' said Rustus, holding out the back of his hand for the beast to sniff. 'Is he friendly?' he asked the Marquis.

'Most of the time.' The Marquis held the rope out to Rustus. 'Here, would you hold his leash for a minute? I just need to get one more thing.' He climbed back up into the wagon. Rustus took the leash excitedly, crouching down to become better acquainted with the beast.

Kayla was looking at the mountain in the distance. 'The rock looks pretty sheer.'

'It's probably not so bad when you're up close,' said Rustus, not taking his eyes off Ernie. 'There are always faults in the rock you can make use of once you start looking.'

'I know,' Kayla quickly retorted. 'I wasn't suggesting I would find it difficult. I was just making conversation.'

Rustus caught Alethea's eye. Had Kayla always been this irritable, Alethea wondered, or was it something to do with the illness spreading?

'Rustus is a great climber,' said Alethea, trying to dispel

the tension. 'He's a Furi. His brothers hold the all-time speed records for ascending Kahanga Rock.'

'I'm not like my brothers,' said Rustus, looking down at his feet. 'And in case you've forgotten, I failed pretty spectacularly at the last climb I attempted.'

'But that wasn't your fault!' exclaimed Alethea. She didn't know why she felt so keen to reassure him, but it seemed like he needed to hear it.

'No? Whose was it then?' he replied.

Alethea didn't know how to respond. Perhaps he hadn't acted as most Scorched Ataris would have, but in her eyes there was no denying he had done the right thing. His actions didn't make him any less of a warrior. If anything they made him more of one.

'Being kind isn't a weakness,' she said.

'Being kind doesn't get you to the top of mountains though,' said Kayla, scratching at her arm again. It was looking redder than ever. 'I'm going to the toilet.' She walked off into the heathland, ducking through the places where tall fronds of arrowsedge had grown right over the pathway.

Rustus struggled to hold onto the grunthog's rope as it strained to follow her. 'Do you think Ernie needs the toilet too?' he asked as the beast almost pulled him over.

'Maybe.'

'I'll just walk him up to the edge.'

A few seconds later, the Marquis returned, rubbing some kind of oil into his beard. 'Where are the others?' he asked. 'Where's Ernie?'

'They walked down there to go to the toilet,' Alethea said, pointing to the heathland.

'What?' The Marquis turned sharply in the direction she was pointing, a look of horror on his face. 'They can't go down there, it's dangerous!'

'You just said this was the safest place to stop,' said Alethea, panic starting to roil in her gut.

'No, no, no,' said the Marquis. 'I meant right *here*, by the wagon. The heathland itself is a death trap. Kayla! Rustus! It's not safe! Come back!'

But they either couldn't hear him or weren't interested in what he had to say, because neither Kayla, Rustus nor Ernie returned.

'This is lavabear hunting territory,' said the Marquis, glancing around on high alert. 'They really shouldn't have strayed from the wagon. Rustus will be OK as the lavabears won't go near Ernie, but Kayla . . .'

'Should we go and find her?' Alethea asked, about to head towards the tall patch of arrowsedge.

The Marquis yanked her back. 'And give the lavabears twice as many victims to choose from? No, we stay here. Let's just hope they don't take too long.'

'My da used to tell me a story about lavabears,' said Alethea, 'but I was never sure if they really existed.'

'Oh, they exist all right,' said the Marquis. 'Fascinating beasts. Have you heard about their coats?'

Alethea shook her head.

'They express lava melanism, which means in areas where there's been a recent lava flow and the earth is black, their coats become very dark so they can camouflage. But where the ground is covered by plants, they are grey, with dappled green spots.'

'They sound beautiful,' said Alethea, thinking about plants that exhibited similar traits, 'but I'm guessing they're also pretty dangerous.' Just like the arrowsedge seed pods that surrounded them, which looked cute and fluffy if you left them alone but would explode in your face if you tried to eat them, releasing hundreds of needle-sharp barbs that lodged themselves in your eyes and nose, causing temporary blindness and making you itch for days.

'They haven't always been dangerous to people,' said the Marquis. 'The Beastlands in your realm once looked very different to the way they do now. Before the Turquoise Jungle became covered with webs it was home to all kinds of creatures – featherwings, reptillites, warmbloods, even phaegras! But when the phaegras were all killed, populations of obsidian webspinners – which had once been a favoured snack of the phaegras – skyrocketed. Now the webspinners reign and little else survives. Lavabears still prowl the outskirts of the forest, but with the interior covered in webs it's impossible for them to hunt, so they had to relocate to find new prey.'

'People.' Alethea felt a pang of sadness at all the life that had been lost. What wonders might have existed in that forest before it was overrun by webspinners? What incredible plants and life-changing medicines?

'Precisely,' replied the Marquis. 'People.'

Suddenly a yell from the heathland interrupted their conversation. It was Kayla and she sounded terrified.

'Kayla?' the Marquis shouted. 'Are you all right?'

The reply came loud and clear and was just two words. 'IT'S COMING!'

A moment later, she crashed through the undergrowth, and barely an arm's length behind followed a huge hairy beast with a mouthful of sharp teeth.

'Rustus!' the Marquis ordered, suddenly pale. 'Bring Ernie back here RIGHT NOW!'

Alethea realised she had never seen the Marquis without the hint of a smile on his face before. The situation must be serious.

As Kayla and the lavabear barrelled towards them Kayla stooped to pick up a rock and flung it back at the creature. It was momentarily deterred, but soon continued its chase. If Alethea and the Marquis didn't do something soon, it would crash straight into them.

Alethea's gaze fell on the arrowsedge seed pods. She plucked two of them from their stems and ran towards Kayla and her pursuer.

'Close your eyes!' she shouted, throwing one of the seed pods towards the beast's head. She kept her own eyes open just long enough to see if her plan would work, and sure enough, as it hit the lavabear, the pod exploded in a cloud of white, dispersing thousands of tiny barbs. The beast abruptly stopped its chase and began pawing at its face.

'Don't open your eyes yet!' Alethea shouted at Kayla,

her own now squeezed tightly shut. 'Marquis, can you guide us back to you?'

But before he could reply she heard the sound of hooves thundering towards them, accompanied by a loud snorting.

'Ernie!' Rustus called. 'Come back!'

She heard a crash, a roar, some more snorting and then a cheer from Rustus. 'Take that, lavabear!' he said.

'Can I open my eyes yet?' asked Kayla hesitantly.

'I think so,' said Alethea, tentatively opening her own. She saw the lavabear sprawled on the ground and Ernie pawing the ground next to it. Ernie retreated, preparing to charge again, but the lavabear didn't stick around to fight and turned on its heel, disappearing into the undergrowth. Alethea slipped the second arrowsedge seed head into her satchel.

'Well done, hog,' said the Marquis, strolling up to Ernie and looping another leash around his neck. He led the grunthog back to the children. 'That'll teach you all not to wander off into the Beastlands!'

'Is that it?' Kayla yelled. She looked furious. 'We were just almost eaten by a rampaging beast! You said it was *safe*! I thought it was meant to be a toilet stop, so I went to the toilet. Did you think I was going to do that here in front of you all?'

Hard as it was to be annoyed at the Marquis, Alethea could see Kayla's point.

'You didn't exactly make it clear that lavabears were wandering through the heath,' Rustus agreed. His voice was scolding but his eyes sparkled. He could barely tear his gaze away from the retreating beast.

'I thought that was obvious,' said the Marquis. 'I forget how sheltered you've been. Anyway, good thing is we're all safe now.'

'No thanks to you,' grumbled Kayla.

'That's not entirely true,' said Rustus. 'If it wasn't for Ernie protecting us we'd –'

'If it wasn't for *him* –' Kayla jabbed a finger at the Marquis – 'we wouldn't have *needed* protecting.'

A squawk from above drew Alethea's attention. A white-winged beast was descending rapidly towards them, without any apparent intention of slowing down.

'Er, should we be worried about that?' Alethea pointed at the feathery torpedo.

The Marquis lifted his hand to shield his eyes. 'Milabar!' he yelled. 'At last, she's back.'

He held an arm aloft, watching lovingly as the creature landed gracefully on his outstretched finger. Once it was comfortable, to Alethea's great surprise, the beast began to speak. The voice that emerged was so human-like Alethea actually looked around to check nobody had joined them.

'You were right,' the featherwing said in a rolling and beautiful accent, 'a boat with green sails has been spotted sailing towards Port Royal. Due to dock in two days. Take care – a blizzard is coming. I will await news of your arrival.'

'Thank you, Milabar,' said the Marquis. 'You must be very hungry. Let me get you some food.'

'Did you hear what it said?' asked Kayla. 'The boat *is*

headed for Port Royal.' She seemed equal parts excited and worried. Alethea knew this confirmation would do nothing to ease her desire to get there quickly.

As the Marquis wandered back to the wagon the children hounded him with questions.

'Can that beast really speak?'

'Who was the message from?'

'What type of creature is she?'

'No,' the Marquis replied, addressing their questions one by one. 'Milabar is a fantastic beast with many talents, but she can't speak. She's just a brilliant mimic. The voice you heard was my friend Aquamarine, owner of the Salty Seadog – a public house in Port Royal. And Milabar is a heraldwing from the Fjordlands.'

'How long will it take you to get to Port Royal via the coast road?' Kayla asked, weighing up her options.

'Two more days.'

'But if you come with us you can get the doctor to have a quick look at your wound on the way – and probably still be there before the Marquis,' said Alethea.

Kayla scowled and rubbed her wrist. 'I told you, I don't need to see the doctor. How long will it take if I go over the mountain?'

'Maybe a day,' said the Marquis, feeding Milabar from his hand. 'Assuming you don't come into any problems, like avalanches or rockfalls.'

'Then that's what I'm doing. The fastest option,' Kayla said firmly.

The Marquis sighed and raised Milabar aloft again.

'I'm so sorry, my girl,' he said. 'I know you've just had another long journey, but I'm going to send you on one last errand. This time to Frostfall Mountain.'

Milabar cooed softly. The Marquis cleared his throat and then spoke to her loudly and clearly. 'Start message. Three children coming up the east face, expect them shortly. Finish message.'

The featherwing opened her mouth and repeated, 'Three children coming up the east face, expect them shortly.'

The impersonation was so extraordinary Alethea could hardly believe her ears.

'Quite something, isn't it?' the Marquis said, eyes twinkling.

'How does she know which bit to repeat?' Rustus asked. 'Why isn't she copying *everything* you say?'

'I've taught her the commands "start message" and "finish message",' said the Marquis. 'It was getting ever so tedious hearing her repeat every screech and squeal she heard inside the wagon.'

Alethea watched Rustus as he digested this information in open-mouthed astonishment.

'To the hospital at Frostfall Mountain!' the Marquis commanded, before letting Milabar go.

They all watched as she soared into the sky and disappeared among the clouds that clung to the snowy peaks.

'If only it were that easy for us,' said Alethea, smiling in Kayla's direction. But Kayla's face was set, resolute and determined. She had no time for joking and she would not rest until she found her pangron, no matter what got in her way.

'If only.' The Marquis laughed. 'Come on, everyone, back in the wagon. We don't have far to go.'

15

RUSTUS

After another hour or so they poured out of the Marquis's wagon for the final time, this time at the foot of Frostfall Mountain. They were so close now, it was impossible to see its crown of ice and snow; all they could see from here was the rock face looming over them, steep and foreboding. Rustus was relieved to see that the rock wasn't as flat and smooth as it had seemed from a distance, but instead was jagged, sharp and covered in fungi and tendrilous plants.

'This is where I leave you,' the Marquis said. 'For now at least.'

'Let's do this,' said Kayla, marching towards the rock face.

'Goodbye, Kayla,' said the Marquis, and Rustus thought he looked a bit sad.

'Bye,' she replied, looking over her shoulder. 'I'll see you in a couple of days at Port Royal.'

'See you there.' The Marquis smiled, but there was concern in his face too. 'I hope you see sense enough to visit the doctor.'

She just rolled her eyes. 'Next time I see you, I'll be with Faro!'

Rustus held out his hand to shake the Marquis's. 'Thanks for bringing us here.'

The Marquis swept him into a hug. 'It was my pleasure. I hope we'll meet again one day.'

'Me too,' said Rustus. He really meant it. He would have loved to have stayed longer with the fascinating bestiarist and his hoard of extraordinary creatures. When he pulled away from the embrace, he noticed a small head poking out from the Marquis's beard. 'Bye, Lillypeg.' He gave her chin a little scratch. 'Keep the old man safe for us.'

'Less of the old!' said the Marquis with a tut, then he turned to Alethea. 'Good luck, Alethea. I hope you manage to find the cure.'

'Thanks,' she said, also giving him a hug. 'Me too.'

'Now go on – you mustn't linger too long here at the base. You need to get to the top before it gets dark and the cliffcreepers start to wake up.'

Rustus looked nervously up at the rock, trying to spot any caves where these cliffcreepers might be hiding. 'What are they like?'

'Hard on the outside and soft on the inside,' said the Marquis. 'They don't mean any harm, but if you disturb them after dark they can be a little grouchy.'

Rustus suspected that if the Marquis said they were

grouchy, they definitely weren't to be trifled with.

'Promise me you'll be careful,' the Marquis said, looking Rustus right in the eyes.

Rustus nodded and promised, then he and Alethea followed after Kayla, waving to the Marquis as he rolled off down the track.

When they reached Kayla, she was looking up at the rock face.

'How are we going to get up?' Alethea asked nervously. 'I've never climbed anything before. I don't know where to start.'

'I can help you,' said Rustus. 'It's not as hard as it looks and there are plenty of jagged bits that will make excellent handholds.' He might not have passed the Scorching, but Rustus tried to remind himself he was still a good climber. He scanned the rock face, mentally picking out the best route and making note of ledges where they could rest.

'All right,' said Alethea. She smiled gratefully at Rustus and he felt a pang of pride. It felt wonderful to be useful.

'Right,' he said, 'I'm not sure how much you both know about this stuff, but the first rule of climbing expeditions is to carefully plan the route. So –'

'I don't need your advice,' snapped Kayla before he could finish.

'Rustus does have experience with this kind of thing,' Alethea said. 'Maybe we should listen.'

'Experience in how to fail when trying to climb something, you mean?' Kayla said. 'I don't know if you realise who you're talking to, but I'm a Sky Cadet, enrolled in the Sky Academy. He –' she jabbed a finger at Rustus's chest – 'is a failed warrior and an exile. If anything, he'll only put me in *more* danger.'

Rustus glanced at Alethea. Kayla seemed even shorter-tempered than usual. Alethea's worried expression suggested that she had noticed it too. Was this cantankerous attitude something to do with the Scourge?

'I don't have time for this,' Kayla said. 'Every wasted minute is a minute I'm further from Faro. You guys can make your own way up.' She marched over to the rock.

Rustus bit his lip to stop himself from replying. She was impossible!

'Please look after yourself, Kayla,' said Alethea, reaching out towards her, but Kayla was already stretching up to begin her climb. 'You need to get that wound seen to as soon as you can. The Scourge is serious.'

Kayla didn't reply as she began to ascend the mountain, grappling with the smooth rock overhanging her head. The shiny stones slipped under her palms as she tried to grab onto them.

'I don't think you should go that way,' Rustus couldn't help himself from calling out. 'There's a better foothold over there.' He pointed to their left.

'Stop it,' Alethea said. 'You'll just wind her up. I'm sure she'll work it out.'

'Not if she keeps going that way,' Rustus muttered to himself, as Alethea approached the rock face and touched it with her hand.

'This rock looks really slippery,' she said.

'We can put something onto our hands for grip,' Rustus suggested. He'd done that before when climbing rock columns in Ataria.

'These would've been useful,' said Alethea, pointing to where the sleeves of her shirt had once been. 'Unfortunately I had to use them already.'

Rustus caught sight of a flash of blue threaded through Alethea's hair.

'How about that?' He pointed to the cloth woven into her plait. 'The material is rough enough to give us a bit of grip but flexible and light enough to wrap easily around our hands.'

'Perfect,' said Alethea. As she began to untie her plaits, he saw her glance at his own hair, probably wondering where his cloths had gone.

'They made me take them out,' he said. 'Before I left the city.'

Alethea gave him a consolatory smile. 'I think that should be enough,' she said once there was a small pile of blue cloths by her feet.

Rustus watched as she wound the cloth deftly between her fingers. He was impressed by this unassuming girl from the Blue District. Alethea was kind, capable, resourceful and every bit as talented as his now-Scorched comrades.

'It's not fair, is it?' he asked. 'How different things were for you in Ataria.'

'What do you mean?'

'I guess I thought that Blues were somehow different from Reds,' he said, feeling ashamed as soon as the words had left his mouth. 'Not that we were better or anything,' he added quickly – though in reality, he reflected that he probably had believed that. All of the Unscorched had been encouraged to believe they were more special than the rest of Ataria. 'Just . . .' He didn't know how to articulate his thoughts and wished he hadn't said anything.

'Ataria isn't run fairly,' said Alethea matter-of-factly. 'It's a lottery, based on which district you are born into.'

'Exactly,' said Rustus. It seemed so simple when she put it like that. 'But it shouldn't be like that.'

'No,' she agreed. 'It shouldn't.'

Above them, Kayla had still not managed to grab hold of the overhang.

'Would you like some finger wraps?' Rustus called up to her. 'It will be so much easier with a bit of grip.'

She glanced in their direction before huffing audibly and reaching again for the overhanging rock. But once more she failed to grab on. Eventually she jumped down and stalked over to where Rustus and Alethea were seated on the ground.

'Here,' said Alethea. 'Wrap these around your hands.'

Kayla tied the cloths quickly, continuing to scowl while she did so.

'Which do you think is the best way up?' Alethea asked.

Rustus pointed at a large crack that extended about twenty strides up the rock face. 'We'll follow that fault in the rock. You should be able to push your hands and feet deep into the gap. Then we can clamber across to that big green plant. But don't pull on it for support – you never know how well these things are rooted.'

'Oh!' Alethea laughed, studying the plants above. 'That's anchorweed. You can hold onto that for as long as you like – even a bardebeest couldn't pull it out.'

Rustus smiled. Of course she would know what the plant was.

'OK, that's good to know. After the anchorweed we can traverse across to where those brown boulders are, with the weird dangly tendrils growing from them.' He paused to consult Alethea. 'Do you know what they are?'

She shook her head.

'Never mind. Then, do you see that horizontal crack? We can put our feet in there while holding onto the ledge above – Alethea, I'll help you with that bit if you need me to. Once we get to the end of the crack there's a little ledge, do you see? We'll stay there a while to catch our breath and plan the next section.'

'Right,' said Kayla, pausing for a moment as if she was about to say something else, then thought better of it. 'Shall we make a start?'

They approached the cliff together, climbing as a group. The fabric helped them to grip on to the slippery rock. A couple of times he heard Alethea squeal and flinched as her nails scrabbled at the rock, but overall she did remarkably well. Kayla too was a good climber, even with her bad arm.

After a while Rustus found Alethea had stopped. He assumed she needed a break. 'That isn't the best place to rest,' he called down to her. 'If you can make it a bit further there are some decent handholds where you'll feel much safer.'

'Oh, I'm not resting,' Alethea said. 'I'm just intrigued by this orange moss.'

Rustus hadn't noticed the plant, but now that he looked, he saw it was dotted all the way up the cliff face.

'I've never seen it before,' she said. 'I wondered what it was. It's OK, we can carry on.'

So on they went, until they found themselves almost at the ledge by the anchorweed. Kayla was already sitting there with her legs dangling over the edge, rubbing her arm.

'This is safe to grab on to, you say?' asked Rustus as they ducked under the plant.

'Yes,' said Alethea. 'Look.' She tugged hard on the plant and it was stuck fast.

Rustus used it to guide his way across and then plonked himself down next to Kayla. 'We can rest here for a while. How are you finding it?'

'All right,' Alethea said, joining them. 'I just tried to copy exactly what you did. I'm starting to feel a little bit sick now we're so high though.' She glanced at the ground far below them, swallowing nervously.

'That's normal,' he said. 'Try not to look down. Look over there instead.' He pointed at the horizon where the sun was low in the sky. 'It's going to be a beautiful sunset. The last time I saw one was when I was on lookout duty with my cohort.' His heart hurt a little as he remembered his fellow Unscorched. *Scorched now*, he had to remind himself. Would he ever see another Atarian sunset again?

Alethea hugged her knees to her chest. 'I remember seeing a sunset just after my youngest brother was born,' she said. 'All of us – Ma and Da, Grandma, Lilian, Padma, Elvira, Cassio and baby Digby – had climbed to the rim of the caldera. We snuggled under one holey old blanket and told stories until the sun disappeared entirely from the sky. We had to carry Cassio and Digby home.' She laughed. 'It's one of my favourite memories.'

'Are you close to your siblings?' Rustus asked.

Alethea nodded. 'They're my everything. Aren't yours?'

Rustus sighed. 'We're quite different people. I know we look alike and everyone expects me to be just like them, strong and brave. But I'm not.'

'I don't know,' said Alethea, nudging his shoulder. 'I think you're strong . . . and brave. Maybe just in a different way.'

If only his father could see that.

'How about you, Sky Cadet?' He looked over at Kayla, who'd been uncharacteristically quiet. 'When was the last time you saw a sunset like this?'

Kayla shrugged. 'Probably when I was out flying with Faro.' She didn't elaborate, but instead stared intently out at the burning sky before asking, 'Why can't I remember who shot us down?'

He could understand why it was so frustrating for Kayla. The most important thing in the world had been taken from her and she couldn't remember how it had happened. But he didn't have any answers.

'It's not your fault,' said Alethea kindly. 'The poison they used on their arrows probably had amnesic qualities to make you forget.'

Kayla's head snapped round. 'Do you think so?' She looked almost relieved. 'Anyway, I'll soon find out when I get to Port Royal. Which is where I should be now, not sitting here chatting to you two.'

Alethea and Rustus shared a look.

Kayla got to her feet and turned to face the wall again. 'The Marquis said we need to reach the top before nightfall. We'd better get moving if we're going to make it.'

'All right.' Rustus got up to assess the next stage of the climb, taking time to weigh up the various options. When he looked across to Kayla, she was already on her way towards a ledge ten strides above them. 'Oh no.'

'What is it?' asked Alethea.

'She's gone the wrong way,' he said. 'Once she's traversed across that ledge, there's nowhere else to go – the rock above it is as smooth and flat as glass.'

Alethea paled. 'Kayla!' she called. 'That's the wrong way! You need to come back!"

'This way looks quicker!' Kayla shouted back.

'It's not!' Rustus replied. 'It's a dead end!'

But Kayla was either too far up to hear or didn't want to listen.

'Wait here,' Rustus told Alethea. 'I'm going to go and tell her. She's nearly at the end now. I can at least help her get back down safely.' He scurried up towards Kayla, who had now reached the point where the handholds stopped and was scrabbling against the slippery rock. 'You can't go any further that way,' he shouted. 'You have to come back. I'm coming to help you!'

'I don't need your help!' she yelled back. 'Go away. I'm fine.' She grappled at a hanging plant just above her head.

'Don't trust the plants unless you know what they are,' he said. 'Some of them aren't well anchored.'

'I told you I'm fine! I need to get up there quickly! You go back to Alethea!' A clump of earth fell from a crevice above her and the plant she had been tugging on slid clean out of the rock. She gave a little squeal and desperately grabbed on to a smooth brown boulder hanging over her head.

As Rustus approached her, he saw movement on the wall above. He blinked and squinted but couldn't make out what it was. The light was fading rapidly now, so perhaps it had been a trick of the shadows, but for a moment it had seemed like the rock face itself had moved.

'Did you see that?' he asked, drawing close to her.

'What?'

'Never mind.'

Then he saw it again. Just above Kayla, a clump of roundish brown rocks pulled fully away from the wall. The clump was vaguely animal-shaped, with a large triangular head, six chunky legs and a short squat tail. The smooth brown rock that Kayla had tried to grab onto had actually been its tail.

'The cliff is coming alive!' came a yell from below as the creature's head turned towards Kayla and fixed her with a glistening black eye. Alethea had spotted it too. 'Watch out!'

The beast was almost fully detached from the wall now and it was enormous. Was this a cliffcreeper?

Rustus hooked his foot into a gap in the rock and stretched out his arm towards Kayla. 'Grab my hand.'

The stubborn rider was hanging onto the cliff by her fingertips and the cliffcreeper was rapidly approaching, but she still wouldn't accept his help.

'Kayla, that beast is coming for you! Grab onto my hand right now!'

Kayla scrabbled at the wall for a few moments more before realising it was impossible, and at last she leaned towards him.

Their fingers touched and Rustus squeezed tight.

'I've got you!' he yelled, pulling her towards him, away from the cliffcreeper and onto a sturdier footing.

'Why would you help me?' she asked, as they went quickly back down the way they had come. 'Why would you put yourself in danger for me?'

'Because I didn't want you to get hurt,' he said simply. 'Because you're my friend.'

'We're not friends,' she growled. 'I don't need friends. All I need is Faro.'

Rustus frowned. Everyone needed friends. Without Hubert and his fellow Unscorched, Rustus didn't know how he would have got through the training.

He glanced up and saw that the cliffcreeper was following them at speed.

'We *are* friends,' he told Kayla, ducking as the beast thrashed its tail, sending stones crashing down the cliff face. 'At least, I'd like us to be.'

'I don't need your pity,' she replied, leaning into the wall to avoid the falling rocks. 'I could have got out of here without your help.'

Rustus shook his head. Why was she so desperate to prove that she didn't need anyone else? Did she think he only wanted to be friends with her because he felt sorry for her?

'I didn't come up here because I doubted your ability,' said Rustus, pressed against the cliff beside her. 'I came to help you because that's what you do when your friends are in trouble.'

The cliffcreeper lunged towards them and Kayla threw a stone at its snout.

'Why would you want to be friends with me?' she snapped. 'I've never done anything to help you. I'm from Sophiatown, you're from Ataria.' The cliffcreeper recoiled from the hit with a hiss.

'Nice shot,' said Rustus, moving downwards again. 'Let's move quickly while it's hurt.'

As they descended while the cliffcreeper nursed its wound, Rustus considered Kayla's question. What reason had she given him to be friends with her? None, he supposed. And they *were* from different realms. But why should that mean they couldn't get on? Despite what they had been taught, the beasts weren't all bad – perhaps with the exception of the lavabear and the cliffcreeper currently trying to knock them off a mountain – so maybe their preconceptions about the people from other realms were wrong too. Maybe Sky Riders and Scorched Ataris didn't have to be enemies. Even if she was right and she had never done anything to help him, was that how friendship worked? How would anyone ever make friends if they waited for the other person to do something nice for them first?

'Friendship isn't a trade,' he concluded. 'It's a decision.'

They were almost back at the ledge with Alethea when Rustus's foot slipped. He looked down to see that he had overreached and needed to correct his footing. He was just about stable again when Kayla shouted above him.

'Rustus, look out!'

Before he could look up, something whacked him on the back and he lost his footing again, leaving him hanging by his arms. He glanced to the side to see another cliffcreeper had appeared from the shadows beside him. It was gearing up to whip him on the back with its tail again when he grabbed a rock shard and flung it towards the creature as hard as he could, but the beast just launched itself at him. What could he do? If he kept his hands where they were the cliffcreeper would bite them, but they were the only things preventing him from crashing to the ground far below.

'I'm coming!' shouted Kayla.

Rustus looked up just in time to see her aim another

rock at the beast's head. It hit its target and the beast recoiled with a squeal, losing its footing. Rustus didn't have a chance to move out of its way before it hurtled past him, so he braced for impact and clung on to the rock face as tightly as he could. But the creature missed his back and arms. Relieved, he thought the danger had passed, but as the reptillite tumbled by his foot it latched on with its powerful jaws and tugged. The sensation took Rustus by surprise and his right hand slipped.

'Argh!' he said, battling to hold on.

'Grab my hand,' yelled Kayla, moving quickly towards him and reaching down with extended fingers.

His muscles burned as he strained to reach her. The memory of falling from Kahanga Rock flashed through his mind. *No*, he thought, *this can't be happening*. He heaved up towards Kayla and their fingers met, but then the cliffcreeper still attached to his foot gave a wiggle and he felt Kayla's fingers slip from his grasp. Suddenly the ground was rushing towards him and he felt the familiar sensation of freefall. There was no denying it now; he was falling. *Again*.

16

KAYLA

Kayla stared open-mouthed at the spot where Rustus lay far below, her eyes wide and her heart hammering.

'Rustus!'

She heard Alethea's panicked screaming from the ledge. 'Rustus, are you OK?'

He wasn't moving. A cliffcreeper was sprawled out next to him. She couldn't believe what had happened. It was all her fault. How had things gone so wrong? Just a few hours ago, Kayla had been well on her way to rescuing Faro. She had a good idea where he was and knew how to get there – nothing but time had stood in her way. And now? Not only did she have a toxic wound that would kill her if she didn't get it seen to, she was also responsible for hurting someone whose only crime was trying to save her life. No one had asked Rustus to come and help her, but he had, because he was a good person. Why had she been so mean and difficult?

Further down the rock face, Alethea was also leaning over the edge, looking at Rustus. Kayla needed to get down there and help her. She wasn't going to let another person get hurt on her watch. 'Alethea,' she shouted. 'Are you OK?'

'I'm fine,' she cried. 'What are we going to do about Rustus?'

Darkness was descending rapidly, stretching long shadows beneath the pointy crags and swallowing the details that would guide them up safely. Kayla looked up. There was a hospital at the summit. If they could carry Rustus up there then they could get him seen by a doctor. She continued her descent towards Alethea, but as she did so the wall lurched strangely before her eyes and her stomach rolled. Was it the low light or another cliffcreeper? Or had the Scourge affected her vision? She didn't want to find out the answer.

'I'm coming to you,' Kayla called to Alethea, who was reaching for the anchorweed. 'Don't move. It's getting really dark.'

'I can't wait. I have to go down to help him,' said Alethea.

'No!' shouted Kayla. 'It's too dangerous. Wait for me!' She clenched her teeth. She was the stronger climber, so she should be the one to go to save Rustus. 'Hang on – I'm nearly there.'

'All right,' said Alethea. 'But hurry!'

Kayla clambered nimbly down the rest of the way to where Alethea waited on the ledge, running her hands over the rock to find a good route down.

'Watch out for shiny brown patches,' Kayla said. 'They're cliffcree—'

The advice came too late. One of the beasts had peeled itself from the rock face and was stalking towards Alethea.

Kayla lunged, ready to protect Alethea, but the healer girl was quicker.

'Get away!' she yelled, throwing a handful of red powder at the cliffcreeper's face. It skittered backwards and disappeared off the ledge.

'What was that?' Kayla asked.

'Powdered fire thistle,' said Alethea. 'Seems cliffcreepers don't like it!'

'Nice work,' Kayla said, panting. She was impressed by the girl's ingenuity. She spun around to look for any other cliffcreepers lurking nearby and was suddenly overcome by a wave of nausea. It hit her with such force she had to sit down on the ledge.

'Are you OK?' Alethea asked, hurrying over to her side.

'I'm fine,' Kayla said, though she didn't feel it. The world was spinning around her and she felt as if she was going to throw up.

'What's wrong?' Alethea asked.

'Nothing. I'm all right. Come on. If we're going to help Rustus, we've got to keep moving.' She stood back up, but the feeling didn't go; instead it got worse, building inside her like a swirling vortex until she could contain it no longer. She took a deep breath and closed her eyes, leaning against the rock, then her stomach heaved and its contents forced themselves out.

'You're OK,' Alethea said, rubbing her back. Her voice was muffled and sounded far off. 'Here, chew this.' She gently pushed a tarry black pastille between Kayla's lips. The flavour was so strong and spicy she thought she might be sick again.

'I feel terrible,' Kayla said, as she sank to the ground. 'What's happening to me?'

'It's the Scourge. It's normal. Don't try to fight it. The herbs will soon make you feel better.'

I can't die, or who will rescue Faro and Rustus? Kayla tried to tell her, but the words wouldn't come.

'That's it,' said Alethea gently. 'Just relax.'

Relax? This was no time to relax. She would relax when Rustus and Faro were safe and not before. She looked blearily at Alethea, but found her vision too blurred to make out the girl's face. She pushed herself groggily forward, fighting the urge to vomit again.

'Kayla,' said Alethea, 'can you lie down for me?'

No! Kayla screamed inside. This was no time to lie down. But the world was closing in on her and her head felt so, so heavy. Maybe she could just rest for a second . . .

17

ALETHEA

Alethea reached to cushion Kayla's head as it crashed onto the hard rock, but she was too slow and crimson blood bloomed on Kayla's forehead. It was a superficial cut, but enough to give her quite a headache when she awoke.

Alethea cast around to see if there was anything to stem the bleeding. Her eyes fell on a patch of the orange moss she had noticed earlier. What *was* it? Moss was generally great for dressing wounds, so she reached for it, pressing her fingers deep into its wet sponge. As she did so there was a tiny pop – the sound of air being ejected forcefully. A puff of small particles emerged from the moss, and as they took to the air they began to glow. Alethea's mouth fell open in surprise.

'Candlemoss,' she whispered. It was the Realms' only known fluorescent moss, but she had never expected to see it with her own eyes. The cloud of orangey light drifted into the night, its brightness growing dimmer as the particles dispersed.

In the glow, she looked up and down the mountain for signs of more cliffcreepers, but she couldn't see any. She turned back to Kayla, who looked pale and small, just how Da had in the days before he passed. She hoped the doctor at the top of the mountain really did have a cure.

Please get better, she thought. *Because if you don't, maybe Grandma won't either.* Not wanting to dwell on that thought, she focused her mind on the present. Rustus. She could save Rustus.

Alethea got to her feet and rolled Kayla close to the wall so she would be safe on the ledge while Alethea descended. 'I'll be back soon,' she said.

Climbing down was no easier than going up had been, especially in the dark. But she soon found that the route was lined with patches of candlemoss, which she could press to light up and guide her way. After Kayla's earlier warning she was careful to avoid shiny brown patches. Once she started to notice them, she realised the cliffcreepers were everywhere, but like many of the beasts she'd come across, they were content to leave her be if she did the same to them. As she was nearing the bottom she heard a familiar voice and relief pumped through her body.

'Alethea? Is that you?'

'Rustus!' she shouted. 'You're OK!'

'It *is* you!' he called back. 'How are you making the cliff glow like that?'

'Candlemoss! Are you hurt?'

'I think I've broken my ankle, but otherwise I'm all right. How are you two?'

'Kayla's passed out. We need to get her to the hospital as soon as we can.'

'Passed out is probably the only way we were ever going to get her there,' he joked. 'At least we won't have to fight her now.'

Once Alethea was close enough to the ground, she hopped down beside Rustus and immediately began assessing him. His foot was badly swollen. She knelt and touched it gently.

'Not broken,' she said. 'Just sprained. But it's going to need some support. Let me strap it up for you.' She pulled the remaining cloth from her hair braids and bandaged his ankle to support it as best she could, then handed him a tuber of taxacum from her satchel. 'It won't take the pain away completely,' she said, 'but suck this.'

Rustus put the root in his mouth and then spat it immediately out again. 'That's disgusting!'

'Perhaps,' Alethea replied, 'but if you're going to climb this mountain with a sprained ankle, it's necessary.'

Reluctantly he put the taxacum back into his mouth.

In the light of the moss, she saw the colour in his face change, flushed from the pain relief. His jaw loosened and his shoulders fell.

'Wow,' he said. 'That's pretty effective.'

'Magic, isn't it?' said Alethea with a smile. She loved this part of healing – when it worked how it was supposed to.

Rustus nodded. 'Would it work on animals too?'

'I guess so,' said Alethea. 'What did you have in mind?'

Rustus pointed to the gloom beside him and Alethea squinted at a pile of rocks. When she realised what it was, she recoiled in horror.

'The cliffcreeper that nearly killed you?' she said.

'It also hurt itself in the fall. Now it's injured it's not aggressive at all. Look.' He leaned over and stroked the beast on the head. It made a little murmur.

Alethea hesitated.

'Please, Alethea,' he said. 'I've already killed one beast this week.'

'The lavabear?' Alethea frowned. 'We didn't kill that, we just –'

'Not the lavabear,' he said. 'A webspinner. It was before the Scorching. We all had to kill one. We weren't allowed to take part in the Scorching unless we did.'

'Oh,' said Alethea, remembering how peacefully the webspinners had sat in their webs. Killing one must have been awful. 'Well, you didn't have a choice,' she said sympathetically. 'You had to do it.'

'We always have a choice,' said Rustus gravely. 'I see that now. And we have a choice here too. We can help this cliffcreeper or we can leave it to suffer.'

Something about his words reminded Alethea of her da: *We cannot choose how the ash falls, only what we build with it.* Rustus was right. She chucked him another small tuber. 'Give it that,' she said. 'But let's get out of here before it's well enough to chase us.'

Once he'd fed the taxacum to the beast, Alethea helped Rustus to his feet and they stepped up to the rock face.

'How do you make this stuff glow?' he asked, pointing at the candlemoss.

'Press down on it,' said Alethea. Rustus tried it and another cloud of orange spores floated into the air. 'But watch out for the shiny brown patches. They're sleeping cliffcreepers.'

Rustus nodded and started his ascent up the wall, making a series of grunts and groans each time he needed to put weight on his bad ankle.

Slowly but surely they made it back to the ledge, carefully avoiding disturbing any more beasts. Kayla hadn't moved. Alethea checked her over and was glad to find she seemed no worse.

'How are we going to get to the top?' Rustus asked. 'With my ankle working I might have been able to carry Kayla, but now I'm going to struggle just to get up there myself.'

'I could carry her,' Alethea said. Rustus laughed. 'Don't look so surprised! Healing is very physical work. People who are unconscious or can't walk need transporting, and that job usually falls to me. And it's no better when I'm at home. I have five younger siblings and one or more of them are permanently attached to my legs or torso.'

'Carrying someone up a mountain is different though.'

Alethea looked up and begrudgingly had to admit he was right. Climbing had been hard enough without injuries and patients to carry, let alone in the dark.

'Maybe we should sleep here for the night,' she said, 'and continue climbing in the morning?' She glanced down at Kayla. The girl desperately needed to get to a healer, but they risked getting lost or injured if they tried to find their way by moss light alone.

Rustus nodded in reluctant agreement. 'We can start again at first light.'

Alethea pushed herself to standing and looked about the ledge, trying to decide where the safest place to sleep would be. It was then she noticed the night sky was peppered with tiny brilliant flecks of white.

'Well, isn't that something,' she whispered. 'Snow.' She thought it was the most beautiful thing she'd ever seen until she remembered Aquamarine's warning about the blizzard and shivered.

'We need to keep warm,' said Rustus, as the flakes began to land in his hair and on his face.

Suddenly Alethea remembered the blanket in her satchel. 'Come here,' she said. 'This blanket is old but it's better than nothing. It will keep a layer of air between us and the snow.'

They moved either side of Kayla and huddled together, shuffling close to the rock and covering as much of their bodies with the blanket as they could. It was going to be a long night.

Alethea wasn't sure how much time had passed when she was shaken awake. At first she thought the cliffcreepers had returned and she jerked upright, before remembering what a precarious position she was in, perched on a narrow rocky ledge halfway up a mountain.

'It's OK,' a calming voice said. 'We're here to help you.'

Alethea blinked and rubbed her tired eyes, waiting for them to focus. It was early morning and the sun was still below the horizon. In front of her was a man, his body covered in a thick white fur.

'My name is Sami,' he said. 'I'm a nurse working with the doctor on Frostfall Mountain. A heraldwing came to tell us that you were on the way. When you didn't arrive, we came looking.'

Alethea's eyes travelled up the rock face to see two more figures making their way down. Attached to ropes, they moved in huge bounds, lighting up the candlemoss as they passed.

'Is it safe?' Alethea asked.

'We're well-practised at this,' Sami said with a smile. 'Come on – we don't have much time. Your friend is already in the second phase of the Scourge. We need to get her to the hospital.' Sami pulled a silvery cloth from beneath his furs and handed one end to Rustus. They'd clearly woken him first, as they had already rebandaged his ankle. 'Stretch this out, please.'

The cloth was long and narrow, with loops at either end. *A stretcher*, Alethea realised.

'Help me lift her on,' Sami said, as he gently lifted first Kayla's head and then her shoulders. Alethea lifted from under Kayla's knees, and together they moved her onto the stretched fabric. Her skin was cold to the touch and she looked deathly pale. Alethea cursed herself for not waking earlier to check on her. Sami must have noticed.

'You did the best you could. Keeping her safely on this ledge and putting her to sleep – it probably saved her life.' He unhooked two silver ropes from his belt and attached them to the loops at either end of the stretcher.

'Is that –'

'Webspinner silk.' Sami nodded. 'The stretcher is made of it too. Strongest material known to man.' Once he had finished, he tugged twice on the ropes and they pulled tight, lifting Kayla into the air. Alethea guessed there must be more people at the top of the mountain, holding onto the other ends of the ropes.

By the time Kayla was out of sight, the other two people had landed on the ledge. They tied Rustus and Alethea into silk harnesses and soon they too were being lifted up to the summit of Frostfall Mountain. It was a long way. Alethea could barely believe they had attempted to climb it. What would have happened if Sami and his colleagues hadn't come to rescue them? If the Marquis hadn't sent Milabar with a message? How foolish they had been.

As they neared the top, they passed enormous icicles that dangled from the rock like streams of water cascading over a waterfall.

'Frostfall Mountain,' she murmured to herself.

At last a gloved hand appeared above her, accompanied by a shout. 'Hold on!' Nervously Alethea reached up, and with a yank she was lifted over the edge.

The world atop the mountain was vastly different to

that which they had left behind at the base. Everything around them was white; snow coated every surface, like glimmering diamond dust. She noted a large winch, which had been used to help lift them up the rock face. Rustus crunched into the snow beside her, groaning as his foot made contact with the ground.

Alethea looked around for Kayla. 'Where's our friend?' she asked between shivering breaths.

The woman who had pulled Alethea over the edge wrapped a fur around her shoulders and pointed straight ahead to where Alethea could just about make out the outline of two people trudging through the snow with a stretcher.

'Where are they taking her?' Alethea asked. 'We need to get her to the hospital.'

'You're at the hospital,' the woman said. She pointed again.

Alethea peered into the swirling snowflakes, and the outline of a large building came faintly into view. Was it a trick of the snow, or was it made entirely of ice? She blinked and looked again. It *was* made of ice! Her eyes travelled over its towering spires, vast ice pillars and sparkling arches. It was a breathtaking construction, majestic and foreboding, nothing like the rundown House of Healing where she worked.

'Come on,' said the woman.

Alethea pulled the edges of the fur close around her and pushed forward through the snow and biting wind. It wasn't far to the door of the hospital, but fighting against the elements made every step a struggle. She wondered how Rustus was managing with his ankle.

At last, somehow, she made it. Close up, the walls of the building were as smooth as glass. They changed colour from blue to white, depending on how the dawn light was reflected off them. She stumbled inside through a doorway lined with icicles. Rustus followed behind, supported by Sami and another nurse.

'You can wait here,' Sami said, leading them down a tall icy corridor to a room containing two fur-covered beds. 'Have a rest. Someone will send for you when they're ready.'

'Where's Kayla?' Alethea asked, desperate to know how their friend was faring.

'She's gone for treatment,' said Sami. 'That's all I know for now.' He made to leave and then seemed to think better of it, turning back to face them. 'By the way,' he asked, looking nervous, 'how did you hear about the doctor?'

'Tas told us,' said Rustus. 'In The Silk. And then Marquis Macdonald brought us to the base of the mountain.'

'And did you tell anyone else that you were coming? Or let anyone else know about the existence of the doctor?'

They shook their heads.

Seemingly appeased, Sami smiled and turned away again. Alethea had wanted to ask about the cure, but before she could, everyone was gone. She glanced anxiously at Rustus.

'It's OK,' he said with a smile. 'Kayla's going to be fine.'

Alethea took a deep breath and tried to tell herself he was right. She could find out about the cure once Kayla was better. But something about the wild remoteness of the hospital, about how hard it had been to get here and about Sami and the questions he'd asked, made her feel uneasy. She pushed her doubts to the back of her mind and tried to think instead about the grand purpose of her mission. For Grandma – and all their sakes – she hoped her suspicions were wrong.

18

RUSTUS

Rustus sat on his bed, finishing a bowl of cereal and warm milk. Alethea paced up and down the room. They had been so exhausted when they had arrived that it hadn't taken them long to fall asleep, but after almost a full day of sleeping they were bored of waiting around for news about their friend.

'This is ridiculous,' Alethea said. 'Why haven't they given us an update? I'm a healer, I could help them.'

'I don't know,' Rustus said. 'But I'm sure they know what they're doing.'

'How am I meant to learn how to cure the Scourge if they won't show me?'

'Let them focus on Kayla first,' Rustus said. 'They'll explain everything to you once they're finished.'

'I can't just wait here any longer,' Alethea said, her voice tinged with frustration. 'I'm going for a walk.' She strode up the corridor and out of sight.

Rustus watched quietly as she left. Following her would do no good. Besides, his ankle was hurting a lot and someone needed to be here when the nurses returned with news about Kayla. And he trusted that news would come – some things just took time. Rustus had spent most of his life waiting: waiting to be Scorched, waiting to be accepted by his family, waiting to find his purpose. He was comfortable with his own company. As an Unscorched he had spent hours on lookout duty, staring out over the Beastlands from the edges of Ataria. Nothing of note had ever happened, but he had found comfort in those long quiet nights. Time to watch and think, away from the critical eye of his father.

Rustus let his mind wander, as it had when he had sat on watch. He thought first of the events on the mountain. He couldn't believe he had fallen again. Failed to achieve his goal for the second time in as many days. Maybe his dad and his brothers were right. He had never been good enough. He pondered what the Marquis would have made of it. Would he think less of Rustus? Somehow Rustus couldn't imagine he would. With a smile, he wondered whether Topaz had managed to escape again and how far the travelling menagerie had travelled by now. What a journey they had shared. He still couldn't believe that there was a whole city in the Beastlands he had never known about. He was surprised by how exciting the world outside Ataria was. Why had the Ash Bishops kept it from him? Why had they lied to him about the source of the Scourge?

He had spent so long learning how to kill webspinners, only to discover they didn't even carry the disease they were all so frightened of. It was a lot to take in. Especially when he remembered Tas's warning about the return of the phaegra and wondered if the theft of Kayla's pangron really did have anything to do with it.

He wasn't sure how much time had passed when a tall figure dressed in white furs came into the room. It was a boy, whose face was half-covered in intricate purple tattoos. He was bigger than Rustus, but he looked young, maybe even the same age as him. His skin was unlike anything Rustus had ever seen – so pale it was almost blue – and he had bone-white hair that stuck straight up along the middle of his scalp and was shaved to the skin on the sides. But the most striking thing of all was that although the boy's leg was bandaged and he walked with a limp, his footsteps didn't make a sound.

'Hello.' The boy grinned widely. 'I'm Maaka. You new?'

'Just arrived,' said Rustus, instantly put at ease by the boy's warm welcome, despite his intimidating appearance. 'I'm Rustus. How long have you been here?'

'Two weeks,' Maaka replied.

'Two weeks?' said Rustus, surprised. He figured people would be in and out quickly once they'd received the cure. 'Are you ill?'

'Not any more.'

'So it's true then? The doctor can heal the Scourge?'

Maaka nodded. 'You got it too?'

'No, my friend has.'

'Well, she's come to the right place.'

Relief surged through Rustus's body.

'Course,' continued Maaka, 'she may have to stay here for the rest of her life, but at least she won't be sick any more.'

Rustus wasn't sure whether to laugh. Was that meant to be a joke? 'What do you mean?'

'Ice therapy,' Maaka replied. 'It's the only thing that stops the toxin from damaging the body. We have four ice baths a day and it keeps us more or less normal.'

'Is that the cure everyone has been talking about?' Rustus tried to imagine how they could carry a bath of ice back to Ataria without it melting. He didn't fancy their chances.

'I suppose so,' said Maaka. 'Although I'm not sure I would call it a cure. We still carry the toxin inside us – it just doesn't hurt us any more. I feel much better than I did though. I could barely stand when I arrived.'

'Well, that's something,' said Rustus, trying to stay positive while also wondering if Alethea had already discovered this information. 'Have you seen a girl in blue dungarees walking about?'

'Can't help you there,' he said. 'Lia'Oua are colourblind. In our language we don't even have words for the different colours.'

'Lia'Oua,' said Rustus, rolling the word around his mouth. 'Is that what your people are called? I've never heard of you. What realm do you come from?'

'That's what we call ourselves,' Maaka replied. 'And we belong to no realm, only the island. But you probably know us as Shadow Ghouls.'

Without thinking, Rustus recoiled. A Shadow Ghoul? He'd heard the legends. Shadow Ghouls were said to be violent and dangerous people, to be avoided at all costs. Before now, Rustus had never been sure they actually even existed, and this smiling, friendly boy in front of him was not what he had expected.

'You're . . .' Rustus struggled to find the right words, 'different than I had imagined.'

Maaka laughed. 'You've heard the legends we invented then.' He caught Rustus's perplexed expression. 'It can be useful for people to be frightened of you,' he explained. 'Keeps curious explorers from investigating too closely.'

Rustus had many questions he wanted to ask in response to that. He settled on, 'What are you doing away from the Shadowlands?'

'Even Lia'Oua can get the Scourge,' said Maaka. 'I live here now. Nobody who has the Scourge can leave this place. If we don't have ice baths regularly then the toxin starts to work again and we'll die.'

'But surely you can't stay here forever. What about your family?'

Maaka shrugged. 'I don't exactly see eye to eye with my dad. He'll be glad I'm gone. And my sister left a few moons ago, so there's not really much to miss about home.'

Rustus could sympathise with some of that. 'My dad

isn't my greatest fan either,' he said. 'He disowned me a few days ago.'

'That's great,' said Maaka, grinning again.

Rustus was so surprised by the response he choked out a laugh. 'What?' Officially losing his dad's approval was the worst thing that had ever happened to him.

'You're free,' said Maaka. 'You don't have to worry about pleasing him any more. The day I realised that I didn't have to live my life the way my dad wanted was the best day of my life.'

'Actually,' said Rustus, 'I think I've found a way I could impress him. If I take back the cure for the Scourge to Ataria, he'll realise –'

Maaka held up a hand. 'Let me stop you there,' he said. 'I've been where you are, and trust me: nothing you ever do will be enough. He's already made his decision about you.'

Rustus frowned. Was that true? Was it too late to change his dad's mind?

'I didn't wait around for my dad to disown me,' Maaka said. 'I told him he could accept me as I was or find himself another son. It's his problem to deal with now, not mine.'

'But all I want to do is make him proud.' Rustus struggled to imagine what his life would be like without that motivation to guide him.

Maaka sighed. 'That will never make you happy. You think it will; you think it's what you want. But do you really want to spend the rest of your life doing things just because your father wants you to?'

Rustus had never thought about it like that before.

'At some point you have to start doing things that *you* want to do and things that make *you* feel proud.'

But what did Rustus feel proud of? What made him feel good? That was really hard to answer. He knew his father had wanted him to pass the Scorching, but would Rustus actually have enjoyed being a Scorched Atari? He certainly didn't feel good after killing the webspinner. So what *did* he enjoy doing? The last couple of days out in the Beastlands had been pretty great: visiting The Silk, getting to know the Marquis and his wagon of wonderful beasts, meeting Kayla and Alethea. Come to think of it, he had been happier these last few days than he could remember ever being at home. But he couldn't just run off into the Beastlands . . .

'I'm not sure what I want to do,' said Rustus finally.

'Well, that's the challenge,' said Maaka. 'Find out what it is that makes you happy and then spend your life trying to do that. Make your own path.'

Rustus was reminded of his mum and what she had said just before he left Ataria. About his path not being in the city. Was this what she had meant?

It was too much for Rustus to process in one go. For as long as he could remember, becoming a Scorched Atari had been his goal. In Ataria there was no space for dreaming or imagining any other kind of life. He had no idea what other options were out there.

'What do *you* like to do?' he asked Maaka.

'Me? I love to dance!' Maaka lifted his arms above his

head and let them fall as gracefully as snowflakes. 'But Dad – our clan chief – thought it wasn't becoming of a person of my status, so I left my clan and was planning to join another, but before I could decide on a new home I contracted the Scourge. Anyway, you thought taking the cure to the Scourge back to your homeland could win your dad's approval?'

Rustus nodded.

'Well, unless you're going to take the ice pools home with you, you're going to struggle with that plan.'

'I guess I am,' Rustus replied. He had a lot to think about. But one of those things was more pressing than the others. 'Do you have any idea what's taking so long? We've been here ages and I haven't heard a thing about my friend Kayla. Surely she's had a bath by now?'

'Kayla . . .' said Maaka thoughtfully. 'I heard one of the nurses saying that name. She was in a pretty bad way when she came in, wasn't she?'

'She was unconscious,' said Rustus, remembering how frail the ferocious Sky Cadet had looked on that stretcher.

Maaka grimaced. 'The further the Scourge has progressed, the harder it is to treat.'

'Do you think she's going to be all right?' asked Rustus, starting to worry.

'Hard to say,' said Maaka. 'But one thing's for sure, if anyone can help her, it's the doctor. Your friend is probably on a ward right now, waiting to be assessed. You should ask Nurse Oskid.'

'Who's that?'

'The man with a mouthful of scalefish.'

Rustus was thoroughly confused. 'Always?'

'What do you mean?'

'He always has a mouthful of scalefish? His breath must stink!'

Maaka laughed loudly and deeply. 'Have you never heard that saying before?' He sounded surprised. 'It means his teeth are sticking out in all different directions like this.' He held up his hands to his mouth, fingers pointing every way possible to demonstrate.

'Oh!' said Rustus, laughing too. Maybe it was the lack of sleep or just the absurdity of the phrase, but once Rustus started laughing he couldn't stop. When their stomachs were both cramping from all the giggling, Maaka offered his hand to Rustus.

'I can help you look for your friends if you like.'

Rustus grabbed the boy's hand and stood up. 'Yes, please.' Perhaps the time for waiting was over after all.

19

KAYLA

'Faro!' screamed Kayla, salty water slapping her face and burning her eyes. Bobbing ahead of her, Faro's head dipped under a wave. She pulled him back up. 'Are you OK?'

Blinking at the boat in the distance, Kayla trained her eyes on the person who had done this to her pangron. Purple and yellow tattoos covered the girl's pale face.

I'll kill you for this, *Kayla thought,* I'll kill you.

The girl threw back her head and let out a cackle of laughter, her long white hair fanning out behind her. Anger bubbled through Kayla's veins. She tried to swim towards the girl but the water pushed against her, preventing her from making any progress. Kayla screamed in frustration. Why wasn't she moving? 'You won't get away with this!'

Suddenly the girl stomped her glimmering silver boots and her writhing hair morphed into a mass of white snakes that rose like a halo hissing into the wind and darted towards Kayla. She recoiled in horror. In the same moment, the water around her started to spin like a whirlpool, tugging her backwards, pulling Faro from her grasp. Kayla fought against the current and held on tightly to her pangron's head.

'It's all right,' she whispered, 'I've got you.' But as she held him the pangron started to disintegrate, slipping through her fingers like sand until he had disappeared into the waves.

'Faro,' she screamed again. 'Faro, where have you gone?'

She looked around wildly as the ocean distorted, colours fading from blue to black. Now Kayla clung to a rock face amid a raging blizzard. A small blonde-haired girl appeared in front of her.

'Am I going to die?' Kayla asked her. 'What about Faro?'

'Eat this,' the girl said. She opened her palm to reveal a handful of snow.

'No,' said Kayla. 'I don't want to. I want to find my pangron.'

'It's for your own good,' the girl said. 'Trust me.'

Kayla clamped her mouth shut, so the girl rubbed the snow on her face. It was so very cold. The icy feeling travelled all over her body. She shivered wildly. Was it possible to be this cold and still be alive?

Please someone help me, she thought. I can't die like this. I need to find my pangron. I need to find Faro.

20

ALETHEA

Alethea hurried down another corridor, desperate to find Kayla and to learn more about the cure. For a long time, there were no doors or turnings, but at last she came upon a rectangular doorway where two white furs hung in place of a door. Alethea pulled the furs back to reveal an old woman, neck deep in a round pool of water.

'Is it time to get out?' she asked.

'No, sorry.' Alethea backed out of the room quickly and closed the furs.

That was weird. Why were people here taking baths? Across the corridor was another set of hanging furs. This time she spoke before barging in.

'Excuse me?'

There was no reply.

She opened the furs to find another round pool, this time empty. Intrigued, she entered the room and scooped up a handful of water. It was freezing cold. An ice bath!

She lifted the water to her face, taking a sniff. It smelled fresh, so there didn't seem to be any spices or medications added to it.

She continued down the corridor until she reached a door made of wood and carved with a pattern of pasqueflowers. She pushed the door and it opened with a loud creak. Alethea looked around to check she wouldn't be seen, then slipped into the room, gently closing the door behind her. Inside it was wide and beautiful. The icy walls were carved floor to ceiling with shelves filled to bursting with books and technical-looking instruments. In the centre was a desk made of large square blocks of ice. Piles of papers covered its surface.

Alethea was drawn to a small metallic object that sat on a low shelf. She lifted it from its place, intrigued by its delicate structure. It looked vaguely like one of Grandma's knitting needles. She felt certain it must be some sort of medical device, but she had absolutely no idea what it could be for. What *was* this place?

She eyed the books on the shelf and ran her finger over their spines.

Anatomy and Physiology of the Snogart
A Brief History of Healing Beasts
Wetskins: Medical Marvels
Surgical Techniques in Bardebeests: Revised Edition
Teeth to Toxins: The Complete Reptillite Handbook

These books all seemed to be about healing or the use of beasts in human healing. Alethea hadn't been aware that knowledge like this existed. She moved to another section of the bookshelf, where one title in particular caught her eye: *A Healer's Guide to the Flora of Ramoa*.

She pulled the book from the shelf. It was the old edition. When she opened the cover, a slip of paper fluttered to the ground. She stooped to pick it up.

Level — 7, Experimental Laboratory

Experiment 265

Lead scientist: Dr Ophelia Kalima Everhart

Species: Shadowy stinger X Southern bardfly

Chimaera name: Shadowy bardfly

Description: Bardfly with four wings — blue and silver. Indistinguishable from other bardflies in all ways, except a small stinger on its abdomen

Experimental laboratory? Was that here at the hospital? And chimaera . . . Did that mean a cross between two animals? She vaguely recalled Rustus reading out something about a shadowy stinger from the bestiary, and she was familiar with bardflies. They were everywhere in Ataria. She was sure she'd heard the doctor's name before too, but she couldn't put her finger on where . . .

None of it made sense. She flipped the paper over and noticed a scrawled note on the back.

Unexpected outcome — venom dangerous to human life.

Do not repeat.

Just then she heard voices at the door. She stiffened, looking around for a place to hide. As the latch rattled, her eyes fell on the ice desk. She slammed the book shut, shoved it onto the shelf and threw herself behind the desk just as the door burst open and two figures hurried in. The first she recognised as Sami, but the second was a tall woman in a long green coat. The woman leaned over the desk and picked up a pile of papers before handing them to Sami. Alethea pushed her head into her knees, hardly daring to breathe.

'Don't let anyone else see these,' the woman said.

'Of course not,' said Sami. 'How did you get on with the new patient?'

'Fine. Treatment has been initiated.' She spoke with authority – was she the doctor they had been told about?

'Did you notice anything strange about her?' Sami asked.

'Not particularly. Why?'

Sami didn't answer.

'You're worried she might have been sent by the professor.'

Sami paused. 'It doesn't hurt to be vigilant.'

'I didn't notice anything,' said the woman. 'But I'll keep it in mind. How are you getting on with the latest experiment?'

'Ready to go,' Sami said. 'Whenever you are.'

'Excellent,' replied the doctor. 'I have to do the rounds in Ward Four and then I'll join you.'

'Fingers crossed for this one.'

'Yes,' replied the woman in a flat voice. Alethea thought she sounded tired. 'Fingers crossed.'

After the door creaked shut, Alethea waited a few moments to ensure the coast would be clear, then jumped to her feet and exited the room. She saw the woman disappearing one way down the corridor, her coat billowing out behind her, and Sami striding off in the opposite direction. If she was suspicious of this place before, it was nothing compared to how she felt now. She had to find out more.

She followed Sami to another wooden door, which had a lopsided 'KEEP OUT' sign hanging on it. He slipped

240

inside, leaving the door open a crack. Alethea waited a moment then peered through into a large rectangular room filled with long rows of square glass boxes. Sami rushed across the room and disappeared through some white fur curtains covering a doorway on the far side. Keeping her distance, Alethea waited until the furs fell back into place behind him and then let herself in.

She was intrigued to know what was in the boxes. She hurried up to the nearest one, hoping it would hide her from view if Sami returned. Inside she saw a tall purple-stemmed plant. Taxacum. It was a common herb. She always carried its tubers as they were useful painkillers. She moved up to the next box, and the next, all full of plants, mostly familiar though some she had never seen before. In the next row, instead of plants, the boxes contained beasts. The first held a tightly coiled ball of grey-blue snakes.

Hypnos snakes, read the label. *Venom causes paralysis and amnesia – neutralised by leaf of frostwort applied on mucous membranes.*

Alethea moved up to the next enclosure from which a small pink animal with enormous eyes and a striped tail peered out at her.

Tamaranian, said the label. *Venom affects the nervous system – neutralised by skyberries.* The beast looked just like Lillypeg, and Alethea wasn't at all surprised that a cute-but-deadly venomous creature was just the kind of companion the Marquis would choose to keep about his person.

She moved to the next cage, which was slightly bigger

than the previous two, and recognised this creature even before reading the label.

Obsidian webspinner. Venom neutralised by mist violets.

That was interesting. Alethea had never heard of mist violets before, but it could be useful knowledge to take back to Tas. She moved along the row, but before she could examine any further, she was interrupted by the furs at the far end of the room opening again and Sami returning. Alethea crouched quickly behind the boxes. She noticed that he now wore thick leather gauntlets. He walked over to a cage, took something from its enclosure and went back out through the door. Its cage mates buzzed loudly. As soon as Sami was gone, Alethea hurried over to look.

Shadowy bardfly, the label read. *Venom neutralised by – ???*

She recognised the flies inside immediately. They looked just like the bardflies that liked to lay their eggs in the blue lakes. Although, now she thought about it, whereas the wings of the bardflies around the lakes of Ataria had always been red before, over the last year she'd seen plenty of blue-and-silver-winged ones like these too. Her heart rate rose. She hadn't known they were venomous.

Just then the wooden door to the corridor opened and the green-coated woman walked in. Alethea flung herself to the floor once again, hoping she hadn't been seen.

The woman hurried across the room, then paused to

call out to Sami, 'Have you extracted the venom already?'

'Doing it now, Doctor,' Sami replied, confirming Alethea's suspicions about the woman's identity. 'Can you grab the clawleaf?'

The doctor moved to a box containing sprigs of scythe-shaped leaves, pulled one out, then strode across the room and slung open the furs just strides from Alethea. Through the gap in the furs, Alethea saw Sami coaxing something green from the fly's sharp pointed stinger into a vial. That must be the venom. The furs flapped shut and Alethea had to rely on the sound of their voices to understand what was going on.

'Pass me the vials,' said the doctor. There was a clinking of glass. 'OK, experiment 103. Combining clawleaf with Scourge venom.'

Scourge venom?

It took Alethea a moment to connect the dots. It seemed unthinkable, and yet . . . She thought back to Ataria and how those small innocent-looking flies had flitted freely through the district. They were everywhere! It could easily have been them that had transmitted the Scourge. She considered the tiny spike on the end of the fly's abdomen and remembered her confusion at seeing the webspinner's two fangs. Alethea couldn't believe she had never considered the flies before. How had she been so blind?

'I'm applying the serum now,' said the doctor. 'Sami, note down the time, please. Now we wait . . .'

The room fell silent apart from the occasional noises

made by the beasts in their cages. Eventually Sami spoke. 'Time's up.'

'Bring me the indicator, please,' said the doctor.

Alethea wondered what they were doing. Trying to find a way to neutralise the Scourge venom with a plant? There was a pause, then, 'Arrrrgh . . . it hasn't worked.'

There was a loud thump and the wall beside Alethea shuddered, a web of cracks lacing its way through the ice. Alethea slithered away.

'Never mind,' said Sami consolingly. 'Onto the next one. We'll get there eventually.'

'But when?' the woman asked. 'How long has it been now? How many moons have we been searching?'

'We're close, I know it,' said Sami. 'We can keep the patients stable here until we find the cure. No one here is going to die while they wait.'

So they *didn't* have a cure yet. Alethea's mouth went dry. She had travelled all this way – and for what? The marshwort hadn't worked, she was further away from Grandma than ever and she still had no idea how to cure the Scourge.

'But what kind of life do they have here?' said the doctor. 'We're failing them.'

'They're alive,' said Sami. 'The ice baths keep them that way. That's more than any of them could have hoped for.'

'They're prisoners,' the woman replied. Alethea swallowed nervously. 'And we're running out of space. The Scourge is spreading through the Realms so fast now. New patients are arriving every day.'

'We'll find the solution, Doctor. I believe in you. We're nearly there. What's next?'

'That's the other problem,' said the doctor. 'I'm out of ideas. That was my last suggestion. Nothing but frostwort has neutralised the toxin, and that's far too aggressive to apply directly into the blood.'

So the doctor *had* tried using frostwort. Alethea wondered if she had experimented with firewort and marshwort too. And what did she mean about applying it into the blood?

'Well, back to ward rounds,' said Sami. 'And back to reading and thinking. The answer has to be out there.'

Alethea rolled out of sight, realising that Sami and the doctor were about to leave and praying they wouldn't notice her in the shadows. Sami walked right past her as he replaced the bardfly in its cage. Alethea held her breath and squeezed her eyes tight.

'I think I'll go and read in my office,' said the doctor.

'All right,' said Sami. 'I'll get the afternoon bathers into their pools and meet you there.'

Alethea heard their footsteps retreat and the door close, then breathed a deep sigh of relief. She waited for a couple of moments, to be sure they wouldn't return, then got to her feet and crept over to the furs. She was desperate to see what was going on inside.

The next room was much smaller, barely more than a cupboard. Littered around were vials of liquid in a rainbow of colours and pinned to the wall was a chart.

Treatment	Effect on Scourge Toxin
Hypnos venom	no effect
Obsidian webspinner venom	no effect
Tamaranian venom	no effect
Frog root	no effect
Taxacum	no effect
Frostwort	neutralised but too potent to inject
Ice thistle	no effect
Fire thistle	no effect
Mist violet	no effect
Skyberry	no effect
Arrowsedge	no effect

On and on it went. Next to the chart was a picture of a hand with a sharp-tipped object pressed against it. She recognised it as the knitting-needle-like tool she'd seen in the doctor's office. The tip penetrated through the skin and into a vein. A stream of coloured dots moved through the needle and into the patient's blood. Alethea frowned.

The image and the doctor's words seemed to suggest she was applying medicines directly into her patients' bloodstreams.

The thought of it sent a little thrill of excitement down Alethea's spine. Was that possible? Da had been famously innovative with his healing, always trying new potions and combinations, but he had never suggested something as audacious as injecting medicines into a person's blood. Could it work? It offered an incredibly direct way to get medicine into the body. And if a shadowy bardfly had a sharp-pointed stinger for delivering venom, then delivering a treatment in a similar fashion made perfect sense.

In her excitement she forgot to be vigilant and so didn't hear the door to the outer room open and then shut.

When the furs to the small room flapped open it was too late for Alethea to jump out of sight so all she could do was stand open-mouthed in astonishment. The doctor had returned. She stood in the doorway, the outline of her silhouette glowing green with the reflected light from the ice behind her.

'Who are you?' The doctor fixed Alethea with an icy stare.

'Um . . .' said Alethea.

'Do you have the Scourge?' she asked.

'No.'

'Did the professor send you?' The doctor's nostrils flared slightly.

Alethea shook her head. Who was this professor they kept talking about? 'No,' she said. 'My name is Alethea.

I'm just a healer from Ataria, looking for a way to cure my people of the Scourge.'

'Well, you won't find that here,' said the doctor, and Alethea noted a tinge of sadness in her voice.

'Is this your work?' Alethea asked, pointing to the writing spread around the walls. 'It's fascinating.'

The doctor nodded. 'We've been working hard, but the answer still eludes us. I currently have a passable treatment, which prevents afflicted patients from dying, but it's far from a cure.'

'The ice baths,' said Alethea. 'I saw. And you've tried frostwort too, haven't you? I used another plant in the tasselbaggia family, firewort, to treat some patients in my district.'

The doctor quirked an eyebrow. 'Did it work?'

'Only if it was applied while the wound was still very fresh; otherwise the venom had spread too far into the body.'

'Sounds similar to the experience I had with frostwort,' said the doctor. 'Did it slough away the infected skin?'

Alethea nodded. The doctor's expression had changed ever so slightly – she looked more receptive and a little intrigued.

'It looks like you inject medicines directly into the veins,' Alethea said. 'Is that right?'

'Not the frostwort,' said the doctor. 'It's far too strong. Damages any flesh it touches.'

'Oh,' said Alethea, eyes travelling back to the picture on the wall. 'But you've tried it with other plants?

I've never even considered applying potions directly into the bloodstream. Barely seems possible . . .'

'Extraordinary, isn't it?' said the doctor, a hint of pride in her voice. 'I developed the technique myself, inspired by the needles used by the weavers back in Freyavik. Intravenous injection is the most effective way of treating disease if you have the right potion.'

'But you haven't found the right one yet,' said Alethea.

'Thank you, child, for reminding me of my shortcomings,' said the doctor, her tone souring.

Alethea's brain whirred. Like firewort juice, frostwort juice was dangerously corrosive. But there was another member of the tasselbaggia family, wasn't there? The new edition of the botany textbook had told her so. She remembered applying the marshwort to Kayla's skin – nothing had happened. It wasn't damaging to flesh, so it hadn't been strong enough to slough off the infected skin; in fact Tas had told her that in The Silk they drank the liquid as an antacid. But what if the marshwort juice was still able to neutralise the Scourge venom? If it was, and they injected the marshwort into the blood instead of applying it to the skin . . . Alethea's heart began to race with the possibility.

'Did you know that there's another plant in the tasselbaggia family?' she asked.

'No, there's not,' said the doctor, 'I have a botany textbook in my –'

'There's been an update,' said Alethea, rummaging in her bag to find her copy. She passed the book to the doctor, the page already folded down. 'Marshwort! I went to collect some from the coast of the Ashlands before I came here. I tried applying it directly onto the wound, but it didn't work, but maybe if it was injected . . .' She scrabbled in her bag and held up one of the stems for the doctor to see.

The doctor stared at Alethea dismissively. 'That's pickleweed.'

'It was,' said Alethea, 'but it's been reclassified. Now it's called marshwort! Look at the book,' she said. 'Please.'

A strange expression passed over the doctor's face as she took the book from Alethea, but it soon disappeared as she began to read. Her eyebrows twitched as she took in the new information. 'Fascinating,' she said.

Alethea passed the plant to the doctor, who held it up to her nose and sniffed.

Meanwhile Alethea lifted the vial containing the green liquid she'd seen Sami collecting from the shadowy bardfly.

'This is the Scourge venom?' Alethea asked.

The doctor nodded.

'OK, and then you add some kind of indicator to it, to see if it's been neutralised?'

The doctor jerked her head to indicate a vial of viscous purple liquid. A pipette floated in the top. 'Just a drop.'

Alethea added a drop of the purple liquid to the toxin, and the resulting solution was deep violet.

'So if I were to add frostwort to this,' said Alethea, 'what would happen?'

'It would turn pink,' said the doctor.

'And that would mean the toxin had been neutralised?' said Alethea. 'That it was no longer dangerous?'

The doctor nodded.

'Shall we try the marshwort?' Alethea asked, holding out her hand to the doctor.

The doctor shrugged. 'You can try.' She handed Alethea the plant back. Her words were disinterested but Alethea could see a glint of curiosity in her eyes.

Alethea made a small hole in the bladder beneath the flower and squeezed a few drops of the marshwort juice into the purple liquid. She held her breath as she waited, counting to ten. After so much disappointment she barely dared to hope. And yet . . .

Slowly the colour began to change. Beside her, Alethea felt the doctor shift her weight. They both watched in silence as gradually the violet disappeared. Alethea braved a glance at the doctor, who couldn't look away from the vial, which was now a vivid pink.

'It worked,' she whispered eventually, looking up at Alethea with wild, disbelieving eyes. 'After all this time. You did it.' The corners of her mouth twitched upwards. 'You found the cure to the Scourge.'

21

RUSTUS

Maaka and Rustus searched the hallways until they found a nurse. The man smiled when he saw them, revealing a mouth full of teeth that did indeed point in all directions.

'Nurse Oskid!' Maaka said. 'Have you seen a girl called Kayla?'

'Hello, Maaka,' the man said warmly. 'I think she's still sleeping. Would you like me to take you to her ward?'

The boys nodded.

Nurse Oskid led them to a large room of ice that contained eight beds. Only one of them was occupied.

'Kayla!' Rustus spotted his friend and rushed up beside her. She was asleep, or unconscious still. He wasn't sure which. Her face was pale and her lips were cracked with the cold, and when he held a hand up in front of her face, her skin was freezing but he was relieved to find her breath was warm. 'Hey, Sky Rider,' he said. 'It's good to see you.'

At the sound of his voice, Kayla's eyelids fluttered, then opened wide and she looked around. She grabbed at her necklace.

'Faro,' she croaked. 'Where's Faro?' She tried to sit up.

'Whoa.' Rustus rushed to steady her. 'You're all right, just take it slow.'

'The girl,' she said. 'The girl with the snakes for hair. It was her. She shot Faro.'

'You were having a bad dream,' said Rustus. 'You've had a fever.'

'No, it was her!' yelled Kayla. 'I remember now. I remember it all. She was tall, with white hair and such pale skin. She wore big silver boots . . .'

Rustus didn't know what to make of her revelation. Was it just a dream or had she really remembered what had happened to Faro? Either way, getting this agitated in her delicate state would do no good for her recovery.

'Kayla,' he said, more forcefully than before, 'slow down. Breathe. Look, it's me, your friend Rustus.'

For the first time she seemed to realise who Rustus was.

'You're alive,' she said. The relief in her voice was so palpable it brought a lump to Rustus's throat. 'I thought I'd killed you.' She took his hand and squeezed it. It was the friendliest Kayla had ever been to him. She must be feeling better.

'Takes more than that to kill Rustus Furi,' he said with a grin.

Kayla laughed. 'I'll try harder next time then.' She

looked around the ward. 'Where's Alethea? She is all right, isn't she?'

'Last time I saw her she was fine,' said Rustus. 'But I'm not sure where she is now.' He lowered his voice. 'She's gone off somewhere in search of the cure.'

'Sounds about right.' Kayla shivered. 'Why is it so cold? Where are we?'

'We made it to the hospital,' said Rustus, wondering how she would react to this news.

Kayla's expression faltered. 'No. I told you I wasn't going to come here. I need to get to Faro.' She tried to sit up again.

'Kayla, you were unconscious.' Rustus gently pressed her back into the bed. 'The nurses brought you here by stretcher. If they hadn't rescued us, you would have died on the mountain. Maybe we all would.'

'He's right,' said Maaka, who had joined him at Kayla's bedside. 'You were in a really bad way when you arrived.'

Kayla's eyes travelled to Maaka and went wide. 'Who is this?' Her face contorted in terror and then fury. 'He looks exactly like the girl who shot down Faro.'

'Who's Faro?' Maaka looked to Rustus.

'Her pangron.'

'A Lia'Oua shot down your pangron?' Maaka said, looking disbelieving.

'Were you in on it too?' asked Kayla, trying to clamber out of bed towards Maaka. 'Where is he? What have you done with him?'

'Kayla, no!' Rustus jumped between them. 'He's a friend. He's got the Scourge like you. He came here to be treated, that's all.'

'What's a Lia'Oua?' Kayla asked.

'A Shadow Ghoul,' Rustus replied.

Kayla let out a high-pitched noise. 'A *Shadow Ghoul*?'

At that moment Sami rushed into the room. 'You have to relax, miss,' he said, forcing Kayla back onto the bed. 'Your body's been through an awful amount of stress. You can't get out of bed yet.'

Kayla batted his hands away. 'I'm fine,' she insisted. 'Am I healed?' She looked down at her arm, where there was now a large purple bandage. 'Is it gone?'

'Not gone,' the nurse said. 'But its effect is less. You'll feel a little weak for a while, but you will grow stronger with continued treatment.'

'I *can't* continue treatment,' said Kayla. 'How long have we been here already? Faro will have reached Port Royal by now. I need to go!'

Rustus could see the pain in Kayla's eyes. He had once found her insistence and defiance annoying, but now, after all they'd been through, he just felt sympathy for her.

'You can't leave, Kayla,' said Sami softly. 'The cold is all that's keeping you alive.'

Kayla stared at the ice surrounding her. She looked small and vulnerable in her bed.

'I'm sorry, Kayla, but it's true,' Rustus said. 'The cold reduces the effect of the Scourge, but it's still inside you.'

'What are you suggesting?' Kayla asked. 'That I stay here forever?'

'Only until we find a cure,' said Sami. 'We're very close.'

'Close isn't good enough,' said Kayla. 'I have to rescue my pangron.' She tried to climb out of the bed but was restrained by two more nurses. 'I would rather die than stay here without Faro!' she yelled. 'Let go of me!'

At that moment a tall woman with dark brown skin swept into the room, wearing a long green coat, with a badge that said 'Dr Oke'. At her side was Alethea – so *that* was where their friend had got to.

Alethea wore an expression that Rustus couldn't place, but her eyes were sparkling. What in the name of Ash had she been up to?

'This is Kayla,' said Alethea to the doctor, giving Kayla and Rustus a little wave.

'Hello, Kayla,' said the doctor. 'I'm Dr Oke.'

Alethea's expression changed slightly when the doctor introduced herself, like she was trying to recall some long-forgotten memory.

'I thought you were meant to have found the cure,' said Kayla, scowling.

'I'm afraid you were misinformed,' said the doctor. 'I have not found the cure. But luckily for you, it looks as if your friend Alethea has.'

Rustus couldn't believe his ears. Alethea? *Their* Alethea had found the cure for the Scourge? But as he thought about it, Rustus realised it made perfect sense.

Alethea was the most skilled healer he'd ever met, and determined at that.

Kayla, on the other hand, looked doubtful. 'That's pickleweed,' she said. 'We've already tried that.'

Rustus's eyes travelled to Alethea's right hand, which clutched the familiar woody stem.

'And it turns out it *is* the solution after all,' Alethea said. She gave them a bright smile. 'We just needed a slightly different method of application.'

'For the first time since the creation of the Scourge,' said the doctor, 'we've discovered a treatment that can neutralise the toxin and be safely injected into the body. We know the theory, but this treatment is still highly experimental and could result in all sorts of unexpected side effects, up to and including death.'

'And you want me to try it?' Kayla asked, raising an eyebrow.

The doctor nodded.

'What's the other option?' Kayla said. 'Stay here until someone else volunteers?'

'Yes,' said the doctor. 'That's about it.'

'Well, I haven't got time to wait.' Kayla turned her gaze to Alethea. 'Do you think this is going to work?'

Alethea paused to consider her answer, taking a deep breath before speaking. 'I believe that the marshwort is the cure we have been looking for,' she said, 'but I've never administered drugs directly into a vein, so I don't know exactly what to expect.'

She looked quietly confident though. Rustus thought

about everything they had been through: how committed Alethea was to finding a cure, her ingenuity with the arrowsedge in the heathlands, the way she had cared for Kayla when she had become really sick. He knew he would trust Alethea with his life.

'I trust Alethea,' said Kayla, clearly drawing the same conclusion. 'I'll try it.'

The nurse brought in a wheelchair and tried to lift Kayla into it, but she hissed like a draggard and flung herself from her bed into the chair without assistance. Rustus smiled. Their Sky Rider certainly hadn't lost her spirit.

Alethea and the doctor led the party, followed by Kayla, who wheeled herself as the nurse hovered awkwardly behind her. Rustus walked alongside Kayla, and Sami and Maaka brought up the rear. After a short walk they came to a room with a flat ice table in the middle. The nurses covered it with blankets and Kayla allowed them to help her up onto it.

'All we're going to do,' said Alethea, 'is inject the marshwort here.' She touched the crook of Kayla's arm. 'You'll feel a little scratch and that should be it. I'm going to clean your arm now, OK? Hold still.'

Kayla didn't flinch as Alethea poured icy water onto the inside of her elbow. She cleaned the site with something foamy and white. Once she had finished, the doctor picked up a pointed implement. It looked like a tiny spear.

'This is the needle,' said Alethea. 'It's what we'll use to inject the marshwort. You ready?'

'Ready,' said Kayla. The doctor had already moved towards her when suddenly she said, 'Wait!' She reached out to grab Rustus's hand and looked him directly in the eye.

'I'm sorry,' she said. 'For not listening to you on the mountain.'

Rustus was taken aback. Of all the things he had expected her to say, that was not it. 'It's OK,' he replied. 'I shouldn't have followed you up there. I know you can look after yourself.'

'I can,' Kayla agreed, 'but it's still nice to know I have friends who care.'

Rustus's heart swelled.

'And as my friend,' she continued, 'I want you to promise me something.' She pulled off the necklace she'd been wearing ever since he first met her and pressed it into his hand. The pendant looked like it was made of a shard of eggshell. 'If I die, rescue Faro for me.'

'You're not going to die.' He squeezed her palm. 'But in case anything happens, I promise.'

'All right, Kayla, lie back,' said Alethea, taking Kayla's other hand in hers. 'You're going to be fine.'

If Alethea was worried or uncertain about the procedure, she didn't show it. Rustus watched in awe as she placed her thumb over Kayla's arm until a blue vein rose up under the surface. The doctor moved the tip of the needle towards it and Rustus closed his eyes. This kind of thing made him squeamish.

'Deep breaths in and out,' Alethea reminded Kayla.

Rustus peeked at his Atarian friend and noticed she was watching the doctor intently. After all, if it worked, she would be the one doing this procedure when they went back to the city. The doctor slowly depressed the plunger, her eyes darting from the needle, to the vein, to Kayla's face and back again. What was she expecting to see? How would they know if it had worked?

'How do you feel?' Rustus asked Kayla. His heart was in his mouth.

'Fine,' she said and began to open her eyes.

'Does it hurt?'

'Not really, it just feels a bit cold. How will we know if it's worked?'

'See that vial over there?' Alethea pointed to a conical flask of purple liquid. 'We'll take a sample of your blood and test it. If the purple solution turns pink, we've neutralised the toxin.'

'And if it doesn't?' said Kayla.

The doctor withdrew the needle and pressed a cloth to Kayla's elbow. 'Hold this here,' she said, ignoring the question. 'Sami, prepare the second needle.'

Rustus smiled at Kayla. Was he imagining it, or was colour returning to her cheeks?

'Why do I need to have another injection?' asked Kayla.

'This one is just for a blood sample,' Alethea replied. 'But we have to wait a little while for the treatment to travel around your body first.'

The wait was unbearable. Nobody spoke. Rustus tried many times to think of something to say to break the silence, but everything that came to mind seemed too flippant, too insignificant. So like the others he just waited.

'I feel different,' said Kayla eventually.

'You look different too,' said Rustus. Her face was definitely less pale and her eyes had regained their sparkle.

'Shall we test it now?' Alethea asked.

The doctor nodded.

Sami passed Alethea another cloth and she cleaned the skin in the crook of Kayla's other elbow.

The doctor held out the needle to her. 'Do you want to do this one?'

Alethea's face lit up. 'Do you mind?' she asked Kayla.

'Go ahead.'

Alethea took the needle, pressing it to Kayla's skin as the doctor had done.

'Gently and slowly,' said Doctor Oke. 'That's it. Now pull back on the plunger. Good, now gentle backwards pressure and let it fill nice and slowly.'

When she had completed the task, Alethea's face relaxed and her look of intense concentration was replaced with one of elation. She caught Rustus's eye and gave a proud smile.

'Well done,' he mouthed.

Sami brought over the vial of purple liquid and Alethea squirted Kayla's blood into it. Rustus held his breath.

Slowly swirls of colour appeared. At first just a splash, then gradually the whole contents of the vial turned bright pink. Rustus, Alethea and Kayla looked at one another and all let out a nervous laugh, not daring to believe what they were seeing.

Kayla was the first to speak. 'Am I cured?'

Alethea glanced at the doctor, who gave a tiny nod.

'I think you are!' Alethea said.

Rustus pulled both girls into a hug. It lasted about two seconds before Kayla said, 'That's enough hugging. I need my personal space back now, thanks.' But she was smiling.

Rustus broke away and out of the corner of his eye saw the doctor, who had tears pouring silently down her face. 'Are you all right?' he asked her.

She pulled a handkerchief from her sleeve and dabbed at her cheeks. 'I've been waiting for this moment for a long time,' she said. 'Ever since the Scourge was created.'

Alethea's head snapped towards the doctor. The joy that had been there moments before was replaced with a quizzical look, just like earlier when the doctor had introduced herself. Before she could say what was on her mind, a quiet voice spoke from somewhere near the doorway.

It was Maaka. In all the excitement and anxiety of the treatment, Rustus had forgotten the Lia'Oua was even there with them. 'Would this cure work on me too?'

The doctor wiped her tears on the sleeve of her coat. 'I think it just might,' she said, a hopeful and determined look on her face. 'Sami, let's prepare the rest of the patients. Kayla, do you feel well enough to go back to your ward?'

Kayla nodded and Rustus went to help her clamber

down from the bed, but she pushed him away.

'Your strength and temper have returned too, I see!' He tried to catch Alethea's eye, but she wasn't listening. Her brow was furrowed and she was chewing furiously on her lip. 'Are you all right, Alethea?'

She looked up, as if disturbed from the deepest of thoughts. 'No,' she said quietly so only they would hear. 'I'm not. Something fishy is going on here.' Rustus had never seen Alethea like this before – she looked angry. 'I need to talk to you,' she said. 'Both of you. But not here. Follow me. I know just the place.'

22

KAYLA

Kayla hobbled after Alethea as quickly as she could. Her legs felt tingly and numb, as if Faro had been lying on them. Instead of going back towards the ward, Alethea led them down a new corridor until finally they reached a wooden door carved with flowers, which Alethea heaved open before ushering them into an office.

'Are you going to tell us what's going on now?' Rustus asked once they were inside.

'OK,' said Alethea. 'Earlier, when the doctor was talking, she said "for the first time since *the creation* of the Scourge". At the time I couldn't put my finger on why it felt wrong. I pushed it to the back of my mind. But then, when she was talking just now, she said it again, and I realised . . . That's not the language we usually use when we talk about disease. We say a disease was discovered or appeared, but we don't say it was *created*.'

Alethea was right. It *was* a strange thing to say.

'What do you think it means?' asked Kayla.

'I'm not sure.' Alethea shook her head. 'But I think it has something to do with this.' She pulled a book from a shelf, opened it and handed them a slip of paper. It contained information about something called 'Experiment 265'.

The words made little sense, but the name of the lead scientist seemed familiar. Kayla narrowed her eyes as she read the paper over again. Suddenly she realised why she recognised it. 'The doctor just now said her name was Dr Oke, right?' she said. The others nodded. 'Well, look.' She pointed to where it said *Lead scientist: Dr Ophelia Kalima Everhart.* 'That makes her initials O.K.E.'

Rustus and Alethea gasped.

'But what does it mean?' Rustus asked. 'What was the point of the experiment?'

'To make a chimaera?' asked Kayla, stumbling over the unfamiliar word. 'What's that?'

'I think it's a new type of beast,' said Alethea. 'A cross between two existing creatures.'

'Yeah, look, it says so right here,' said Rustus, pointing at the paper. 'Dr Oke crossed a shadowy stinger with a southern bardfly to make a shadowy bardfly.'

The description of the chimaera sounded like the flies Kayla and Faro often chased over the city.

'Oh no,' said Alethea, looking suddenly horrified. 'I didn't realise when I first saw the note. I didn't put it together! I was so busy trying not to get caught!'

'Put what together?' Rustus asked.

The healer gulped. 'I saw the shadowy bardflies in the doctor's lab earlier today. They look just like normal bardflies, but they have blue wings and a venomous sting.'

'Did you get stung by one?' asked Kayla, trying to understand why Alethea looked so panicked.

'No,' said Alethea. 'But *you* did, Kayla. And so did my grandma and da and Maaka. Shadowy-bardfly venom is what causes the Scourge!'

'*What?*' exclaimed Kayla and Rustus together. 'How do you know that?'

Kayla found it hard to believe the harmless-looking flies she had often chased around Sophiatown could really be the cause of such a devastating illness.

'Because I found a secret lab here in the hospital, where I saw Sami extracting their venom – it was what he and the doctor were using to test their Scourge cures,' Alethea replied. 'I used a vial of it to test the marshwort.'

Kayla's chest went tight. Rustus stared, open-mouthed and unblinking.

'So if the shadowy bardfly causes the Scourge . . .' said Rustus.

'And Dr Oke created the shadowy bardfly . . .' continued Kayla, barely believing what Alethea was saying, 'then that means . . .'

'Dr Oke created the Scourge,' finished Alethea.

The children had a few seconds to stare at one another in shock before the door burst open and Dr Oke herself entered. She stopped in surprise when she saw them all.

'What are you doing in here?' she demanded. 'This room is private.'

Kayla, Alethea and Rustus took a step towards one another, forming a united front.

'We know the truth,' said Kayla.

'We know what you've done,' said Rustus.

Dr Oke blinked slowly. 'What are you talking about?'

'I found this,' Alethea said, handing the paper to Dr Oke.

'We've worked out that *you* are Dr Ophelia Kalima Everhart,' said Kayla.

'You created the shadowy bardfly,' added Rustus.

'And the Scourge,' finished Alethea accusingly.

Dr Oke looked at the paper and back to the children and gave a heavy sigh. 'It's not what you think,' she said. 'Not entirely.'

Anger coursed through Kayla's veins as she watched the doctor walk over to a cupboard on the far side of the room and pull out a glass decanter and a tumbler. She tipped in a sharp chunk of ice, poured a glug of a gold-coloured liquid then took a sip. She looked pensive. Eventually she said, 'We never meant it to happen.' She swirled the glass. 'We never even considered that it could be a side effect of what we were doing.' Another sip. 'We thought what we were doing was good.'

'What *were* you doing?' asked Kayla distrustfully.

'I think you need to start at the beginning,' said Alethea.

Dr Oke sighed again and downed the rest of the glass before replacing it in the cupboard.

'In the realms, we're taught to fear the Beastlands and the beasts that live within them,' she began. 'But that's never felt right to me. I've always been fascinated by the beasts. Drawn to them. In the Fjordlands, where I grew up, I used to study them – in secret of course. One day my father found out about my obsession and I was terrified that he would punish me. Instead he put me in touch with a naturalist whom he had met through his work as a ferryman. The naturalist told me she was gathering a team of experts to work on a top-secret beast-conservation project on an island called Polliflora, off the northern coast of Ramoa. She invited me to join them. I soon discovered that there were others like me, who also loved the beasts and wanted to help them. People who believed that humans and beasts could live together, outside the walled cities. I was overjoyed. I left Freyavik without looking back.'

The faraway look in Dr Oke's eyes reminded Kayla of her mother, who had also believed that people should live alongside beasts rather than enslaving them.

'We made some exciting progress,' Dr Oke continued. 'But after a couple of years, things took a turn.'

'What kind of a turn?' asked Rustus, but Kayla was pretty sure she could guess.

'Professor Penn – the naturalist who was the leader of the programme – won our trust by letting us work on projects that interested us – like studies on how we could reintroduce the animals from the Beastlands into the cities. At first it seemed like she was only interested in the beasts that already existed. But after a few years she unveiled her great plan: to replace the extinct beasts the first settlers had wiped out.'

'Replace them with what?' asked Alethea, shooting a nervous look at Kayla and Rustus.

'With new beasts,' said Dr Oke, her expression pained. 'As soon as she suggested it, we should have refused, but she told us that it would be the ultimate way of rewilding the island – and at that time the idea made sense to me.'

'Where did you get new beasts from?' asked Rustus.

The doctor gave a heavy sigh before continuing. 'We created them.'

The children looked at one another, confused.

'How?' asked Kayla.

'Through a process the professor called merging,' the doctor explained. 'She found a fungus growing deep under the surface of the island, and she discovered that when you put two creatures in contact with this fungus it breeds a new creation, with the characteristics of both beasts swaddled into it. We called the new beasts chimaeras.'

The children exchanged glances.

'It was the whole reason she had taken us to the island,' the doctor said. 'At first we all assumed that we were based on Polliflora because it was too risky to carry out our work in the realms – if we were found out, we'd have been thrown into jail.' Kayla thought of her mum again. 'But it soon became clear that we were on Polliflora because of the fungus and that the professor's plan had always been to create a whole collection of new beasts.'

'And that was your job?' Kayla asked.

'Indeed,' said the doctor. 'The professor suggested starting with the winged beasts, which had been the most feared and therefore most hunted. She set up a "sky-beast division", which she put me in charge of. Our job was to merge beasts from across the Realms to make new beasts that could fly.'

'Is that where the shadowy bardfly came from?' asked Rustus.

Dr Oke winced at the mention of it. 'The shadowy bardfly,' she said with a sigh, 'was my greatest mistake.' She laid a hand against her breastbone before continuing. 'We merged many different animals of many different types, with varying degrees of success. Even though some of the new beasts were astounding, the professor was never satisfied. She always wanted beasts that were bigger and better. One day we tried combining a shadowy stinger, an enormous veniscorp, with a southern bardfly, a small agile winged hexapod. We hoped we might create a giant flying hexapod, but as so often happened with these experiments, instead of the southern bardfly taking on the size of the shadowy stinger, or the shadowy stinger taking on the wings of the southern bardfly, the new beast simply took on the shadowy stinger's venom and kept the size and shape of the southern bardfly.

'The resulting chimaera was small and seemingly harmless – so when it zipped out of the lab before we could catch it, we didn't think too much of it. Not until about a week later,' Dr Oke said, face grave, 'when my best friend fell sick. He started with a fever, then the sickness, the hallucinations . . . then more people at the facility started to become ill. I was certain it had something to do with the experiments, but I couldn't work out exactly what. Then we heard that people on the mainland were getting sick too. They called it the Scourge, on account of the suffering it caused.'

They all sat quietly, thinking about the way the disease had ripped through the Realms.

'Eventually I traced the illness to the bardfly we had created. By that time, the reports were too widespread to have been caused by one individual, so I deduced it must be able to reproduce asexually, like the shadowy stinger. Finally I captured a shadowy bardfly and was able to isolate its venom. It wasn't the same as the venom of the shadowy stinger – merging had altered it somehow. Made it stronger.' The doctor hung her head in her hands. 'I couldn't work out how to treat it. I felt so guilty. I had unleashed this creature on the world and I vowed that I would dedicate my life to finding a cure. But I wouldn't have been safe searching for answers on the island, so I ran away with my colleague Sami. That was when we came here and set up the hospital.'

The children looked at one another. It was a lot to take in.

'Did you tell anyone about what was happening on Polliflora?' Alethea asked.

'I was too frightened. I thought they might lock me up, and then I would never find a cure.'

'So no one else in the Realms knows that the bardflies cause the Scourge?' said Rustus.

The doctor shook her head.

There was still one detail about the story Kayla found confusing. 'We have those bardflies in Sophiatown,' she said. 'So why is nobody there getting the illness?'

To Kayla's surprise, it was Alethea who answered.

'Didn't you say you wash with marshwort?' she asked.

Remembering that marshwort was the new name for pickleweed Kayla nodded.

'Well, if marshwort works against the shadowy-bardfly venom, then maybe it repels the flies too. It would explain why hardly anyone in The Silk has been affected too – they use marshwort all the time.'

Kayla thought about it for a moment. She cleaned herself with pickleweed juice all the time, but after she was shot down into the ocean, the pickleweed she had used that day would probably have washed off.

'Did the other people working on the experiments stay on the island after you left?' Rustus asked, returning to their original line of questioning.

'They did at first,' Dr Oke replied. 'But more and more people were becoming ill and the professor was increasingly fixated on creating bigger and more ferocious beasts. Everyone was beginning to question her motives. The workers gradually disappeared back to the realms. From what I've heard, there's hardly anyone left now.'

'What do you mean, questioning her motives?' asked Alethea.

'In the early days, we all believed we were helping to restore the balance of the island, but the professor was *so* fixated on creating large and dangerous beasts, we started to consider whether she might have another goal.'

'What kind of goal?' asked Kayla.

Dr Oke shook her head. 'I don't know,' she said. 'But if I were to make a guess, I would say she wants to take over the Realms. She once told me that when she first left Sophiatown she dreamed of returning and destroying the city.' Sophiatown? The evil mastermind was from the same city as Kayla? She wondered how long ago she had left. 'I suspect her goal was never really to do with supporting the ecology of the island – rather she just wanted an army of beasts and a huge flying steed to ride to war and ensure her victory.'

An army of beasts . . . It was an unnerving thought, but one that was soon replaced by an even more horrible one, that made Kayla sick to the pit of her stomach. 'Do you think she's the one who's taken Faro?' she asked. 'So that she can experiment on him and try to make a new flying beast for her army?'

Rustus and Alethea looked at her wide-eyed.

'Who is Faro?' asked the doctor.

'My pangron,' said Kayla.

The doctor looked at her as if noticing her for the first time. 'You're a Sky Rider?'

Kayla nodded.

'And your pangron has been taken?'

'Yes,' said Kayla. 'Three days ago. By a Shadow Ghoul on a boat, along with another pangron from the city.'

'So she finally recruited a Lia'Oua,' the doctor mused. 'She's been trying to do that for a long time. She believed the Lia'Oua knew secrets of the island that no other human did.'

'We do,' a voice said from the doorway.

They all turned to see who it was. A tall figure stood by the door, a central brush of snow-white hair standing high atop his head like a frozen crown. It was Maaka, the Shadow Ghoul who had been with Rustus when Kayla had woken up. He was good at sneaking about without being heard. Kayla didn't trust him at all, and not just because of where he came from. When had he come into the room? From the looks on Rustus and Alethea's faces, they hadn't noticed him enter either. 'We Lia'Oua have sworn to protect the secrets of the island,' Maaka continued, 'and until recently I didn't believe any one of us would ever break that promise.'

Kayla scowled at him.

'Do you know something about a Lia'Oua going to work for the professor?' Rustus asked.

'Perhaps.' Maaka padded soundlessly towards them. 'A few moons ago a woman found her way down to our home. She asked many questions about Banahiki, as well as about our prophecies.'

'Banahiki,' Rustus asked. 'What's that?'

'That's what we Lia'Oua call the process the professor

refers to as merging,' said Maaka. 'We've known about it for many generations. It's a natural ritual, but the professor was asking questions about using it in unnatural ways. In exchange for answers she made big promises, but we declined her offers, so she left.' He paused. 'Shortly after that, my sister Gabba disappeared. The other clans accused Gabba of leaving to sell our secrets. I didn't want to believe that it could be true, but after what you said earlier, Kayla, about the girl who shot down your pangron – and what I've just heard you talking about – I fear Gabba must be working for the professor.'

Kayla felt hatred bubble up inside her. So Gabba and this professor wanted to experiment on her pangron, did they? Wanted to use him to create some kind of beast of war? Kayla wouldn't stand for it. 'I will kill her if she's damaged a hair on Faro's head.'

Maaka didn't respond to Kayla's threat. 'I don't know which of our secrets Gabba has shared,' he said, 'but based on the questions the professor asked, I have my suspicions. And if you are to stop her, I think I have to share one of them with you too.'

Kayla, Alethea and Rustus exchanged worried glances.

'What is it?' Kayla asked, still cautious of anything this Shadow Ghoul had to say, but too curious to resist asking for more information.

Maaka took a deep breath, a serious expression on his face. 'The professor was fixated on the prophecies and legends regarding one particular beast,' he started, 'a beast that was killed off long ago.'

Kayla's heart quickened, remembering the prophecy Tas had revealed to them.

'The professor didn't want to create just any beast, did she?' asked Alethea, pale-faced. She had made the connection too.

Maaka shook his head and Rustus's hand went to his mouth in shock.

'She wanted to make a phaegra.'

Maaka nodded.

'I can't believe I never considered this myself,' said the doctor, sinking into a seat by the desk.

'The phaegra is a chimaera,' Maaka continued, 'created when two beasts are combined in Banahiki. If Gabba has divulged our secrets to the professor, then she probably already knows which beasts she needs for the ritual.'

Kayla's stomach churned. Was this why the professor had chosen this moment to steal a pangron? After finding out the recipe to make a phaegra, she had sent Gabba to Sophiatown to collect one half of the ingredients?

'One of the beasts is a pangron, isn't it?' she asked, voice quaking.

Maaka turned to look directly at her, fixing her with piercing purple eyes. 'Yes. I'm sorry, Kayla.'

She felt the familiar anger bubbling inside her again. *At least if the professor wanted to use Faro for Banahiki she would have to keep him alive*, she told herself. *And as long as he's alive, there's still a chance to save him.* But could Kayla get him back before the professor created a phaegra?

'What's the other creature?' Rustus asked. Kayla held her breath, listening for the answer. What if the professor already had the other beast? Was it on Polliflora, waiting for Gabba to return with Faro and Ezra to complete the ritual? But then why would Gabba need to stop in Port Royal on the way?

'A salinka,' said Maaka.

There was a sharp intake of breath. 'Impossible,' said the doctor. 'They're extinct.'

Maaka shook his head. 'No, they're not. No more than the Lia'Oua are. They live with us, in the Shadowlands.'

Kayla didn't have time to dwell on this revelation; locating Faro was now more urgent than ever. 'I need to get to Port Royal as soon as possible,' she said. 'Before Gabba can find a salinka.'

To her surprise Rustus spoke up immediately. 'I'm coming with you.'

Kayla gave him a wide smile. Then, without realising what she was doing, she felt her eyes flick to Alethea.

'I can't,' Alethea said. 'I'm sorry.'

Kayla felt embarrassed. Of course she shouldn't have expected Alethea to join her. 'I know,' Kayla said. 'You have to get back to your grandma.'

'If I had more time –' Alethea began, her brow furrowed and expression pained, but Kayla interrupted.

'It's fine,' she said. 'I get it.'

Before either girl could continue, the doctor spoke. 'Please,' she said. 'I should be the one to take the cure to Ataria.'

Kayla rounded on the doctor. 'Wait, you're not coming with us to stop the professor?'

Dr Oke shook her head. 'I can't,' she said. 'Alethea has achieved something extraordinary today. Something that I have been trying to do for a long time. Now I must take her discovery and right the wrong I committed many years ago. I will not rest until every patient in all the Realms is cured of the Scourge, starting in Ataria.'

Alethea chewed her lip uncertainly. 'That's really kind,' she said. 'And it's not that I don't trust you, I do. It's just that I promised Grandma . . .'

'It's my fault that your grandmother ever contracted the Scourge in the first place,' the doctor replied, 'the least I can do is to make her better. If I travel by sled I'll be there in two days.' She stopped suddenly, her hand going to her mouth.

'What's wrong?' asked Rustus.

'The sled,' said Dr Oke. 'We only have one. If you take it to Port Royal . . .'

She didn't need to finish the sentence. If Kayla and Rustus took the sled then the doctor would be forced to walk to Ataria, and goodness knows how long that would take. But what choice did the children have? If the professor brought back the phaegra, it would mean the end of life as they knew it. The entire fate of the Realms was in their hands.

Kayla glimpsed Alethea out of the corner of her eye. For the first time since Kayla had known her, the Atarian healer looked defeated. It broke Kayla's heart and she wished there was a way she could take Alethea back to Ataria in time to save her grandma. If only she had –

'Faro!' Kayla exclaimed, shocked it had taken her so long to think of it. 'As soon as we rescue Faro I can fly you straight back to Ataria. You'll be there even faster than if you had taken the sled!' She didn't allow the idea that they may *not* find Faro to form in her mind. Failure wasn't an option. Too many people were relying on her now.

Alethea's expression brightened. 'How long do you think that would take?'

'Not long at all,' said Kayla. 'Faro's really fast.'

'Kayla's right,' the doctor agreed. 'A pangron would get you to Ataria much more quickly than my snogarts would. And Port Royal is only a few hours by sled. If you find Faro today then you could be back in Ataria by nightfall. You'd be better off going with your friends – I'll join you there as soon as I can.'

'Then it's settled,' said Alethea, her usual expression returning. 'I'm coming with you after all.'

A few days ago there was no way Kayla would have accepted any help on her mission. For as long as she could remember it had just been her and Faro. She liked it that way; it meant she didn't have to rely on anybody else. But despite Kayla's reluctance, Rustus had already proven himself to be a great friend, and Alethea had literally just saved her life, so she simply said, 'Thank you.'

At that point Maaka spoke up. 'I'd like to come too,' he said. 'The phaegra cannot be allowed to return, and if my sister's involved, I want to help set it right.' Kayla was about to voice her disapproval about the Shadow Ghoul joining them when he continued. 'But something tells me there may not be space for me in this quest . . .' His voice carried a hint of hesitation, as if unsure about what he was saying. 'Three must unite,' he murmured. 'Three must unite. But three *what*? If it's the three of you . . .' He glanced up at them, rubbing a hand over his face. 'With me you would be four. I can't risk going with you and upsetting the balance. The fate of the island is too precious to gamble.'

'I don't know about three uniting,' said the doctor. 'But even if you wanted to go, I wouldn't let you leave the mountain. I might be able to cure your Scourge, but you still have a nasty infection in your foot. It's going to be a week or so before you're well enough. Come, I'll take you back to the ward on the way to get these children to the sled.'

They all followed her out of the office and through the hospital, dropping Maaka off with a nurse at one of the wards. What had he been talking about? Another prophecy? Kayla didn't spare it much thought, she still didn't trust the Shadow Ghouls and besides, they needed to get on the road.

'Good luck, Maaka,' said Rustus, shaking his hand.

'You too,' Maaka said. 'All three of you. And if you see my sister, tell her that she still has her little brother to reckon with.' Kayla grunted a reluctant goodbye. She didn't quite trust the Shadow Ghoul, but a grudge against

Gabba was one thing she and Maaka had in common.

Kayla, Alethea, Rustus and the doctor travelled down a long ice corridor that looked much like all the others. At the far end, they encountered Sami.

'These children need the snogarts urgently,' said the doctor. 'Can you get them ready?'

He rushed off to do as she bid while they stopped off at a room that looked like a small store cupboard. Dr Oke pulled out six thick furs, handing the children two each. 'Wrap up warm,' she said. 'We're at the tail end of a blizzard and the sled provides little shelter.'

Once they were ready the doctor led them to a large door made of ice. As soon as it opened the frosty air took Kayla's breath away. She pulled the edges of the fur close around her. Never in her life had she felt such cold, as painful and as biting as if she had been burned. They made their way to a small stable, where six shaggy white beasts were already hitched to a cart, Sami at their side.

'What funny creatures,' said Alethea.

'They're snogarts!' said Sami, smiling. The creatures had long white hair and four curled antlers, with slender legs that ended in cloven black hooves, which reminded Kayla of the sophisticated slippers worn by the Sophiatown royals. 'Their tiny hooves allow them to navigate the narrowest of edges and steepest of slopes. Come on,' he said. 'Let me show you how to guide them.'

The children clambered up into the sled and Kayla looked around for the reins. Alethea and Rustus settled into the cushioned seats on either side of her.

'How do you steer this thing?' Kayla asked.

'With your voice,' said Sami. '*Shum* means go. *Yo* means stop. Say *kish* to turn left and *haka* to turn right.'

'Seems simple enough,' said Kayla. 'But how will we know the way to Port Royal?'

'Follow the path down the mountain to the coast,' the doctor said. 'You'll know when you've arrived. Leave the sled at the Salty Seadog. I have a friend who can collect it.'

Sami gave the children a quick lesson in how to change the sled's runners for wheels once they were out of the snow, and soon they were ready to go.

'Shum,' said Kayla, testing the command out. The snogarts responded immediately, jerking the sled forward. At her 'Yo!' they halted abruptly, nearly catapulting Alethea out of her seat.

'You're going to need to work on your tone,' said Sami. 'They're very sensitive.'

'Shum,' said Kayla, more softly this time, as if she were speaking to Faro. The snogarts sprung forward again, but this time the movement was more controlled. 'Yo.'

'Better,' said Sami. 'You can use the journey to work on your technique.'

'Don't let them go too fast,' warned Dr Oke, 'or the sled will topple. If it breaks, getting down to Port Royal will be much more difficult.'

'All right,' said Kayla. She was desperate to find Faro and whisk him off to safety, but she knew the doctor was right. There was no point in rushing. Look where it had got her when she'd tried that on the climb up. 'Thank you for saving my life.'

The doctor smiled. 'Good luck,' she said, and then took Alethea's hand. 'I cannot thank you enough for bringing the marshwort to me.' As they pulled away, Kayla saw she had left something in Alethea's hand. 'A token from my home, the land of healing, for you. You'd like it there, I think.'

'A pasqueflower.' Alethea studied the delicate bracelet that had a single flower engraved on it as she fastened it around her wrist. 'It's beautiful, thank you. But really, I couldn't have solved the problem without your help. Until I saw your work, I had no idea how to use it.'

'Let's agree that you're both brilliant,' said Kayla, and everyone laughed. 'Now can we get on the road?'

'One last thing,' said Sami, passing them a cage with a familiar featherwing inside.

'Milabar!' said Rustus.

'We should send her to the Marquis,' said Alethea. 'Tell him to keep an eye out for a salinka.'

Rustus took the heraldwing from the cage, spoke the message and then let her fly off down the mountain. Kayla hoped she would reach the Marquis before he got to Port Royal.

'Be careful,' said Dr Oke, 'Professor Penn is very dangerous.'

'We will,' said Rustus.

Kayla gave a final wave and then turned her attention to the beasts ahead of her. 'Shum,' she said, and the snogarts took off. They seemed to know exactly where they were going, heading straight for the path down the mountain. Kayla turned to look back at the ice building one last time.

It was a pretty extraordinary place. If she hadn't been so busy almost dying or searching for a pangron who had been stolen by an evil professor who wanted to bring back a terrible monster and take over the world, she would have liked to explore it further. Alas.

After a while, the doctor, Sami and the hospital faded out of sight. Finally Kayla felt like she was on her way to Faro, and surprisingly it felt good to have friends by her side.

23

ALETHEA

Alethea gripped her seat, struggling to stay upright, as the sled lurched wildly down the mountain path.

'Shum!' yelled Kayla. The snogarts picked up the pace.

'Kayla,' Alethea warned, 'remember what the doctor said. Not *too* fast or we'll overturn.'

'We need to get to Faro,' Kayla said, face set. 'We can't let the professor create a phaegra.'

'She may not even have a salinka yet,' Rustus reasoned.

'But what if she does?' snapped Kayla.

Alethea bit her lip. She really hoped the professor didn't have a salinka. If she was still searching for the other beast then she would probably be storing the pangrons somewhere – and now that a pangron was her ticket back to Ataria, Alethea was as keen to rescue Faro as Kayla was. Even so, it would do no good for them to crash and have to walk the rest of the way. Ahead of them the path curved steeply.

'Haka!' yelled Kayla. The snogarts leaped immediately into a right turn and the sled tipped precariously onto one runner, sending Rustus crashing into Kayla and both of them on top of Alethea. Her chest was crushed under the weight.

'Slow down!' shouted Rustus. 'We're going to crash.'

But Kayla didn't listen. As the sled levelled out and the snogarts galloped down the mountain road, she commanded them to go faster still. The sled hit a rock and took to the air, landing back on the path with a heavy thump.

The impact brought Alethea's head crashing into Kayla's and she squealed in pain.

That was the final straw for Rustus, who bellowed 'Enough!' before shouting 'Yo!' at the snogarts, who responded immediately, coming to a sudden halt.

Kayla shoved him, hard. 'How dare you undermine me like that!'

'I'm sorry, Kayla,' said Rustus, holding up his hands. 'We know you're worried about Faro, but we won't make it to Port Royal at all unless we drive sensibly. Look at the snogarts – we can't push them any harder.'

She shot a glance at the panting beasts. Their fur was slick with sweat, white froth collecting at the corners of their mouths. Rustus was right, they looked exhausted.

Kayla turned to Alethea. Was she looking for support?

'It was a bit fast,' Alethea conceded, rubbing her head.

Kayla scowled. 'I'm just trying to get us there quickly.'

'We know,' said Alethea, placing a hand gently on her

arm. 'We want to get there quickly too.'

'I could command the snogarts for the next bit of the journey if you like,' said Rustus.

Kayla bristled. 'You think you can do a better job than me?'

'I just thought you might like a rest,' he replied.

For a moment Alethea thought they were going to start bickering again.

Kayla glared at Rustus before her expression thawed and she slumped back in her seat. 'Fine,' said Kayla. 'Let's see how well they listen to you.'

Alethea and Rustus shared a look. Kayla had been the only one to command the snogarts since they had left, which wasn't a problem, but she still hadn't perfected the art of smooth transitions and they had found themselves thrown from their seats whenever there was a change in speed or direction.

'Shum,' said Rustus evenly. The snogarts shook their heads, snorted and then gently broke into a smooth and even walk. Rustus looked at the girls out of the corner of his eye. He seemed to be fighting the urge to point out his success. Alethea pursed her lips to stop herself laughing, but a little squeal managed to escape.

'OK,' said Kayla, smiling despite herself. 'I admit it – that was way better than any of the times I did it.'

Rustus and Alethea burst into fits of giggles.

'Can we agree that Rustus gives the commands for the rest of the journey?' Alethea said.

Kayla rolled her eyes and nodded.

As the sled glided down the mountain path, Alethea was fascinated to see the scenery change. The dense snowdrifts thinned and the thick layers of ice gave way to brittle dirty patches. Kayla and Rustus's appearances changed too. The diamond frosting on their eyelashes and nostrils melted and their cheeks were no longer quite so red from the cold. Alethea was relieved to find that the icy air no longer crackled in her nose and she had feeling back in her toes.

If the circumstances had not been urgent, Alethea would have spent hours investigating the flora of the slopes. As it was, they could not get to Port Royal fast enough. After Maaka's revelation the mood was sombre. They hadn't spent much time discussing what the Lia'Oua had said, but Alethea could tell from Kayla's hunched shoulders and frowning face that she was worried about the implications for Faro.

'What are these plants?' Rustus asked, pointing at a tall thorn-covered stem with a spiky white flowerhead.

'Oh!' exclaimed Alethea. 'That's frostwort.' She desperately wanted to take a sample, but it didn't seem an appropriate request when they were in such a rush.

Whether Rustus noticed the expression on her face or it was just a coincidence, he chose that moment to ask, 'Should we stop and change the runners?' Alethea glanced at the ground. It was a good point – the snow was already patchy and would soon disappear completely.

'All right,' said Kayla, 'but let's be quick.'

Rustus ordered the snogarts to halt, and they did so

immediately. For the first time, Alethea was not almost deposited to the ground by the force of it. She clambered out of the sled and headed over to the plant.

'While we're here I'm just going to take a sample,' she said.

'OK,' said Kayla. She and Rustus worked together to remove the runners and replace them with wheels while Alethea cut a few stems of frostwort. When she had finished, Alethea sat and watched as Kayla and Rustus completed their job.

'Sami said that bolt goes here,' said Rustus, pointing at the wheel. Kayla frowned and peered closely at the mechanism.

'It looks like it goes here to me,' she replied, pointing to a different spot.

Rustus shook his head. 'Why would we put it there when we were told it went here?'

'Fine,' said Kayla, practising her patience. They tried Rustus's method, and when it didn't work, it was Kayla's turn to look triumphant. Despite the circumstances, Alethea stifled a giggle. Kayla and Rustus were getting on much better now, but it wouldn't feel right if they agreed all the time.

'See?' said Kayla, grinning.

'Well, that's not what Sami said,' grumbled Rustus.

When they were finished, they both jumped up onto the sled again.

'Hop up, Dr Bashoa,' said Kayla, patting the seat beside her, which Alethea happily slid onto. As they continued their journey, Alethea's thoughts drifted to home. She desperately hoped that they would find Faro quickly and that she would be back to help Grandma soon. Without another healer in the Blue District there were sure to be plenty of other patients waiting to see her too.

She wondered how big Port Royal was. Big enough to keep a pangron hidden from sight? That was assuming Faro was even *in* Port Royal. She didn't want to say it, but part of her wondered if Gabba would have taken Faro straight to Polliflora. She knew the message from Aquamarine had said the ship was due to dock in Port Royal, but it didn't make sense to hang around in the port if the professor had a whole secret island she could take him to. Besides, hadn't the doctor said the fungus only grew on the island? If the pangrons were already on Polliflora, the children would struggle to find them; beyond being off the north coast, they had no idea where the island was – they hadn't thought to ask the doctor for more details. And if Faro wasn't in Port Royal then it could be days before Alethea was back in Ataria. The thought tied her stomach in knots.

'Do we have a plan for when we get down there?' she asked.

'The first thing to do is try and find the Marquis,' said Kayla. 'He should already be there by now because of our delay at the hospital. For all we know, he's got Faro already.' Her voice was painfully hopeful. Alethea really wanted her to be right.

'Do you think the professor has a salinka?' Alethea

asked. Thus far they had skirted around the topic, perhaps because the implications were so dire.

'I don't know,' said Rustus. 'I'm sure the Marquis's bestiary said they were extinct, but Maaka seemed pretty convinced they weren't. I've been racking my brain trying to remember what else the book said about them.'

Alethea vaguely remembered Rustus reading about the salinka as they were travelling from The Silk to Frostfall Mountain. 'Didn't it say it was green?' she asked.

'Yeah, I think so,' said Rustus, but he didn't sound sure. 'I'm sure there was something about the food it liked to eat too . . .'

'When we find the Marquis we can ask him about it,' said Kayla. 'He'll know as much as anyone.'

'It was nice of him to go to Port Royal to look for Faro for you,' said Rustus.

Kayla's head snapped round. 'He's not going there for Faro,' she said. 'He's going to meet some naturalist. They've been talking about Topaz. The Marquis thinks the naturalist might know what species she is.'

A naturalist? Wasn't that what Professor Penn had told Dr Oke she was before she'd gone to Polliflora? As soon as the words had left her lips Kayla seemed to make the connection too.

'Oh no,' said Rustus, also joining the dots. 'Do you think the Marquis's naturalist is the professor?'

'Got to be, hasn't it?' said Alethea. It was way too much of a coincidence to be anything else. They all shared a worried glance. What did the professor want with

Topaz? And what kind of terrible beast might she use her to create? Reaching the Marquis was more urgent than ever. Alethea just hoped he would be easy to find.

It was late afternoon when Port Royal appeared at the end of the road. The town was built around a cup-shaped bay, with a port right in the centre. Even from this distance they could see that it was bustling with activity. The streets of the town radiated in a semicircle out from the harbour – all roads leading to the sea.

'Looks like quite a big place,' said Rustus. 'How are we going to know where to look?'

'The boat carrying Faro should already have docked.' Kayla squinted to make out the boats in the bay. 'It had green sails.'

'Can't see it in the port,' said Rustus. 'What about the Marquis's wagon – can you see that anywhere? We need to warn him before he goes to meet the professor.'

The three of them looked out across Port Royal, but their view was obscured by the overhanging roofs of the buildings and the lines of washing drying in the breeze.

'Let's find the Salty Seadog and get rid of the sled – we can get around the town more easily on foot,' said Rustus.

That reminded Alethea of something. 'That's where the Marquis's friend Aquamarine works, isn't it? Maybe the Marquis is there.'

'It's as good a place to start as any,' said Kayla.

As they rolled down the stony pot-holed road to the

centre of town, Alethea was surprised by how easy it was to enter Port Royal. It was so unlike Ataria or what she'd heard of Sophiatown, with no high walls or locked gates. The buildings, which were mostly wooden, were squeezed tightly together and in a poor state of repair – devoured by brine after years of exposure to the salty sea air. Alethea could hear unfamiliar beasts bellowing in the distance and street vendors chattering in an accent that was totally alien.

'Pasties! Pasties! Git ya seawort pasties!'

'Buy moy fat mudrats! Tasty fat mudrats!'

'Six furra sovereign, eleven furra laurel!'

'Old rags! Old rags! Any old rags!'

They pulled up next to a stall.

'Excuse me,' Kayla asked. 'We're looking for the Salty Seadog.'

'Not from around these parts?' the seller said, regarding them curiously. 'You want to go up there –' he pointed along the road – 'then take a left at the bakery.'

'Thanks,' said Alethea, and Rustus urged the snogarts on.

They trundled past a boat-repair shop, a funeral parlour and a bakery and took a left as the man had told them. They turned down a dark road, where the second floor of the buildings stuck out above them, creating a kind of tunnel. Once they narrowly avoided being covered in a smelly liquid that someone poured out of one of the open windows.

'Watch out!' said Kayla, wrinkling her nose.

'What was that?' asked Rustus, looking back.

'I think it was a chamber pot,' said Alethea, who very much didn't want to confirm her suspicions.

'You mean that was . . . ?' Kayla's eyes widened in horror. 'That's disgusting!'

'Explains the smell,' said Rustus.

Finally they came to a three-storey wooden building at the end of the road. If the other buildings were ramshackle, this one was utterly dilapidated. Broken beams dangled pendulously from the eaves, the windows, where they weren't broken, were coated in a thick layer of grime and the walls were scarred with scrapes and stains. Rustus pointed to a sign above the door squeaking loudly in the wind. Its black lettering was peeling away from the wood, but Alethea could just about decipher the words.

The Salty Seadog.

She squinted to make out what lay beyond the murky windows and glimpsed brightly coloured silks and warm candlelight. From the decor and the sounds that drifted out, it was clear this was a pub. The sled pulled to a stop outside and the three children jumped out. They crossed the road and approached the entrance, trying their best to avoid the puddles of murky brown water. As Kayla was about to push open the broken door, the three of them were enveloped in a turquoise cloud of sweet-scented silk.

'Arrgh!' screamed Kayla, batting at the air and accidentally hitting Alethea in the eye.

'Darlink,' said a rich exotic voice, 'calm down, there is no need for such dramatics.'

The children recognised the voice at once. It was the voice they had heard Milabar use when delivering the message about the avalanche. This must be . . .

'Aquamarine!' Rustus said.

'The one and only,' said Aquamarine with a little curtsy, cascades of blue silk billowing over their legs.

'Where's the Marquis?' asked Kayla curtly. Alethea shot her a reproachful glare, but Aquamarine didn't seem to be offended.

'He called in for a drink before going to meet some naturalist by the lighthouse on Hookclaw Point,' they said, pushing a strand of soft grey hair away from their face, 'but that was several hours ago. I haven't heard from him since.'

The children looked briefly at one another, wondering whether to explain everything they had learned about the island and how the naturalist was likely to be Professor Penn or Gabba. There wasn't time.

'We have to go,' said Rustus. 'I'm sorry, Aquamarine. We'll explain later.'

Aquamarine did not look perturbed by their immediate departure. 'No problem, darlinks. Always a pleasure to meet friends of the Marquis, no matter how briefly. I'm sure our paths will cross again.'

'Oh, there was one other thing,' said Rustus. 'Our friend Sami told us we could leave his sled with you – is that OK?'

'But of course,' crooned Aquamarine, gliding towards the snogarts and feeding one of them a titbit from their pocket. Something about the way they moved gave the impression of water. 'Leave it with me.'

'Thank you,' said Rustus.

'Which way is Hookclaw Point?' asked Kayla.

'Fastest way is through the beast market,' said Aquamarine. 'Go to the end of this street and then follow your nose. You can't miss it. Take the main road straight through the market and out onto the coast road beyond. You should be able to see the lighthouse from the other side.'

The instructions seemed slightly cryptic, but once the children reached the end of the street Alethea realised Aquamarine had been absolutely right. The only comparable reference she had for the smell that now reached her nostrils was the Marquis's wagon, but this was on another level entirely. Beside her, Rustus and Kayla were covering their faces.

'I guess the market's that way,' said Kayla, voice muffled through the fabric of her sleeve.

On Aquamarine's advice they followed the stench and soon found the entrance of the open-air market, a loud imposing place right on the seafront. Inside, the affront on their senses was overwhelming. The air was thick with the scent of ammonia, and calls of exotic beasts rang through the huge market, with its rows upon rows of fascinating cages and pens. The Marquis's menagerie paled in comparison.

They entered, passing signs for 'reptillites', 'warmbloods', 'wetskins' and 'featherwings'. Alethea could barely believe her eyes. There were giant slimy beasts with flat, arrow-shaped heads, hunched winged ones with long, red beaks, dark-furred creatures with droopy orange ears and many more besides. All of the enclosures were cramped and dirty, the beasts themselves thin and caked with mud. None of them looked well cared for, and if they made too much noise they were flogged by market workers with whips and sticks.

'This is horrible,' said Rustus, voicing what Alethea was thinking.

Kayla didn't speak, but from her horrified expression and the way her fingers trembled, Alethea knew that she was worrying about Faro and what state he might be in.

Just after they passed the featherwings, they saw a sign for 'slimefoots'. A lank-haired market seller stood in front of a towering pile of boxes while having an animated conversation with a hooded figure in large silver boots.

Beside Alethea, Kayla gasped. 'That's Gabba!' she hissed. 'I'm sure of it.'

'Let's get closer,' said Rustus, 'so we can hear.'

The trio ducked behind the neighbouring pen, listening keenly to what Gabba and the seller were saying.

'That's the best deal I can do,' the seller said quietly. 'Take it or leave it. There are plenty of other people will buy these slugs if you don't want them.'

'I only want them as food,' hissed Gabba. 'Your price is extortionate. You should be grateful I want to buy these disgusting beasts at all –'

At that moment a screech sounded above them. They

looked up to see a small black beast cutting through the air like an arrow, its eyes fixed on Gabba. Gabba lifted her head to reveal a pale face covered in purple and yellow tattoos. She bore a striking resemblance to Maaka. When she saw the beast approaching she raised a hand and snatched it from the air. The creature opened its mouth to speak but the girl clamped her fist tightly around its beak, preventing it from making a sound. It looked similar to Milabar, the Marquis's heraldwing, but in place of beautiful white feathers it had jet-black scales. Alethea had never seen anything like it, not even in the Marquis's bestiary.

It must be one of Professor Penn's chimaeras.

'I have to go,' Gabba said suddenly, turning on her heel and stalking out of the market. The seller shouted after her, trying to lure her back with promises of a better deal, but Gabba didn't look back as she marched out onto the coast road. The children followed, remaining a reasonable distance behind so as not to arouse suspicion. Ahead, Alethea could see the road wound onto a headland with a tall red lighthouse at its tip: Hookclaw Point.

When Gabba had got far enough away from the market to be out of earshot of any nosy traders, she released the beast from her grasp. The children were huddled in some bushes around a hundred paces behind her. Realising the beast was about to speak a message, Alethea suddenly wondered if they would be close enough to hear, but she needn't have worried – the roar that burst from the scaled beast's beak was deafening.

'You shipwrecked the boat?' it yelled. 'Can I not trust you to do anything? First you lose the salinka before you even leave the mountains, and now this. If you'd have kept hold of it like you were supposed to, you would never have needed to go to Port Royal in the first place. I'm coming there. Do not move. Do not do anything but wait for me with the beasts. Do not take your eyes off them. Build a fire so I know where to dock. And try not to make any more mistakes before I get there.'

If Gabba was hurt by the message her face didn't show it. She flung the beast to the ground, rearranged her hood and then, after glancing quickly behind her to check she wasn't being followed, strode down the street towards the headland and the lighthouse.

The children stared at one another, mouths agape.

'Gabba had the salinka and then lost it!' exclaimed Rustus.

'I'd been wondering why she needed to stop in Port Royal instead of taking the pangrons straight to Polliflora,' Alethea said. 'Do you think she was trying to buy another one at the beast market?'

'Maybe,' said Kayla. 'Or maybe she's already got it back and that's why she wanted slugs – to feed to it.'

'We mustn't let her out of our sight,' said Alethea. 'Come on.'

They continued along the coast road after Gabba, leaving the sound and smell of the market behind them. The road climbed upwards and soon they were hurrying along a high cliff. There were no buildings now, only a path lined with prickly oceanhedge and a steep drop that led to a stony beach far below. They moved slowly, darting in and out of the oceanhedge in case Gabba turned around again. The coast here couldn't have been more different to the one in the Ashlands where Alethea had collected the marshwort; instead of soft black sand, the beach was covered with round grey stones that clacked and rattled as they were tumbled by murky brown waves.

On the rocks below Alethea spotted something wooden. 'Look down there,' she shouted over the howling wind.

Rustus squinted. 'It's a shipwreck.'

'It's Gabba's boat,' said Kayla sombrely. 'Look at the green sails.'

'That's why the professor's coming here,' Alethea realised. 'To collect Gabba and the pangrons and take them back to Polliflora.'

'That must be her.' Rustus pointed out over the waves, where a rowing boat, much smaller than the wreck on the beach, bobbed on the waves.

Alethea gasped. They had to get to Gabba and save the pangrons before it was too late! She glanced back at the headland, eyes scanning the road for the Lia'Oua, when suddenly her breath caught. She let out a squeal and pointed down the road.

'The Marquis's wagon!' said Rustus.

They broke into a run.

24

RUSTUS

As they sprinted towards the wagon, Rustus saw Gabba disappear beyond the lighthouse. For a moment he considered following her, but then he heard the bardebeests snorthonking and stamping their feet in distress, so he turned his attention to the wagon. The rear door hung off its hinges and was swinging in the wind. Inside, the beasts were squawking and screeching. All three children clambered up the ladder in a hurry.

'Marquis Macdonald!' Rustus yelled once inside. 'Are you there?'

He ran through the wagon, hoping to find the Marquis safely sipping a hot cup of varja. He passed the beasts, which were squawking and pacing, and arrived at the sofas. The Marquis was there, but he was not sitting comfortably on his seat as Rustus had hoped; instead he was spreadeagled on the floor and there was blood on the rug beside his head.

Alethea reached down to check his pulse. 'He's been knocked out,' she said.

'I bet it was Gabba,' said Kayla, her voice bubbling with anger.

Rustus felt furious too. How could someone do this to the gentle and peace-loving Marquis? 'Is he OK?'

Alethea nodded. 'He will be.'

Rustus glanced around the wagon to see if anything was missing. It seemed mostly in order, except the door to one enclosure, which stood ajar.

'Topaz is gone,' he said, pointing at the needlejaw's open cage. Had she been taken or had she escaped again?

'That's the least of our problems right now,' said Kayla. 'We need to follow Gabba and see what she's done with the pangrons.'

Kayla made to leave and Rustus was about to follow her, but his eyes fell on something that stopped him in his tracks. It was the bestiary, open on the sofa. He moved over to it.

'Someone was reading the entry about the salinka,' he said. Kayla paused, waiting to hear what the book had to say about the extinct creature that was the other half of a phaegra. 'Listen to this: "A large, green, long-bodied reptillite that lives in the Shadowlands. Only ever seen by Shadow Ghouls, who have described them as having 'a mouth full of scalefish'".'

'What does that mean?' asked Kayla.

'It's a Lia'Oua saying,' said Rustus, remembering his

302

conversation with Maaka in the hospital. 'Means its teeth point all over the place, like this . . .' He splayed his fingers out in front of his mouth.

The realisation dawned on all of them at the same moment.

'Like Topaz,' they said in unison.

Rustus's heart raced.

'But it says that salinkas are green,' said Alethea, clinging to the hope that they were wrong, that Topaz couldn't be a salinka. But Rustus was already remembering something else Maaka had told him. His stomach dropped.

'I think it's a mistake in the description,' he said. 'The book says the salinka has only ever been seen by Shadow Ghouls, which means it must have been the Lia'Oua that gave the bestiarist this description, but Maaka told me that his people are colourblind. They don't even have words for colours.'

'Meaning the salinka could easily have been blue,' Kayla concluded with a grimace.

Rustus nodded. So Topaz wasn't a new species after all; she was a salinka. Presumably the same one the professor had told Gabba off for losing in the mountains when she left Maaka and the rest of her clan. Hadn't the Marquis told them he had found the beast in the foothills, right by the edge of the Shadowlands? If only he'd left her there, she might have stayed safe. But the professor had tricked the Marquis into bringing Topaz to Port Royal and sent Gabba to pick her up. That meant she now had everything she needed to make a phaegra.

Just then a screech sounded outside.

'That's a pangron!' exclaimed Kayla, her head whipping towards the door.

The three children rushed back outside and looked around frantically. A dense plume of smoke rose from behind the lighthouse.

'I think it came from over there,' said Rustus, pointing towards the fire.

'I'm going to investigate,' said Kayla, breaking into a run.

Alethea glanced back at the wagon, where the Marquis still lay unconscious.

Rustus knew what she was thinking. 'You look after the Marquis,' he said. 'I'll go with Kayla.'

His thoughts raced as he rushed along the headland after Kayla. Where had Gabba taken Topaz and the pangrons? What would happen when Professor Penn arrived? Surely they would have to take the beasts back to Polliflora if they needed the island's fungus.

They approached the lighthouse, pressing close to the curved wall and staying out of sight. As they peered round its side, the fire came into view, large and ferocious, and in its dancing flames they saw Gabba leaning over the cliff, silver boots glinting in the firelight. She took a step backwards, pulling something up. Suddenly Rustus realised it was an arm!

As the rest of the figure emerged onto the headland it was revealed to be a woman. She was dressed in trousers and a jacket, her hair in a short bob, and she dragged something large and purple behind her. As the two women approached the fire, Rustus saw that the purple object was composed of thousands of tendrils, like a web or a net.

Was it the Banahiki fungus?

Gabba and the woman were talking animatedly. As the wind whipped around his ears and featherwings screeched above them, Rustus strained to listen.

'You've wrecked my ship!' the woman said viciously. 'Now we can't take the beasts back to the island.' It *was* the professor – he recognised her voice from the chimaera that had flown to Gabba at the market. Her accent reminded him of Kayla's. He wondered if his friend had identified her too. He shot a glance at Kayla; she was glaring daggers at the professor, which he took to mean she had.

'I'm sorry,' Gabba said miserably. 'But at least you managed to bring the fungus here. We can still create a phaegra.'

'One measly phaegra? I could have made infinite phaegras on the island, not to mention the other chimaeras I could have created. You've ruined everything!'

'I didn't mean to,' Gabba wailed. 'The lighthouse wasn't working and there was a storm. I didn't see the –'

'I don't want to hear your excuses,' snarled the professor. 'Where are the beasts?'

Gabba pointed up at the lighthouse. 'Will the fungus still work here on Ramoa?'

'You'd better hope so,' said the professor. 'Now, bring me the salinka.'

Gabba moved away from the fire and into the shadows

at the base of the lighthouse, only ten paces from where Rustus and Kayla stood. They flattened themselves against the wall as she unlocked the door and disappeared inside. She was gone for several minutes, and when she reappeared she was dragging a muzzled and shackled Topaz by a rope. Gabba pulled Topaz over to the professor, who jabbed her with something that looked a lot like Dr Oke's needle. Topaz squealed and rolled to the ground. Together Gabba and the professor covered Topaz with the now glowing fungus.

Rustus and Kayla watched, awestruck, while Gabba returned to the lighthouse. Again she was gone a long time. Was she keeping the beasts right at the top?

There was another screech, and Kayla clasped a hand to her mouth. It was the sound she had identified as a pangron just moments ago.

Sure enough, when Gabba emerged this time, she was yanking a large winged beast behind her, shackled and muzzled just as Topaz had been.

'Is that Faro?' Rustus whispered.

Kayla shook her head. 'No, that's Ezra. Faro is darker.' She peeled herself away from the wall, preparing to run towards the fire, but Rustus quickly grabbed her arm and pulled her back.

'Have you lost your mind?' he said. 'Did you see what they just did to Topaz? If you go over there, they'll jab you with that poison and you'll soon be out cold too.' As if to prove his point, the professor injected Ezra before stretching out the fungus to cover him too. The purple tendrils seemed to reach around him and pull him in towards Topaz.

'They're making a phaegra,' Kayla hissed. 'What are we supposed to do – just sit here and watch them? The professor said this was their only chance – they can't get the beasts back to Polliflora without the ship.'

Rustus knew she was right – they had to do something. But what? He watched as the fungus, now covering both beasts like a cocoon, started to quiver, glowing pink, then blue, then purple, then red. His heart raced. If they didn't do something to stop the professor, then the fate of the Realms was about to change. But who were they, two children, to save Ramoa?

It was then he recalled his mother's prophecy. It hadn't made sense to him at the time – he'd been so sure his destiny was in Ataria – but maybe she'd been right all along. What was it she'd said? *There are others like you. You must find them before the return of the* – She'd been cut off by the Cardinal, but he'd bet anything she was talking about the phaegra. And maybe she'd been thinking of Alethea and Kayla too. What was it that Maaka had said? *Three must unite.* Maybe the three of them *were* destined to meet. Maybe it *was* up to them to save the Realms. They might be just children, but was anyone ever too small to make a difference? Look at the shadowy bardfly; it was small enough to fit in Rustus's hands, yet it had caused untold destruction across the Realms.

Rustus caught Kayla's determined gaze and nodded. It was time to act. Without a word they sprinted out of their hiding place and towards the mound of fungus, cloaking the beasts.

But it was too late.

As they drew closer Rustus heard a deafening *boom!*

A mushroom of white light whooshed up from the creatures and for a few seconds completely obscured them. Then a wave of energy threw Rustus and Kayla violently backwards. The next thing Rustus knew, he was flat on his back, wind knocked from his lungs, ears ringing. Beside him he heard Kayla coughing. He pushed himself up frantically, worried what he might see. Through the haze of smoke he could see Topaz and Ezra stirring. The purple fungus was no longer glowing, but there atop it sat a glistening golden egg. His heart dropped.

'She did it,' he said. 'She made a phaegra.'

Beside him, Kayla blinked and rubbed her eyes. She looked desperate. 'It's still just an egg. We can –'

'Who are *they*?' a menacing voice cut Kayla off. The professor. 'Don't let them get any closer, Gabba.'

What happened next occurred so quickly Rustus barely had time to take it all in. Gabba began striding towards them, but Kayla was already on her feet, making a dash towards the fungus. Gabba launched herself towards the egg, but before she could reach it Ezra lunged forward, breaking through his bonds, snatched it in his jaws and took to the air.

'The egg!' wailed the professor. 'Stop that pangron!'

Gabba and Kayla both flung themselves at Ezra. Kayla jumped higher, grabbing onto the beast's legs as it rose to

308

the sky. Ezra flapped and screeched, trying to bite Kayla and throw her off, but she clung on. Through a blur of wings and teeth Rustus saw her force her way onto the pangron's back, clinging tightly as it rolled and zipped through the sky over the headland.

From beyond the fungus, he heard the professor scream, 'They're getting away! Stop them!'

'It's OK,' Gabba said. 'Keep hold of the salinka. I have another pangron – we can do it again!'

At this news the professor's face lit up. 'Well, go! Go get it! Now!'

In the chaos Rustus had totally forgotten about Faro. Was he in the lighthouse too? From the way Gabba was sprinting towards it, Rustus suspected he was.

Rustus chased after her, but Gabba was too far ahead. Just as he thought he would be too slow to close the gap between them, he saw Alethea running across the headland, a beast galloping along on a leash beside her. Ernie! She pulled the leash from around the grunthog's neck and patted him on the rump, sending him barrelling towards Gabba. The ground shook with the force of his thundering hooves.

Rustus watched in amazement as Ernie ran full pelt towards the Lia'Oua girl. When Gabba realised what was headed her way, she changed course to try to avoid the rampaging beast, but Ernie swerved too, crashing into the back of her legs and sending her tumbling backwards, dangerously close to the cliff's edge.

'Arrgh!' Gabba yelled, trying to regain her footing,

but Ernie stamped his foot and charged again, this time hitting even harder than before and sending Gabba over the edge of the cliff, down to the ocean below.

'No!' screamed the professor, rushing towards the drop.

Rustus didn't hang around to see what she did next – he needed to get to the lighthouse before she did. As he ran he glanced over his shoulder, expecting to see the professor pursuing him, but Topaz had thrown off her shackles and positioned herself between the cliff edge and the lighthouse, barring the professor's way.

Thank you, girl, he thought.

When Rustus finally reached the door to the lighthouse he was panting heavily. 'I'm coming, Faro,' he whispered between breaths.

He yanked the door, but it didn't budge.

'*No!*' he wailed. Gabba still had the key – and thanks to Ernie she was at the base of the cliff. He would have to climb up the outside of the lighthouse instead. He scanned the sheer wall, mentally picking out a route.

I can do this, he told himself, reaching up to grab a metal hook fixed into the bricks. His muscles flexed. *Easy*, he thought. *You are Rustus Furi*. He walked his legs up the wall and looked for his next handhold. He spotted a broken brick – it was further than he could reach without letting go of the hook, but he knew that with a leap he could grab it. He took a deep breath and braced his legs, elastic energy surging within them. Then he let go of the hook, bent his knees and sprang upwards. His fingers found the fault in the wall and every muscle in his hand

and forearm clenched. He planted his soft soles flat on the wall and braced his feet against the stone. His right arm quivered with the strain. He relaxed into the feeling – more confident now, trusting his hands and feet, moving quickly up the wall – and soon he was halfway up. He looked down at the ground, searching for the professor, and saw she was making her way down to the small boat she'd arrived on, far below on the pebbly beach. What was she planning?

Almost there, he told himself, refocusing on the task at hand. He looked up at the lantern room. It was as close as the top of Kahanga Rock had been when he had fallen. He felt a wave of uncertainty. *No*, he insisted, *this is different. You can do this.* He shook his head, focused his mind and continued, moving hand over foot, using all his strength and experience to get him to the top. At last his fingertips hooked over the crumbling brick balcony surrounding the glass-walled lantern room. A loose brick slipped beneath his fingers and fell away from the wall, but he quickly adjusted his grip, and this time the brick held and he heaved himself to safety.

Relief flooded his body. He had done it.

He let himself sit for a moment among the shards of broken brick, his back against the glass of the lantern room, drinking in the cool night air as he regained his breath.

Over the ocean he saw Ezra screaming through the sky, thrashing his body as he continued to try to throw Kayla off, the egg clutched precariously in his talons.

He looked down at the beach and saw the professor there, raising a weapon.

Oh no! She was going to shoot the pangron down.

'Kayla!' he yelled in warning, but it was too late. The arrow soared through the sky, finding its target in Ezra's chest. A few wingbeats later, pangron and rider were tumbling towards the ocean.

Rustus jumped to his feet and ran around the perimeter of the lantern room, searching for a door. He needed to get Faro free and go to Kayla and Ezra's aid. But there was no door. Realising he had no other option, he stooped to pick up a loose brick, took a deep breath and punched it through the glass. Tiny shards fell around him like hailstones, while inside the lantern room something gave out an ear-splitting shriek.

This must be Faro.

The beast was huge and beautiful, with a coat like lavastone, eyes like magma and wings like velvet. In his wonder, it took Rustus a moment to realise that Faro was bound with leather and rope. Rustus moved over to him quickly, but the pangron snarled.

'It's OK,' Rustus murmured gently. 'I'm a friend of Kayla's. She's in trouble and needs our help.' He remembered the necklace Kayla had given him on the mountain and held it up to show Faro. The pangron sniffed the eggshell, then made a rumbling sound that made the whole room shake. 'That's right,' said Rustus. 'I'm a friend. We're going to help her now.' He quickly unbuckled the muzzle and restraints.

Once Faro was free, he shook his wings loose and made that sound again. What did it mean?

Rustus's throat was dry. If he got this wrong, the beast would surely destroy him. He placed a hand gently on Faro's shoulder, holding his breath. The pangron dipped its head to the ground. Was he inviting Rustus to get onto his back? Rustus's heart was in his mouth as he moved up beside the huge beast.

'I'm sorry,' he said, climbing awkwardly onto the pangron's back. 'I'm new to this.' He clambered up onto Faro's shoulders, sliding one leg over the front of each wing. Was this how he was supposed to get on? He had barely got into position before Faro was launching himself through the broken glass and into the open sky. Rustus grabbed handfuls of fur to stop himself from falling, heart in his mouth as he clung on for dear life.

25

KAYLA

Kayla and Ezra crashed into the ocean just as she and Faro had done all those days before. The golden egg bobbed on the surface a short swim away, but in that moment Kayla's priority was Ezra. She knew she had to find the arrow and remove it as it was likely poisoned, so she set about searching his body for a point of impact, all while trying to keep him afloat. She soon found it embedded in his hind leg and gave it a strong tug. 'Sorry Ezra,' she said, giving him an apologetic rub.

Once it was out, she checked her surroundings. Near the base of the cliff she made out a figure swimming. It was Gabba. She had no idea how the Shadow Ghoul had ended up in the water. To her left, closer to the beach, the professor had climbed into a boat and was gliding towards her. Kayla knew she was coming for the egg, but she needed to stabilise Ezra before she left him to retrieve it herself.

Just then a distant howl rose in the cool air. Kayla would have known that sound anywhere. She turned to the source. Through the salty spray of the ocean she saw a rust-coloured beast shooting towards her as if loosed from a knucklebow. Tears pricked her eyes and her chest heaved.

It was Faro, and there was a figure dangling from his back.

'Rustus!' she shouted in relief. 'Get the egg!'

Faro raced towards the water, Rustus clinging desperately to his fur, but they were not heading for the egg. Faro was flying directly to Kayla.

'Not me!' she yelled. 'Get the egg! Before they do!'

'No time!' yelled Rustus. 'Look!'

Kayla turned to find the professor's boat was almost upon her. How in the skies had the boat moved so fast? A plume of water broke the waves ahead of the boat and gave Kayla her answer; it was being pulled by beasts. Probably more chimaeras.

'Watch out, Kayla,' shouted Rustus. 'She's aiming for you.'

Kayla shifted her gaze to the boat and found the professor's weapon raised. 'Faro!' she screamed, one hand on Ezra, the other reaching for her pangron.

Faro was flying at full speed, the space between them growing smaller and smaller until, at last, Faro's talons grasped Kayla's shoulders. As he dragged her up out of the water, Ezra slipped from her grasp.

'Ezra!' she shouted as she clambered onto the safety

315

of Faro's back, squeezing her legs tightly around her pangron's neck. Despite the dire circumstances, gratitude and relief pulsed through her. They were reunited at last. She blinked the tears from her eyes and forced herself to concentrate.

She leaned back and offered a hand to Rustus. 'What are you doing down there?' she asked, heaving him upright.

Rustus looked slightly green. 'It's not as easy as it looks.'

'Hold on round my waist,' said Kayla, 'and squeeze his body with your legs. We need to get that egg.'

Instead of flying forward though, Faro shot up into the sky, away from the professor's aim, but also from Ezra and the egg.

'Go back down!' Kayla yelled. 'We need to grab the egg and Ezra and get out of here!' She tugged on Faro's mane to encourage him back down. Below, the currents were pushing Ezra further out to sea, and both the professor and Gabba were closing in on the egg – one in her boat, the other swimming with long strokes.

'Come on, Faro,' Kayla yelled, but he ignored her. 'We have to stop them!' Faro flapped a couple of times, but instead of dropping towards Ezra and the egg, he rose higher in the sky. He had never been disobedient like this before, and Kayla urged him more forcefully, but still he refused. She could only watch in horror as Gabba snatched up the egg from the crest of a wave and then hauled herself into the boat.

'Bad luck, you lose!' she yelled, looking up at Rustus and Kayla with a wicked grin.

'They're getting away!' screamed Kayla, watching as the boat rocketed across the waves, pulled by unknown beasts below the surface.

'Can't you get Faro to dive down and take it?' Rustus asked frantically.

'He won't listen,' said Kayla, desperately trying to control her pangron. 'I think he's scared of the poison arrows. Faro,' she pleaded, 'we *have* to get that egg.' But still he would not do as she asked.

A splash from below drew her attention back to Ezra. Rustus had heard it too.

'We need to help him,' Rustus said.

Kayla agreed. Now that Gabba and the professor were out of the way, maybe Faro would listen to her again. She squeezed Faro's body with her legs. This time he obeyed, levelling out his wings to swoop just above the ocean surface. As they reached Ezra, Faro extended his talons and grabbed the other pangron, pulling him clean out of the water. Kayla was astounded by her pangron's strength: he was carrying twice his usual number of riders and dragging a weight as heavy as he was.

She looked back at the professor's boat, now just a small speck, travelling rapidly out to sea. Even if he'd wanted to, there was no way Faro could chase after the professor with such a load. Whatever happened next, they would have to take Ezra back to the beach first.

She urged Faro to the shore, encouraging him to glide

low and slow. When they reached the rocky beach Faro landed ungracefully, sending Rustus and Ezra sprawling over the pebbles. Kayla, more accustomed to such landings, leaped off Faro's back moments before his feet touched the ground and landed in a crouch. She rushed to her pangron, pressing her face against his, warm tears pouring down her cheeks as quickly as Faro could lick them away. She was whole again at last.

'I'm so sorry for letting her take you from me,' she sobbed into his fur.

He rubbed his face against hers and she knew that he forgave her.

'I've missed you so much.' She buried herself in his neck. He smelled like home.

For a few blissful moments the overwhelming emotion of seeing her pangron again blocked out all thoughts of the egg, but Rustus's voice brought them all flooding back.

'Well done, Kayla,' he said. 'I thought Ezra was going to drop you into the ocean at one point.'

'But the professor got away,' Kayla wailed. 'And she's got the egg. I have to go and get it back.' She squinted out to sea. The professor's boat was already out of sight.

'She's too far away,' Rustus said. 'Did you see how quickly her boat was moving? It was pulled by some kind of sea beasts. You'd never catch up.'

An empty pit opened in Kayla's stomach. 'She mustn't get away with this. We can't let her hatch the phaegra.'

'But what can we do? We can't go over to Polliflora

and take it back right now. One, we don't know where the island is. Two, even if we did, we're all exhausted, so neither we nor these pangrons are in a fit state for a fight. And three, if those sea beasts were anything to go by, she has a whole chimaera army to protect her.'

'Then that's it? We just let her destroy the Realms?'

Before Rustus could reply, they were interrupted by a familiar voice.

'You found him! Hello, Faro.' It was the Marquis. He offered the back of his hand to Faro, who sniffed it, then dropped his head for a pat.

'You're all right!' said Rustus, rushing to hug the Marquis. The old man was limping on his right leg and had a large painful-looking lump on his forehead, but he looked in good spirits.

Kayla was surprised at the emotion that washed over her. 'It's good to see you.' She allowed him to pull her in for a hug too.

'We saw what happened from the clifftop,' said Alethea, appearing behind him.

'Then you saw the professor escaping with the egg?' Kayla said glumly.

'It wasn't your fault,' said Alethea, joining in the hug. 'You did everything you could.'

'But it still wasn't enough to stop her.' Kayla pulled away, furious with herself.

'It's not too late,' said Rustus. 'After all, she's got to wait for that egg to hatch. We can still find a way to stop her before the phaegra gets too big.'

'If I hadn't brought Topaz here, then the professor never could have made the phaegra in the first place,' said the Marquis, looking abashed. 'Just as I arrived at the lighthouse, Milabar appeared with your message and the pieces fell into place. I tried to leave but then Gabba appeared on the cliff, dragging the pangrons towards the lighthouse. I tried to run, but well . . .' He gestured to the bump on his forehead. 'Alethea has brought me up to speed on everything the doctor told you. I feel such a fool. If I hadn't come to Port Royal . . .'

'We cannot choose how the ash falls,' said Alethea, staring wistfully out to sea. 'Only what we build with it.'

Before Kayla could ask what she meant, Rustus spoke.

'The professor is determined. She would have got Topaz here one way or another,' he consoled the Marquis. 'Speaking of which, where's Topaz now?' He looked around for the needlejaw.

The salinka, Kayla reminded herself.

'Back in her cage,' said the Marquis. 'Munching on slugs. I'll be taking her straight back to the Shadowlands where she belongs. The Lia'Oua will do a better job of looking after her than I ever could.'

A strange look flashed across Rustus's face. 'The Shadowlands . . .' he mused. 'Professor Penn was there looking for information about the prophecies, wasn't she? If we're planning to stop her then maybe we need to learn more about the prophecies too.'

'Are you saying we should all go down to the Shadowlands?' Kayla asked, disbelieving.

'Not all of us,' said Rustus. 'I know you need to get back to Sophiatown, and Alethea to Ataria. But *I* don't need to go anywhere. I'm an exile.' He seemed pleased about that title for the first time. 'So maybe I could go with the Marquis to the Shadowlands?' He glanced at the Marquis to gauge his response. The old man nodded happily. 'The Lia'Oua may be able to give us an idea of how we can stop the professor before she can do too much damage.'

Kayla had to admit, it sort of made sense. It was a better plan than trying to fly across the ocean right now at least. And she'd made a promise to Alethea that she didn't want to break. 'Maybe I'll be able to find out more about the professor in Sophiatown too,' she said, remembering what Dr Oke had told them about Professor Penn's grudge against the city. 'After all, that's where she's from.'

At the thought of home, another memory resurfaced: from the distillery chimney she had heard those two voices discussing how they had hidden Ezra on Gabba's boat. Did the professor have people working for her in Sophiatown? It was something else to investigate, for sure. 'And I'll need to warn the Sky Riders – if she's planning to attack the city they need to prepare their defences.'

'What about you, Alethea?' Rustus said. 'You haven't said much.'

The healer took a long, contemplative breath. 'There's a lot to think about,' she said. 'First of all, I need to get back and deliver the cure to the people of Ataria. Once

I've done that, I want some answers about why the Ash Bishops lied to us about life outside the city.'

Rustus nodded solemnly. 'They've kept so much from us,' he agreed. 'And if anyone has what it takes to challenge them, it's you.'

Kayla noticed that Alethea hadn't mentioned anything about joining them. 'But you'll come with us,' she asked, 'to stop the professor?'

For a moment she wondered if Alethea might refuse. And could Kayla blame her? This had never been Alethea's battle. All she had ever wanted to do was to find a cure for the Scourge. And yet something tugged at Kayla's insides at the thought of completing the next part of the journey without one of her new friends.

'Of course I'll come,' Alethea said. 'I need to make sure the people of Ataria are safe first, but as soon as I've taught the healers there how to treat the Scourge, I'll join you. I promise.'

Kayla felt the grin break across her face, a warmth spreading through her chest like she had just guzzled a steaming cup of varja.

'Thanks, Alethea,' she said. 'I couldn't bear the thought of doing it without you.'

'You know, I have this weird feeling,' Rustus said, 'that Maaka was right. The three of us were always destined to meet.'

Kayla wasn't sure she believed in prophecies, but she knew what he meant.

Alethea was nodding, like she felt it too. 'Maybe the

island brought us together for a reason. How will we all keep in touch while we're apart?'

As if on command, Milabar appeared then, landing neatly on the Marquis's shoulder.

'I think I know of a heraldwing you could borrow,' he said with a smile.

'Then it's decided,' said Kayla. 'Rustus, you'll go and learn more about the prophecies in the Shadowlands; Alethea, you'll deliver the cure to the people of Ataria; and I'll find out everything I can about the professor in Sophiatown. Once we've done all that, we'll reconvene and travel together to Polliflora. Are we agreed?'

Rustus and Alethea nodded enthusiastically.

'Group hug?' Rustus suggested, opening his arms wide.

Kayla sighed. *Another* hug? But she didn't resist when Rustus and Alethea swept her towards them. As they pulled apart, she caught sight of Ezra, unconscious on the beach.

'What are we going to do about him?' She rubbed a long scratch on her arm where he had fought against her.

'Let me see if I can rouse him.' Alethea strode over to the pangron. She pushed a white leaf from her satchel into his mouth and waited. After a few breaths he snorted himself awake.

'How did you do that?' said Kayla, amazed yet again by what Alethea could achieve with her plants.

'I guessed that Gabba was coating her arrows in hypnos-snake venom,' said Alethea with a smile. 'It causes amnesia. And it just so happens it's neutralised by leaf of frostwort.'

Ezra heaved himself to his feet.

'Hey, buddy,' said Kayla, moving slowly over to him. He made a little nose whinny. 'You feeling better now? Don't want to rip me to shreds any more?' He rubbed his head against her.

'I think that's a sorry,' said Rustus.

'Animals always act oddly when eggs are involved,' said the Marquis. 'Now that the egg is gone, he can think straight again.'

'How long till he can fly?' asked Kayla.

At the word 'fly', Ezra flapped his wings.

'I think he's ready to go home right now,' said Alethea with a giggle.

Kayla showed Alethea how Faro liked to be stroked on his ears, giving them a brief chance to be acquainted before letting Alethea climb onto his back. Faro was patient, dipping his shoulders as she scrabbled to get a footing. Once she was comfortably seated, Kayla leaped up in front of her.

'I guess this is goodbye then,' said Rustus, looking up at them.

Kayla felt a pang of sadness. 'Just for now,' she said. 'And we'll keep in touch. We'll be together again before we know it.'

Kayla was about to give Faro the signal to move forward – she didn't want to get too emotional over saying goodbye – when Rustus shouted, 'Wait! Your necklace!'

He held up the shard of eggshell, reaching to pass it over Faro's ears. Kayla took the leather cord and slipped it over her head, pleased to feel the comforting weight of it around her neck once again.

'That reminds me,' said Alethea. 'I meant to give you this.' She pulled a silvery plant from her satchel and passed it delicately to Rustus. 'Be careful, it's arrowsedge – it's what I used against the lavabear. Keep it somewhere safe, and close your eyes if you ever need to use it.'

'Thanks,' said Rustus with a broad smile.

'While we're all giving gifts,' said the Marquis, 'take this.' He tossed a paper bag up to the girls, and Kayla snatched it from the air and passed it to Alethea.

'Varja beans!' she exclaimed, peering inside.

'To get you through the journey,' the Marquis explained.

'Thank you,' Kayla said, the tight feeling returning to her chest and tears threatening to spill. Luckily Lillypeg chose that moment to poke her head out of the Marquis's beard and she giggled instead. 'Bye Lillypeg,' she said with a wave. 'Come on, Ezra.' She turned to Prince Ethun's pangron. 'It's time to go home!'

Ezra trotted up beside Faro and soon both girls and beasts were in the air, waving at Rustus and the Marquis as they rose. Every now and again Alethea would give a little squeal – of delight or fear, Kayla wasn't certain. Either way, it was nice to be flying with her friend. For the first time she had a glimpse of what life could be like if she allowed other people in, expanding her universe beyond herself and her pangron. She found she rather liked it.

'Can you believe it's not even been a week since we left our cities?' Alethea said.

Kayla shook her head. It felt like a million years had passed since the day of the initiation.

'It's been quite the adventure, hasn't it?' said Kayla. And yet somehow she knew it was only the start.

Beasts

of

Ramoa

An Illustrated Guide

By Maltheus Macdonald

Pangron

Beast type: Warmblood
Habitat: Domesticated

Second largest of all the flying beasts, loyal and devoted pangrons once lived near water, feeding mainly on scalefish they caught by diving. Since their domestication by the Southlander army, pangrons have been taught to carry humans on their backs, sometimes forming close bonds with their riders. Unlike most warmbloods, pangrons hatch from eggs laid underwater. After hatching, young pangrons grow rapidly, usually reaching their full size in less than two years. They have impressive teeth, sharp talons and dense fur, which comes in a jolly array of colours and patterns, as well as light, hollow bones, which allow them to take flight despite their size. Pangrons are most active in daylight but also see well in low light conditions due to a reflective layer at the back of their eyes.

Salinka

Beast type: Reptillite
Habitat: Caves

When it runs, the salinka is the embodiment of grace,
its sinuous body weaving side to side like a ribbon
fluttering in a breeze, but take care to avoid being
trodden on by its large feet, which it uses to dig
for worms, slugs and snails. Don't be fooled by its
intimidating fangs, which protrude from its mouth in all
directions – its cumbersome teeth prevent it from biting
and chewing. Instead it slurps its food with the help
of its long muscular tongue. Salinka scales are vibrant
iridescent ~~green~~ blue, save for the fiery orange rings that
surround their pale blue eyes. By way of defence, it has
a long muscular spiked tail and foul-tasting silvery-blue
blood, which is unappealing to most predators. Wild
salinkas were thought to be extinct, but have recently
been rediscovered in the Shadowlands,
where they coexist with the
Lia'Oua.

Grunthog

Beast type: Warmblood
Habitat: Woodland

The barrel-shaped bristly bodies of grunthogs
were once a common sight in the forests of the
Southlands, where they could be seen snuffling their
way through the undergrowth in search of their
favourite food, mushrooms. Sadly deforestation and
hunting have now driven them almost to extinction.
Grunthogs were notably persecuted by Southland
hunters, who held the nonsensical notion that their
corkscrew tusks looked better on mantelpieces than
their original owners. Though they can be trained
to live happily in the presence of humans, even
learning to obey some simple commands, grunthogs
are inordinately strong and never lose the instinct
to charge. If you ever find yourself in the path
of a galloping
grunthog, run!

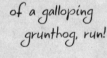

Obsidian webspinner

Beast type: Webspinner
Habitat: Jungle

A beast of immense size and beauty, the eight-legged obsidian webspinner was once a relatively uncommon sighting in the Turquoise Jungle. It is a master engineer, spinning its silk with the precision and patience of an artist, hanging the sticky strands carefully from branches to entrap unwitting hexapods as they pass. Obsidian webspinners were once the favoured food of the phaegra, but since the extermination of the large flying beasts, they have flourished in the Turquoise Jungle, becoming the dominant species there. Their waterproof, fireproof, sunproof, acidproof silk can be harvested and used by people to build everything from rope to clothing. They have a painful but non-fatal bite and their venom is neutralised by the nectar of mist violets.

Lavabear

Beast type: Warmblood
Habitat: Jungle

Lavabears also evolved to live in the jungle on the slopes of Mount Ataria, but after the proliferation of the obsidian webspinners in that area, they were forced out into the foothills instead. Their conspicuous turquoise mottled coat (which turns black after a recent lava flow) makes them relatively easy to spot in any environment other than the Turquoise Jungle, but their speed and strength have allowed them to continue to catch their prey despite this handicap. Lavabears have been blamed for the deaths of a number of nomads and travellers since moving to the foothills, but their preferred foods are magma hares and lavaberries.

Cliffcreeper

Beast type: Reptillite
Habitat: Rocky surfaces

A master of camouflage, the cliffcreeper can go
entirely unnoticed when resting on a cliff or other
stony surface. It often inhabits vertical rock faces,
where it may spend many hours lying in wait for its
preferred prey: the astral ashmoth. The cliffcreeper's
wide head and body are covered with large, lumpy
scales, which are painted in a palette of earthy
tones, making it impossible to distinguish from its
rocky surroundings. Nocturnal and very territorial,
cliffcreepers will fiercely defend their patch of
rock from intruders. When navigating rocky terrain
at night beware, as these armoured reptillites don't
take kindly to strangers in their patch and have an
impressive bite force.

Snogart

Beast type: Warmblood
Habitat: Alpine

The sure-footed snogart is an agile climber that traverses the steep and snowy terrain of the craggy Shivertips with ease. It has a thick white coat with a pendulous dewlap and slender legs that end in small delicate hooves. Male snogarts have four short antlers, which are shed each spring. Snogarts have excellent hearing and can locate the whinnying cries of other snogarts from many miles away. They are very stoical and have been known to walk for many miles with severe injuries, leading people to believe – wrongly – that they have unbreakable bones.

Heraldwing

Beast type: Featherwing
Habitat: Fjord

A beast of unparalleled grace and talent, the heraldwing is a master of mimicry. It can copy almost any sound so perfectly that its imitation is virtually impossible to distinguish from the source. It is a mesmerisingly beautiful creature, with long white feathers that cascade around its neck and a crown of feathers atop its head. Now uncommon in the wild, heraldwings are often used as couriers, carrying messages far and wide. They have an uncanny ability to locate any person they have previously met and can remember hundreds of names and places. The heraldwing's only flaw is its tendency to become transfixed by its own voice; if it hears a beautiful sound it can sit for hours repeating and perfecting its call.

Stained-glass scuttleclaw

Beast type: Exocrust
Habitat: Coast

Rarely seen alone, stained-glass scuttleclaws move together in large groups, often coordinating their movements so they seem to march along as one. Found on sandy shores across the Realms, they are inquisitive and charismatic beasts that seem to enjoy spending time around humans. Stained-glass scuttleclaws are named for their beautifully coloured, slightly translucent shells, which in certain lights allow their internal organs to be seen from the outside. They have two bulbous eyes raised up on tall stalks and twelve legs, the front pair of which have large sharp pincers for catching prey. Stained-glass scuttleclaws hunt at night and are not fussy – they will eat almost anything that gets in their way. For this reason it is highly recommended never to take a nap in known stained-glass scuttleclaw territory.

Shadowy bardfly

Beast type: Chimaera
Habitat: Widespread

The shadowy bardfly is a chimaera created through the ritual of Banahiki and derived from the shadowy stinger and the southern bardfly. It is a roughly fist-sized flying beast, with dazzling blue-and-silver wings and a wide striped body. In appearance it is broadly similar to other bardfly species, aside from one significant difference: a stinger. Apparently the only feature it has inherited from the shadowy stinger, the curved spike on the end of the shadowy bardfly's abdomen delivers a potent venom known to cause a disease in humans called the Scourge. Like other bardflies, shadowy bardflies reproduce asexually, meaning one individual can give rise to thousands within just a few generations.

Acknowledgements

The world and characters of this book have existed in my head for most of my adult life, but without the help of some extraordinary people, this story might never have made it onto paper. I am deeply grateful to the following people, who have been an enormous help and support on this long journey:

Gill McLay, my literary agent and friend. Thank you for believing in me, for having faith in this story, for walking beside me every step of the journey and for reminding me to stop every now and again to rest.

Ella Whiddett, my brilliant and patient editor, who understood my vision from the outset and fought to help me do it justice. Also for enduring untold 'what if . . .' rabbit holes, before gently steering me back on course. It would not be the book it is without you.

George Ermos, for bringing to life the creatures and world that have for so long existed only in my head – and for the cover of dreams.

A book like this doesn't exist in a vacuum. Thank

you to the entire team at Piccadilly Press, especially Amber, Isobel, Talya and Jen. Team of dreams!

A huge thank you to those that have read, championed and supported the books I have written up until this point – you have also been a part of making this happen at last. And thanks to the members of the book community that have welcomed and supported me – on social media and in reality. Too many to list but in particular I'm looking at you, Isabel Thomas, Jules Howard, Ben Garrod, Hannah Gold, Aisling Fowler, Anna James and of course my dear friend Maya. Thank you, Beetle Queen, for your (many) words of kindness and great wisdom at all the crucial moments and for continuing to inspire me.

My dad, who has read every draft I've ever written and provided supportive and constructive feedback at every step. Thank you for your unwavering belief and support – and for continuing to believe in me when I did not.

My mum, the archetypal strong female character. Thank you for a lifetime of inspirational words and actions and for always believing in me – and for the childcare that allowed me to finally get the words down on paper.

Grandad Ronnie, who never got to see the finished product but who deeply believed that one day it would make it into the wild.

Dan, for being my rock. You've anchored me through stormy seas and never stopped believing, helped me unravel plot holes, whittle down word counts and clarify my ideas. Thanks also for the unlimited supply of hugs and for keeping your cool when I repeatedly forget to save my work and spill various drinks over my laptop despite your constant reminders and technical assistance.

Fenya and Ozra for being my North Star and for reminding me what truly matters. It's all for you.

Thanks to all the many friends that have listened to me ramble about this world and story for over a decade without complaint. Too many to list but especially Luke, Toni, Laurie, Hannah and Erin.

Also to the English teachers that inspired my early writing, particularly Mr Wilson, Mr Bailey and Mrs Jacob.

Lastly, an enormous wave of gratitude for the wonderful beasts that I have shared my life with: Claws, Monty, Hector, George, Winston, Marmaduke, Rocky, Dylan, Pip, Rosie, Flower, Ebony, Cleo, Kipper, Savvy, Gonff, Abu, Mica and my dear, dear Taffy, who sat on my shoulder for a decade of draft-writing. They all shaped my life and this story and made the world a great deal better just by existing.

About the author

Jess French has made a career of working with animals. She is a qualified veterinary surgeon with a first class degree in zoology, a naturalist and entomologist. She is the author of over twenty books for children and the presenter of hit wildlife show *Minibeast Adventures with Jess*. She is also a regular contributor to radio and film, presenting, writing and researching animal science as well as working as an animal handler.

Jess spent much of her childhood adventuring outdoors, which inspired her love of nature and animals. As an adult, Jess continues to explore and has worked with animals all over the globe, including at a gibbon rescue centre in Thailand, a monkey sanctuary in Bolivia, a home for orphaned kangaroos in Australia and a dog shelter in India. She currently lives in Norfolk with her family.

REUNITE WITH KAYLA,
ALETHEA AND RUSTUS IN . . .

BEAST LANDS

LEGEND OF THE CRYSTAL CAVES

COMING 2025

We hope you loved your Piccadilly Press book!

For all the latest bookish news, freebies and exclusive
content, sign up to the Piccadilly Press newsletter –
scan the QR code or visit lnk.to/PiccadillyNewsletter

Follow us on social media:

bonnierbooks.co.uk/PiccadillyPress